MY DUTY TO YOU
An Austen Generation Novel

BY ALYSSA MARTIN

First published in South Africa by Kingsley Publishers, 2023
Copyright © Alyssa Martin, 2023

The right of Alyssa Martin to be identified as author of this work has been asserted.

Kingsley Publishers
Pretoria,
South Africa
www.kingsleypublishers.com

A catalogue copy of this book will be available from the National Library of South Africa
Paperback ISBN: 978-1-7764254-7-1
eBook ISBN: 978-1-7764254-6-4

This book is a work of fiction. Names, characters, places, and incidents are either a product of the authors imagination or are used fictitiously. Any resemblance to actual people living or dead, events or locales is entirely coincidental

To my love match

Chapter One

September 1811

Aiden Elliot watched as Eldridge Castle came into view. He'd been traveling for nearly two days from Switzerland, where he'd been living as a diplomat for the past eight years. As the second son to the eleventh Duke of Northumberland, he'd bought a commission to the British cavalry shortly after the war had been declared on Napoleonic France. However, because of his familial connections, the government decided he'd serve the war effort better by working for them in Switzerland.

At the end of its journey, *The Aether*, the Elliots' vessel, laid anchor on the River Eld, and he disembarked. His spaniel jumped ahead of him, while his valet followed with the luggage he could easily carry. Having seen the ship pull up to the dock, Eldridge Castle's butler stood at the door waiting to welcome him. The sight of the black armband on Jameson's coat was Aiden's first indication that his reason for returning home wasn't a mistake.

"Milord." Jameson greeted him with a bow and a smile that didn't quite reach his eyes. "Your family has just sat down to dinner. If you'd like to join them in the dining

My Duty To You

room, I'll have more food brought up from the kitchens for you."

"Thank you, Jameson," he said, taking in his childhood home. He had various memories of him and his older brother running through the halls and sliding down the banisters. Sadly, however, those days were long in the past.

Aiden had always imagined the day he would return to England. In his mind, it would have been after Napoleon had been defeated; he would have returned home a hero and maybe even been given a title based on his service to the crown. While his family had both means and money, he'd never felt like he had a purpose as a second son, which influenced his decision to buy a commission. More recently, he'd come to enjoy his work in Switzerland as a diplomat and intelligence agent. The idea that those parts of his life had come to a quick and irrevocable end before they reached a culmination irritated a part of him, whereas another part of him simply grieved.

He shook his head and took long strides through the castle until he reached the dining room, where he found his family sitting at the dinner table, eating in silence.

"Aiden." His mother, Eleanor, stood and moved toward him as soon as he walked into the room. All the women of the family were dressed in their mourning black, and his father wore a black armband over his tailcoat.

"How?" he asked; the word slipped from his lips due to a need to understand. A letter from his mother had reached him three days prior. Without going into detail, Eleanor wrote that his brother Ferdy had died unexpectedly and requested that he return home as the new heir to the Northumberland Dukedom.

"A carriage accident," his father replied. Seymour's

appearance had changed immensely in the eight years since Aiden had left for the Continent. He remembered his father being staunch and virile, but now Seymour was smaller, his hair was thinning, and his complexion was gray. Aiden hardly recognized him but attributed the change to the grief of losing his firstborn son.

"Aiden, please sit." Eleanor pulled out a chair for him. "I'm sure you must be tired and hungry after your journey."

He blinked at the chair his mother held for him. It wasn't his. He sucked in his lips and took his usual seat instead. Leaving the chair pulled out, Eleanor returned to her place across from her husband. Jameson appeared a moment later and placed a plate in front of Aiden. Before stepping away from the table, the butler pushed the empty chair back in. Dinner reconvened, but Aiden had no appetite. He couldn't stop looking at his brother's place from the corner of his eye.

"Would you like the port brought up, milord?" Jameson asked when it was time to clear the table.

Seymour waved him away. "Not tonight either, Jameson."

Rowena, the Dowager Duchess, rose from the table. "You can have the tea trolley brought to the drawing room since that's where we'll all withdraw to."

"I'm not in the mood for tea this evening," said Matilda, Ferdy's widow. Her bloodshot eyes met Aiden's. "I'm happy you're home, though." Then before he could say a word, she ducked her head and left the room.

The rest of the family resettled and poured the tea in silence. Aiden's eyes flicked around the room, his teacup shaking in his hand.

"Shall we get down to discussing this dreadful

business?" Rowena asked, breaking the silence.

"Yes, let's." Aiden put his full cup down. "How was Ferdy involved in a carriage accident? Where was he going, and why?"

Rowena looked up at her grandson, who towered over her on the chaise. "That's not the business I was referring to, my dear boy."

Aiden's jaw clenched, and he narrowed his eyes. "That's the only business on my mind, Granny."

Rowena sipped her tea. "As distressing as it is, there is nothing to be done for poor Ferdy other than to celebrate his life and mourn his death. But for you, my child, there is much to be done."

"Mother, I hardly think this is the time—" Seymour tried to interrupt his high-handed mother but was quickly overruled.

"No, Seymour, the time is now, and if Ferdy's untimely death should teach us anything, it is that we cannot delay." Rowena discarded her empty teacup on the trolly and fixed both her son and grandson with a stern look. "If anything were to happen to you or you, the family would be without an heir, and the estates would be given to some distant Scottish connection, which is something I will simply not stand for." She thumped her cane on the floor for added emphasis. "Aiden, we bought your commission because you insisted it would help your future, but things have changed. You will now need to take up the dukedom, which means marrying and producing an heir. As such, I will see you married by the end of the upcoming Season, even if it means I must choose your bride myself."

His hands clenched at his sides, his nails digging into the skin of his palms. "I don't see how that'll be possible since I'll be in mourning."

"Society dictates that you be in mourning for six months, which will not hinder your ability to partake in the Season," Rowena said, only concerned with Society's practices.

"He's my brother!" Aiden's arms flew out in front of him. "I shall mourn him for however long I see fit."

But Rowena did not waver. She stared at her grandson while maintaining an impeccable posture. "Of course you can, but it cannot get in the way of social events and courting a future bride."

"You are set on this?" A lump formed in Aiden's throat. "Ferdy has barely been buried, and you're already urging me to take his place."

"Your grandmother is right in this, Aiden," Eleanor finally spoke. "As difficult as it is to think about, you are now Earl Elliot and the future Duke of Northumberland. It is your duty to establish yourself with your peers in Society, which involves installing a countess and future duchess at your side. There will be no time to swan off to clubs as you'll have social obligations and estate business to attend to."

"You cannot possibly believe . . ." He wiped a hand down his face in disgust, unable to finish his retort. He'd barely been home for a few hours, and his family already thought the worst of him. They thought he would squander his time as the heir to one of the wealthiest and most influential dukedoms in Britain, as if they didn't know how seriously he took his responsibilities. But it was becoming increasingly clear that nothing he could say would change his granny's or his mother's mind. "Fine. I agree to find a bride and marry her by the end of the upcoming social Season, thus accepting my position as earl and future duke." He paused to see if his agreement was acceptable before continuing. "Now will you explain to me how Ferdy met his demise?"

If Aiden hadn't been so tired from his journey, he would have caught the look shared between Rowena, Seymour, and Eleanor, but he'd been traveling for thirty-six hours, so it went unnoticed.

He stared at them, waiting for a response. "Was there a problem with the carriage?"

"We found the carriage crashed into a tree," Seymour said after clearing his throat. "Neither Ferdy nor his horse survived."

The reference to Ferdy's horse might have been inconsequential to some, but not to Aiden. The Elliots had bred horses at Eldridge Castle for generations, and it was their foremost source of income. If Ferdy's death also caused the demise of one of the Elliots' prize stallions, then something must have gone terribly wrong. "Ferdy was a good driver . . . I simply don't understand. Was the weather a factor?"

"There has been talk of Ferdy drinking in the tavern in the village," Seymour replied.

"Drinking?" Aiden shook his head as if the movement would help the words to make sense. "You mean to say he'd been driving his carriage drunk?" The idea didn't sit well with him at all, and he couldn't believe his brother would act so irresponsibly. Ferdy had known his birthright, and while he'd also been known to have a bit of a temper, he'd always conducted himself properly in public.

"It's what's being said," Seymour replied but offered no opinion of his own.

"I don't believe it. I won't!" Aiden shouted, grief and frustration overcoming him. Met with blank stares and shrugged shoulders, he felt he had more questions than answers, so he turned on his heel and stalked out of the drawing room.

The month of September was hard for Aiden; grief and a sense of failure consumed him in regard to losing his brother and the Peninsula War. The Anglo-Portuguese suffered a defeat at the hands of the French, and he couldn't help but feel he was partially responsible. Maybe if he'd been in Switzerland in the days and weeks leading up to the battle, he would have been able to help. But instead, he was in Northumberland being instructed on how to run the dukedom by his father.

The Elliots owned four estates throughout England, which dealt with agriculture and leased land to tenant farmers, providing the dukedom with its income. With the help of his stewards and man of business, Aiden's responsibility was to invest the income properly, so the estates remained profitable in the years to come. Ferdy had already accepted the daily running of the dukedom from Seymour, who planned to retire after the upcoming social Season. Not wanting to delay his retirement, Seymour was pressing Aiden to pick up where Ferdy had left off.

After a particularly grueling morning going over estate business with his father, Aiden decided to go for a walk with his spaniel, Winnie, around the inner bailey and gardens. Shortly into his walk, he found Matilda sitting on a bench watching her daughter with her nursemaid. "How is our little Rosie?" he asked while walking up to sit with his sister-in-law.

"As best as can be expected," Matilda replied. "For better or worse, I don't believe she truly knows what's going on."

Aiden nodded since, at just a little over two years old, Rose wouldn't have any real understanding of her father's death. "And what of you? How are you coping?"

Matilda sighed and studied her hands, which lay in her lap. The sound of Rose playing was the only thing Aiden heard as he waited for her reply. Then he noticed her wet palms. "Just as I expected." He reached for her and brushed a lock of hair behind her ear. "Surely at this point, you know you don't have to hide from me."

Matilda was the only daughter of the Earl of Ravensworth, whose land bordered Eldridge to the west. Ferdy, Aiden, Matilda, and her brother were all of a similar age and grew up together. They spent their childhood riding horses, playing games, and swimming in the river. Aiden believed that Ferdy had had a soft spot for Matilda from a young age and that she preferred him as well. Little changed as they got older. Matilda and Ferdy exchanged letters the entire time he was at Eton, and when he returned home, he wasted little time in offering for her. The match was happily accepted by both families, who had shared generations of friendship.

"I feel as though I've let everyone down," Matilda finally explained. "My family, your family, even myself. It took an age for me to be with child, and now it's been two years since I had Rose, and I've been unable to beget an heir for the dukedom. My one and only duty, and I have failed at it."

Aiden rubbed her back. "Matilda, you are hardly the only one at fault for that."

She turned and met his eye. "But that is what Society will think."

He sighed and swallowed his lips. It was true. Society

was not nice to women, especially ones who did not meet their exacting standards.

"I suppose I ought to return to my father's estate." She sniffed. "I'm sure he'll also want to see me married again, much like your granny wants you married."

"For as long as I am lord here, you will always have a place within the Elliot fold," Aiden said. "You are my brother's widow and my longest friend, not to mention Rose is Elliot by blood and the direct descendant of a duke. So you will never have to want for anything for as long as I shall live."

Fresh tears sprang to Matilda's eyes. "Oh, Aiden, you do not know how much relief that brings me."

He pulled her close and held her until all of her tears were spent. She left him then, preferring to return to the castle in search of a distraction. Alone in the garden, he spent some time contemplating his new reality. He'd always wanted a life's purpose and thought he would need to go out and find one as a second son. Instead, a purpose had found him as a result of his brother's untimely death. Inheriting a dukedom was the epitome of a purpose, entrusting him with a duty to generations of Elliots. While Aiden seemed to be questioning everything else in his life, he knew one thing for certain: he would fulfill the duty bequeathed to him.

Chapter Two

April 1812

In early April 1812, the Elliot family, with the exception of Matilda, sailed to London on *The Aether* to prepare for the Season. It took more than a day to reach it, but when they did, Elliot House stood tall and magnificent in Jacobean style on the Strand, just as Aiden had remembered it.

On his first full day in residence, Aiden attended to business in the study formerly used by his brother. Even though he'd resigned himself to fulfilling his duty to his family, the logistics of it grated on him. It seemed to be of the utmost importance that his father retired as planned. He scrawled his name on a letter and sighed. It wasn't that he resented his family's plans; it was just that Ferdy had been raised with them in mind, whereas he had not. While he was excelling at managing the estates thus far, it still felt as though he was under a crushing amount of pressure.

A hard knock sounded at the door, which caused Aiden to look up from his desk. He watched as his grandmother pushed the door open with the end of her cane and entered the study as if it was her right. "Granny." He stood and walked around the desk to greet her. When he reached her side, she looked up and carefully took his measure.

"I wanted to talk with you about our upcoming social engagements," she said, taking a seat in one of the comfortable armchairs.

"What makes it so pertinent that we must discuss it now?" Aiden asked, sitting in the straight-backed chair across from her. "I'm tending to estate business." He gestured to his desk and the papers that littered it. "We can discuss your plans after dinner."

"We are here to get you a wife, not so that you can hide away with your papers and books!" Rowena chastised his suggestion. "Need I remind you that your position as heir depends on you marrying and siring a son? Furthermore, you will need a wife to guide you through Society as your hostess, so I need to see that you are taking this seriously."

"Granny, I promise you that I am," Aiden said in earnest, if only because the faster he found a suitable wife, the faster he'd have his grandmother off his back and one duty in hand.

"See that you are." She huffed. "The first invitations have started arriving, so we must plan our week accordingly." She took out a large piece of paper from her bag and laid it out on her lap. "Now then, tomorrow we'll have Countess Grey's *al fresco* luncheon followed by Viscountess Torrington's ball in the evening. Thursday will be Lady Jersey's afternoon tea and then the Duchess of Rutland's ball. Friday afternoon will be Lady Paxton's afternoon tea and then the weekend is full of coming-out balls. Friday evening is the coming-out ball for Viscount Keith's youngest daughter; Saturday evening will be the same for the Earl of Devon's daughter; and then Sunday night will be the Duchess of Richmond's ball."

Aiden let his grandmother's words wash over him as she prattled on about this tea or that ball. He pinched the bridge of his nose, feeling a headache coming on. Finally, when Rowena seemed to reach the end of her list of engagements, she looked at her grandson expectantly.

"Granny." He smiled tightly and tried to think of a way to word his dispute to avoid offending his dear grandmother. "Do you really think it's necessary for me to attend the afternoon engagements? The only women in attendance will be those aspiring debutantes, and I cannot imagine any will interest me."

"How will you know until you meet them?"

He shook his head. "They'll be too young."

"That just shows that you should have married years ago," she said, forgetting the war he had been taking part in. "Anybody older worth marrying will already be married or widowed. Unless you want a spinster, which you should be careful of since they might not be able to bear an heir due to their age."

Aiden leaned toward her to offer a diplomatic negotiation. "I can agree to attend the balls since there will be a wider selection at those, but not the luncheons and teas."

Rowena squinted at her grandson. "You will escort me to every afternoon tea and luncheon until you begin courting your future wife. Then you can spend your afternoons calling upon her and walking or riding through the park together. I expect I make myself clear?"

"Yes, Granny." His shoulders slumped as he exhaled deeply. There was no fighting with her; she was a force to be reckoned with and always had been. "Now, if you'll excuse me, I really must try to clear my desk before dinner."

Rowena released him with a nod and then reached for her cane to stand, exiting the study in much the same way she'd entered. After running his fingers through his hair, Aiden returned to his desk but had a hard time concentrating on his work. Despite what his granny potentially thought, he wanted to marry quickly, even prior to the end of the Season if possible. Marriage, to him, seemed like the easiest task he'd been given, not like estate management and investment. So regardless of the meeting he'd just had, he was hopeful for the week to come. He was a wealthy, titled gentleman; how hard could finding a bride be?

Chapter Three

Lynette Elphinstone closed her eyes and enjoyed the warm sun on her face as she sipped her tea in Lady Paxton's garden. A soft breeze blew her brown curls as she tried to let her mother's and sister's chatter fade into the background.

Her sister, Kathleen, swiveled across from her. "Who's that?"

"That's Lord Fenn, the Baron of Southampton," replied her mother, Viscountess Keith.

"Oh." Kathleen's lip curled, but her leg kept jiggling. "Why aren't there more gentlemen here?"

Lady Keith placed a calming hand on her younger daughter's leg. "It's still early in the Season."

Lynette opened her eyes. "Even at the height of the Season, these events aren't heavily attended by gentlemen."

Lady Keith's nostrils flared, and Lynette closed her eyes once more.

"Well there better be more gentlemen at my ball tonight." Kathleen sat back and crossed her arms over her chest. "I'm ready to make a match, Mama."

"And you will," Lady Keith said. "As long as you sit

up straight and act as a lady should."

Lynette could see the pointed look her mother directed toward her through her eyelashes. She sighed. "I'm going to take a turn around the garden, Mama."

"Just don't be gone too long," Lady Keith said with pursed lips.

Left to her own devices, Lynette went to admire the surroundings, even though she'd seen them all before. Lady Paxton kept a beautiful garden, and while it wasn't big by country standards, it was truly an oasis in the capital. She followed the path that led to the orangery and smiled when she noticed the doors had been left open. The aroma of exotic plants and fruits filled her as she entered the glass structure. She breathed deeply, savoring the scent as she strolled, and the closer she got to the exit, the less she wanted to leave. Spying a ripe peach, she looked over her shoulder to make sure she was truly alone before plucking it from its stem. She brought it to her lips, bit into it, and moaned as the sweetness filled her mouth.

"I presume it's good then?" asked a deep voice from behind her. Lynette turned, wide-eyed, heat rising from her neck to her cheeks. A gently bred gentleman who must have descended directly from the Norman conquerors stood before her. He was tall, with long legs and broad shoulders. His eyes, which were the color of the sea, stared intently at her while his dark-brown hair only helped to accentuate his perfect face. But the thing that startled her most in his presence was that he wasn't a young gentleman. Of course he was nowhere near her father's age, but he also wasn't so young as to be trailing behind his mother's skirts like the ones she'd seen at Lady Paxton's tea. She thought a gentleman of his age and ilk should be at one of his London clubs and not sneaking up behind her in an orangery.

"I thought I was alone," Lynette replied with her only line of defense.

The man smiled teasingly and took a step toward her. "If that's the case, I must remember to never leave you alone with my peaches."

She took a step back. "I can assure you, my good sir, that your peaches will never be in danger from me." She tilted her chin up, ready to turn on her heel, but the look on the man's face held her in her place. His lips had parted, and his head had fallen to the side. Crisp blue eyes met her brown ones, and she suppressed a shiver. Deciding she shouldn't dally any longer for fear that her mother would notice an extended absence, she turned to leave but was once again caught by the gentleman when she heard him softly say, "What is your name?"

Lynette paused and breathed deeply before looking over her shoulder at him.

"We haven't been properly introduced," she replied and then dashed out of the orangery, leaving Aiden Elliot wondering who the only woman in London to not know him on sight was.

It had been a trying two days—two and a half, to be more precise, since Aiden's presence at Lady Paxton's tea was nearly at an end. Ever since his grandmother had insisted that he accompany her to Society's afternoon events, he'd been bombarded by mothers and their marriageable daughters. He couldn't quite believe how quickly word had spread that he was in the market for a wife and was now the heir to a dukedom. But on the other hand, he thought it likely that it had all been his grandmother's doing since she was acting like an army general embarking on a battle.

But all the ladies touted in front of him thus far were just as he expected, too young. They were fresh out of the schoolroom and knew nothing about the world around them. They had no ability to talk about anything other than their accomplishments and the weather. Furthermore, it was obvious they didn't want him; they wanted his title, a title he hadn't had nearly six months prior. He wanted to laugh at his naïve assumption that money and a title could be used as an advantage in his endeavor to secure a wife. The truth was that being the heir to a wealthy and prominent dukedom bore no advantages. In contrast, it only seemed to bring out the worst in the women around him.

But then he laid eyes upon her. The one woman who hadn't had any inkling who he was. She hadn't spoken to him like he was a future duke, but as a man; a man who startled her in an orangery. The way her eyes caressed him from his head to his toes. He could tell she'd been curious about his age and appearance at the event. That was just as well because once he found her again, his attendance at afternoon teas would be limited once more.

Chapter Four

"The viscount has two daughters; tonight's ball is for the Honorable Miss Kathleen Elphinstone who is the youngest and coming out," Rowena said to Aiden as they waited in the receiving line later that evening. "While she would make you a fine match, there will be countless other ladies present for you to choose from."

Aiden scanned the guests surrounding them. He couldn't care less who Miss Kathleen was unless she was his sylph from earlier. The moniker seemed fitting, based on the way she'd flitted out of the glasshouse, not to be seen for the rest of Lady Paxton's party. He'd tried to describe her to his granny to garner a quicker introduction but was informed that at least half of the ladies in London fit the description. As they moved closer to their host and hostess, he had his first glimpse of the ballroom. It was still early in the Season, but the ball looked well attended, and he could only hope that his sylph was among them.

"Her Grace, the Dowager Duchess of Northumberland and Earl Elliot," the butler announced. The viscount and viscountess bowed and curtsied, as did the young lady by the viscountess's side.

"If you'll allow me to present my daughter, the

Honorable Miss Kathleen Elphinstone." Lady Keith gestured to the young lady to her left. Kathleen wore the traditional white frock that most debutantes wore for their coming out and was one of the lucky young ladies to have the color complement her dark-brown curls. Aiden smiled and bowed while Kathleen curtsied. The young girl was beautiful with hazel eyes and an oval face, but she was also too young, and therefore, Aiden didn't have any inclination to make a match with her.

"Now then, find me a place to sit—oh look, there's a spot right there next to Lady Paxton. Hello, my dear." Rowena took her place next to her friend and touched cheeks with her. "Now, Aiden, you can make your rounds. I expect a full report by the end of the night."

"That's assuming I make it through the night," he said through gritted teeth.

"What did you say, my boy?" his granny asked with raised eyebrows.

"Nothing, Granny." He bent to kiss her cheek before starting his promenade of the ballroom. It didn't take long for him to find an old Eton friend, Dominic Vane, the Earl of Wiltshire, or the future Marquess of Winchester.

"Here to do your duty?" Dominic asked with a smirk after they'd become reacquainted.

"I'd take this over one of those afternoon teas my granny has been dragging me to."

Dominic chuckled. "There's no one at those save the blooming chits."

Aiden shrugged as he sipped his champagne. "Maybe, maybe not."

"Oh?" Dominic raised an eyebrow. "Know something I don't, Elliot?"

He shook his head. "It's too soon to tell." The truth

was, he knew nothing about his sylph except for her face. She could already be married, or worse, be another title-hungry debutante once they were properly introduced. "You'll be the second to know if I do."

Dominic grinned. "Second only to your granny, I take it."

"Of course, anything to get her claws out of my back."

"Then I'll introduce you to the ladies I know. That should earn me some points with her."

"She'll surely be forever in your debt," Aiden replied sardonically and fell into step with him.

Together, the men made the rounds of the ballroom, winding their way in and out of circles, chatting. As time wore on, Aiden began to think his sylph really was a spirit. Then finally, after what seemed like forever, he saw her.

"Vane, tell me, do you know the lady in green standing next to Miss Kathleen?" Aiden asked his friend. From a distance, his eyes roamed her body. He could tell she was some years older than the other ladies and gentlemen of the group because she was wearing a deep green gown and not the pale colors of a debutante. He took a minute to admire her beauty and how her skin seemed to glow in the candlelight.

"She's her elder sister, the Honorable Miss Lynette Elphinstone."

"Unmarried?"

"Been out nearly ten years, I believe." Dominic nodded. "Is she who you've been looking for?"

"Introduce me, and we shall find out," Aiden replied. Dominic looked like he wanted to respond differently, but instead led him through the crush to the Misses Elphinstones' circle.

"Lady Catherine, Lady Mary, Miss Kathleen, and Miss Elphinstone." Dominic greeted the ladies at the center of the circle and then gestured to his friend. "Have you been made known to my friend, Lord Elliot?"

"Lovely to meet you ladies." Aiden bowed to the group as a whole before coming face to face with his sylph. He stepped toward her and met her eye. "Miss Elphinstone, lovely to see you again."

Lynette's breath caught in her throat as Lord Wiltshire and Lord Elliot joined her sister's group of friends. His eyes danced as he invaded her space, a smug smirk playing on his lips. Despite her hammering heart, she forced herself to smile and curtsy appropriately. "A pleasure to make your acquaintance, milord."

"Milord, please let me express my deepest sympathies regarding your brother," Lady Catherine Pole said once introductions were concluded.

Aiden offered her a tight-lipped smile. "Thank you."

"I'm sure it must be hard to step into his shoes." Kathleen moved toward him. "Why, to inherit a dukedom after so long of not expecting such a thing . . ." The young miss suddenly broke off her speech when she noticed the horror on everyone's faces. "I'm sorry, that was rude of me to say." She took a step back, hung her head, and found a scuff on the floor she could stare at instead of the people around her.

"It's quite all right, Miss Kathleen. I'd rather you say such things to my face than behind my back, as so many have been doing," Aiden said in an attempt to brush off the young woman's words. But after a moment of awkward silence, he concluded that his dismissal of Kathleen's faux pas hadn't been accepted by her peers, so he decided to underscore it with a kind gesture. "Would you do me the honor of partnering with me in a country dance?"

Her eyes lit up. "Of course, milord." She held out her dance card for him to view.

Aiden's eyes widened when he saw it was relatively full. He penciled in his name, but his stomach rolled when he considered what her sister's card looked like. When he straightened, he noticed the other two ladies' longing expressions. "And you, Lady Catherine? Would you like to pair with me for a cotillion?"

She bounced on the balls of her feet. "It would be my honor, milord."

"Is the same suitable for you, Lady Mary?" Aiden asked.

She offered him her dance card. "Cotillions are my favorite dance."

Aiden swallowed and claimed the dance. Finally free to do so, he turned to the object of his desire. "I assume you have permission to waltz, Miss Elphinstone?" He reached for her dance card before she had the chance to extend it herself.

"I have." Lynette breathed the words no louder than a whisper.

"Please save the before-supper waltz for me then." Aiden exhaled and wrote his name in the empty space. "Until then, ladies." He smiled at the four women, but his gaze lingered slightly longer on Lynette before he and Dominic walked away.

"Lynette!" Catherine exclaimed with wide eyes as soon as they were out of earshot. "Lord Elliot asked you to waltz!"

"If only I had permission to waltz," Kathleen said wistfully.

Catherine's eyes narrowed at her friend. "Kathleen, it's

a miracle he asked you to dance at all after you had said such things about his brother's death and his inheriting the title."

Lynette's eyes followed Lord Elliot's head as it faded into the crowd. She wasn't concerned with her sister's blunder since they both had the innate ability to put their foot in their mouth. Her skin flushed when she thought of how harshly she dismissed Lord Elliot earlier in the day. If her mother knew she'd met a gentleman without her, let alone given him the cut direct, she'd swoon. She ran her palms over her skirt and turned back to the group. What her mother didn't know wouldn't hurt her.

"Maybe he wishes to court you, Lynette," Catherine said.

She shook her head. "We've just met and have barely spoken."

Kathleen glared at her sister. "He said it was lovely to see you again!"

Lynette waved her hand dismissively. "We met briefly at Lady Paxton's but were not formally introduced."

"You know as well as I that the length of time you've known each other doesn't matter," Mary Courtenay said. "Maybe you made an impression."

Lynette rolled her eyes.

"Mother said he's actively looking for a wife." Kathleen faced her sister. "His family wants him to marry with all possible haste to keep the dukedom securely within the Elliot family."

Lynette sighed exasperatedly. "He asked us all to dance."

"Yes, but he asked only you to waltz," Catherine said with a pointed look.

Lynette lifted her chin. "Probably because I'm the only

one among you with permission to."

But Kathleen and her friends remained unconvinced, and Lynette didn't get any reprieve from their incessant chattering until the dancing began. She watched as her sister moved around the floor, brown curls bobbing along to the music, a smile illuminating her face. She remembered the excitement of her first Season, thinking it would be her opportunity to find love. With a scoff, she looked away. One did not find love during the Season; they found connections.

Lynette saw her friend, Lady Teresa Palhem, the Earl of Chichester's daughter, in the crowd and walked over to her. "Are we allowed to accept the title of spinster yet?"

Teresa shrugged. "I accepted the title last year."

Lynette scowled. "That's because you don't have a mother bent on marrying you off."

"Do you think she'll be as insistent this year?"

"Potentially," Lynette replied. "She has Kathleen to worry about now, so at least all of her attention won't be focused on me."

"Have you been to the bookstore yet?" Teresa asked, changing the subject.

"No," Lynette replied. "I haven't been allowed while preparing for Kathleen's come-out ball. Have you?"

Teresa shook her head. "We only just arrived a few days ago, so I haven't had the chance. I plan to go tomorrow if you want to come with me."

"I'll have to check with my mother." Lynette didn't keep track of the time while talking to Teresa, preferring to lose herself in the conversation. There was a lot for them to catch up on since they hadn't seen each other in nearly a year, so it wasn't until a warm hand caught her elbow that she realized the melody of the music.

"Miss Elphinstone," Aiden said in a low voice. "I believe this is our dance."

Her stomach fluttered like fingers over the keys of a pianoforte. "After you, milord." She took his arm and allowed him to lead her onto the dance floor while her heart fought its way out of her chest. She couldn't understand her reaction to him and thought it had to be because of her mistake in meeting him so casually in Lady Paxton's glasshouse. Surely once she'd apologized, his presence wouldn't cause her heart to beat so quickly. She met his eye as the waltz began. "I'm sorry, milord. When you startled me in Lady Paxton's orangery, I did not address you properly and took my leave rather rudely."

"How can you apologize when you hadn't known the correct way to address me at the time?" Aiden asked, his blue eyes glinting.

Lynette dipped her head and looked at him through her eyelashes. "Still, 'tis my mistake."

"In all truth, I'm not quite used to my new title, so it doesn't bother me when it isn't used."

"Yes . . . I can see how that would be." She nodded thoughtfully. "Are you used to waltzing at such affairs?" she asked, daring to change the subject. The waltz had only just begun, and she had an overwhelming urge to fill the air between them.

"Here and there. I've tried my very best to stay away from the marriage mart until now."

"That's understandable. I'd stay away if I was able." Her cheeks flushed as soon as the words left her mouth, and she silently cursed herself.

"You do not wish to get married?" He arched a brow. "I thought it was every young woman's dream."

Lynette grimaced. "I'm sorry, milord. Forget I said—"

"No, Miss Elphinstone, please humor me." Aiden smiled and tried to meet her eye, but she was determined to look anywhere but at him. "Forgive me, but from what little I know of you, you seem able to speak your mind."

She snorted and finally turned to face him. "That is the rub, though, milord, as men do not want a wife who speaks her mind. According to my mama, I read far too much and am far too smart for my own good. Her dearest hope was to marry me off before I got too set in my own ways and became a spinster. Also, as the eldest daughter, my parents expected me to make an advantageous match to pave the way for my younger sister. If that wasn't enough, as my father has no son, I am to inherit his Scottish barony and am therefore expected to make a match that will extend the family connections." Lynette paused in her explanation to purse her lips. "Obviously I have not lived up to such expectations."

Aiden swallowed, his lips flattening into a straight line. "Family expectations are hard to live up to."

She looked up at him, and the words tumbled out of her mouth. "If anybody would understand, I daresay it would be you." When they reached her ears, she hung her head and bit her tongue. "Milord—"

"Please, Miss Elphinstone, the truth does not necessitate an apology." Aiden wanted to ask her to marry him then and there but suppressed the urge in favor of something a little more appropriate. "Will you allow me to escort you to supper?"

Lynette exhaled until there was no wind left in her lungs. "I'm supposed to be supporting my sister."

"She's heading to supper as well." Aiden discretely pointed to Kathleen across the ballroom on the arm of a gentleman. Lady Keith followed closely behind them, acting as an attentive chaperone.

Lynette bit her cheek. "All right then." She offered him her hand, and they walked to supper with every eye on them.

Aiden couldn't say what food he ate, but it was the most enjoyable meal he'd ever had. He and Lynette spent the time conversing over a number of topics, and by the end, he was sure his instincts were correct. She was smart, maybe even more knowledgeable than some men, and beautiful. Yes, she was older, but that was exactly what he'd expected of his future wife. As for her family, they were wealthy and titled, so he knew he wouldn't get any resistance from his granny in that regard.

"May I call on you tomorrow afternoon?" he asked when guests started filing out of the dining room. They followed along near the rear of the queue.

"Why?" Lynette asked, the word as light as air. Despite her initial reservations, she'd had a remarkably good time with him. But did that mean she should extend their acquaintance to another day?

Aiden cocked his head to the side. "To take you for a drive in the park."

But Lynette still hesitated. A drive in the park was a rather public declaration of interest. Did it mean that he intended to court her? And if so, to what end?

"Miss Elphinstone?" he asked, his mouth suddenly dry.

She nodded jerkily. "Yes, all right."

He bowed over her hand and left her at the side of the dance floor. She watched as he navigated his way through the crowd to where Lady Paxton and another older, matronly type of lady sat.

Once at his granny's side, Aiden leaned in to whisper in her ear. "I have made my choice." The declaration put

My Duty To You

some sprite into Rowena's step as she rose from her chair, leaving behind a very interested Lady Paxton.

She narrowed her eyes at him. "I saw you waltzing with the elder Elphinstone girl."

"I believe she'll make a fine duchess in time," he said, alluding to his intentions.

She sucked in her lips, the wheels turning in her mind. "Yes," she finally said. "I believe she will."

Chapter Five

Lynette descended the stairs of her family's London town house the morning after Kathleen's come-out ball, still reeling from her encounter with Lord Elliot. The whole thing was like a dream, from the moment they met to his interest in calling on her. A small smile tugged at the corners of her mouth as she filled her plate to break her fast. Content with her selections, she had just sat down to enjoy her meal when Kathleen burst into the dining room.

"Have you seen?!" she asked, her chest heaving with every breath.

Lynette continued to butter her toast. "Seen what?"

Without warning, Kathleen grabbed Lynette's arm and dragged her from her chair and breakfast. "The morning room!"

Lynette sighed and tried to reclaim her arm. "Kathleen, couldn't this wait until I have finished my breakfast?"

"Look!" She flung open the doors to the front morning room. Instantly, Lynette could understand her sister's excitement. There were flowers absolutely everywhere, with not a single surface left empty. Mr. Williams, the family's butler, looked frazzled as he held yet another arrangement in his hands, obviously trying to find a place for it.

Lynette's mouth fell open. "Are they all . . ."

"For me? Yes," Kathleen said with a wide-toothed grin and puffed-out chest. "I've been waiting for you to awaken so that you could see!"

And see she did. Lynette walked around the room admiring all the arrangements, which varied in size and shape. Almost every flower one could imagine filled the room, and they gave the room a fresh floral scent that overwhelmed her. Kathleen continued to bounce as she went to look at the cards attached to each of the bouquets. All of them had been sent by a gentleman who'd shown interest in Kathleen the night before, and Lynette tried not to be disappointed that she hadn't had the same treatment in her debutante year.

"Mr. Williams?" Lynette's maid, Milly, beckoned at the door with a footman beside her. "There's another, I'm afraid."

"Another?" both Lynette and Kathleen asked with varying degrees of surprise and excitement. In response, Milly pushed the door open more to reveal a massive flower arrangement that required two footmen to carry.

"We'll have to start putting them in the other reception room." Mr. Williams led the group out of the morning room. Once in the adjacent room, the footmen put the towering display down. Kathleen then took the opportunity to have a look at the card attached to it since it would tell her which of her would-be suitors the arrangement was from.

Kathleen's smile faltered. "They're not for me."

"Then who are they for?" Lynette asked, unable to keep her voice from trembling.

Kathleen shoved the card into her sister's hands. "Look, 'tis your name on the card."

Lynette peeled open the envelope and read the enclosed note.

Let's take a ride around Hyde Park, about one o'clock.
—Lord Elliot

"Lord Elliot?" Kathleen peered over her sister's shoulder. "As in Earl Elliot, the heir to the Duke of Northumberland?"

Lynette swallowed and set the card aside. "There isn't another one, I presume."

"The future Duke of Northumberland is courting you?!" Kathleen's eyes were as wide as saucers. "With all the luck." She dropped onto a chaise to pout. "The moment I come out, you are courted by the most eligible bachelor in all of Britain! My wedding will surely be overlooked now."

"Isn't it a little early to be talking about a wedding? Don't you need a gentleman courting you first?" Lynette asked. "Furthermore, Lord Elliot is not courting me."

"But he is if he's asking you to ride in Hyde Park with him!" Kathleen was aghast. "Mama, tell her she's obviously being courted!"

"It would appear so," Lady Keith said as she stood at the door about to make her entrance. "Oh, Kathleen, you don't know how much it pleases me that you have so many suitors." She held her younger daughter's hands and smiled and then turned to her eldest daughter. "Lynette, I daresay your sister is right; Lord Elliot seems to have the intention of courting you." She pursed her lips before continuing. "And your father and I would like it if you'd give him a chance to do so."

"I shall do my best not to ruin this minor miracle." Lynette resisted the urge to roll her eyes, knowing it would ruin whatever goodwill her mother had for her. "Would it be all right if I went to the bookstore with Teresa?"

"I want you to try your hand at your needlework first," Lady Keith replied.

"Thank you, Mama." Lynette hurried away before her mother could change her mind. After scribbling a quick note to Teresa, saying she'd meet her at the bookshop in a few hours, she returned to her breakfast. She ate quickly, and once her hunger was satiated, she turned her attention to her embroidery. It didn't take long for her to become frustrated that her lines would never be straight, but in the end, she had sufficient work to show her mother, who was content with it enough to allow her to take her pin money and maid to the bookstore.

Going to the bookshop in London was always the highlight of the Season for Lynette since the Temple of the Muses was a booklover's paradise. The shop was immense with multiple floors and carried the best selection of books in London. She breathed deeply upon entering the store, savoring the smell of paper and ink, before starting her stroll through the bookshelves.

Her love of reading first came through poetry, but in recent years, she'd begun to delve into novels. Having first discovered *The Mysteries of Udolpho*, she subsequently read every other novel published by the famous Ann Radcliffe and wished every day that the author would publish another. Until that magical day came, though, she needed another novel to sate her hunger. Her fingers caressed the spines of the books as she walked up and down the aisles.

"Find anything interesting yet?" Teresa asked, appearing before her.

Lynette picked a book off the shelf and opened it. "I've only just arrived."

Teresa did the same. "Your sister's ball went well then?"

Lynette frowned but didn't look up from the novel. "A florist has moved into our morning room."

"Flowers are overrated," Teresa said. "All they do is die after a couple of days."

Lynette shrugged and reshelved her selection, not enamored with the content. She moved down a different aisle but continued the conversation. "I received flowers as well." There was a thud, and then Teresa was in front of her once more. Lynette studied the shelves, unable to meet her friend's steely gaze.

"It's unlikely he's looking for love, you know."

"I know." Lynette nodded jerkily. "But he wasn't put off by my candidness yesterday, and he even asked to call on me."

"I'll admit, that does sound like a good sign." Teresa sighed. "But I'd hate for you to get your hopes up."

Lynette ran her hands down her skirt and then reached for another book. Suddenly, her expression softened. "Look at this. It's new."

Teresa tsked at her friend's change of subject but leaned in nonetheless.

The novel was titled *Sense and Sensibility*, and the premise captured their attention easily. Lynette would have liked to stay and read some of it with Teresa, but she knew her mother expected her home to prepare for Lord Elliot's arrival. So she paid for the book and then returned to her carriage, where she began to read on the ride home. The first chapter hooked her, and she went on to read the second. Soon she was aghast that a son could revoke a deathbed promise because of a wife's persuasion and intrigued by Elinor's feelings for Edward. She also began to appreciate Elinor's sensible nature and Marianne's romanticism, characteristics that she thought she possessed herself. But before she could get too entrenched in the story, a footman pulled open the carriage door, signaling her return home.

Upon entering her house, Lady Keith instructed Lynette to get changed for her outing with Lord Elliot so she wouldn't keep him waiting when he arrived. Once changed into a smart-looking walking gown, she rejoined her family for luncheon where Kathleen babbled about which gentlemen she hoped would call upon her in the afternoon.

Aiden pulled his phaeton up in front of Viscount Keith's town house at exactly one o'clock. Stepping down, he handed his horses off to the footman and then climbed the steps to the front door, which the butler opened promptly.

He gave the butler his card. "Lord Elliot for the Honorable Miss Lynette Elphinstone."

"If you'll follow me this way, milord." The butler bowed and led him to the front reception room, where Lady Keith, Lynette, and Kathleen were waiting.

"Lord Elliot for Miss Elphinstone," Mr. Williams announced before allowing Aiden to step through.

"Lady Keith, Miss Kathleen, and Miss Elphinstone, it's a pleasure to see you all again." He bowed over the matron's hand first, Kathleen's second, and Lynette's last so he could let his fingers linger on hers. Then as he turned, he saw the flower arrangement he'd picked out for Lynette and decided to address it. "I hope the flowers I sent were to your taste. If not, you may tell me your favorite so I can send it to you at a later date."

Lynette smiled and met his piercing blue eyes. "They're beautiful."

"They're bigger than all the arrangements I received," Kathleen said before her mother could stop her.

"That should put your suitors on notice." Aiden laughed at the young lady's quip. "If it's all right with you, Lady Keith, I'd like to take Miss Elphinstone for a ride in my phaeton."

"Of course, I'm sure she'd be honored." She turned to her daughter. "Lynette, get your bonnet and Milly to go with you."

"I shall meet you outside," Aiden said. "It was a pleasure to see both of you." He bowed again to Miss Kathleen and Lady Keith, who curtsied in return.

Lynette went directly to her room and rang for Milly, who was already waiting in anticipation of Lord Elliot's arrival. The two women then descended the stairs and went out the door that Mr. Williams held open for them. Lord Elliot was waiting beside his phaeton and assisted Lynette in the front and Milly in the back before stepping up himself and taking the horses in hand. Then with a flick of his wrists, they were off toward Hyde Park. The weather was mild with spring sunshine to keep them warm, and they rode the distance to the park in a companionable silence.

"Do you enjoy spending the Season in London?" Aiden asked as they started their slow drive around the park.

"I enjoy having access to a major bookshop here

in London," Lynette said, thinking about her recent acquisition. "But I think I prefer the freedom of the country." She shrugged. "They both have their benefits, so it's nice to be able to enjoy them evenly, I suppose."

"I must admit I actually missed London while on the Continent," Aiden said, deciding it was wise to broach the subject of his time there with the woman he intended to wed.

"You were on the Continent?" she asked, unable to keep the curiosity out of her tone.

He nodded with a gleam in his eye. "Aye, you remember I used to be a mere second son."

"I know, but I just assumed . . . your family is wealthy and powerful; shouldn't you have been secure even as the second son?"

"I would have been. I wouldn't have inherited any land, but my father would have granted me an annuity, which I could have lived on. But I wanted to make a way for myself, separate from the family coffers." He looked at her out of the corner of his eye, hoping she might understand. His parents hadn't understood his thirst for more, and his granny had been expressly against buying his commission.

She nodded as she turned the information over in her head. "Was it as terrible as everyone says?"

"War is always terrible, but usually worse than what the general public will say about it," Aiden replied. "Fighting for king and country, while never a passion, was indeed a means to an end."

"Of course," Lynette said. "Just like how marriage is a means to an end for you now." She arched a brow and waited for him to either confirm or deny it.

"I suppose you could look at it that way." He shrugged,

not having thought of it in such a way before. Marriage wouldn't exactly advance him personally, but it would advance his family and the Elliot name. "I hadn't given marriage much thought until now, but I suppose I always expected it to be an eventuality." In a world where his brother hadn't died, he would have come home after the war with a name of his own, which meant the need for succession; the only real difference for him was the time frame.

Lynette huffed. "That's because old bachelors aren't thought of in the same way as spinsters." Marriage could never be considered a woman's eventuality because once they reached a certain age, everyone assumed they were no longer wanted. If she truly wanted to be married, she had to do it soon, and really, the sooner the better for women of marriageable age.

But that was the ultimate question: did she want to marry? Her parents expected her to marry, and at one point it might have been her dearest wish, but then somewhere along the lines, marriage lost its appeal. Her mother thought it was the books she read, and maybe that was true. In fiction, love and marriage went hand in hand, but in reality, love matches didn't have a place in Society yet. Some took place, but they were almost always exceptions to the rule. Most gentlemen still wanted a marriage of convenience: a woman who brought connections, a good dowry, and the ability to beget an heir.

"It really doesn't seem fair, does it?" Aiden said, unable to come up with a better response. "Men can wait to choose their brides, while women have little choice in either."

"Men are lucky in that way as well." She stared at their surroundings, unseeing. "At this point, I'm sure my mother would insist I accept the first gentleman who offers for me."

The idea turned Aiden cold. "Why?" He halted his horses for a moment on the grass under a tree where he thought they could stop and talk before he took her home.

She turned and blinked at him. "Why what?"

"Why would your mother insist you accept the first man who asks?"

"Oh, because I am nearly seven and twenty," she said as if it was the most obvious thing in the world. "If my mother can avoid me becoming a full-fledged spinster, then she surely would. Which would mean me accepting the first acceptable gentleman who asked."

"Would I be acceptable?" Aiden leaned toward her, deciding to play his hand. If he couldn't choose the timing of his marriage, he planned to at least choose the bride since it felt like the only thing left within his control. Lynette had been the first woman he'd met to move him in such a way. Therefore he wanted her; anyone else simply wouldn't do.

Lynette's eyes widened, and even Milly couldn't help but gasp from her spot at the back of the phaeton. "What kind of question is that?"

"A serious one," he replied. He might have been acting too forward, but he refused to lose his chance to a man hastier than him.

"Are you offering for me?"

"Would you accept?"

Lynette looked upward thoughtfully, then sighed. "I suppose I would have to."

Aiden remained silent because it wasn't the response he wanted. He wanted her to want him in the same way he wanted her, freely and without family or societal pressure.

"I think 'tis time that you take me home, milord." She focused on her gloved hands. Whatever hopes she had of Lord Elliot's potential dwindled as soon as it was clear she would be the same as the war once was—a means to an end. His family expected him to marry, and quickly, according to the gossips, so he found the first acceptable woman to offer for. He wasn't interested in her; he was interested in fulfilling family expectations, and she was simply a woman who could beget him an heir. Thus she was being offered a marriage of convenience, and if she had the choice, she'd prefer no marriage at all to a marriage without love.

"Miss Elphinstone, I hope you didn't find me too forward." Aiden pulled at his cravat, which had suddenly become too tight. "I'm sure you are aware I am in London for the Season in search of a wife at my family's behest."

"I am." She inclined her head without meeting his gaze.

"And given how well we have been getting on, I assumed you would appreciate my courting you."

She lifted her head and straightened her spine. "I'd prefer you wouldn't."

"Whyever not?" he asked, taken aback. He believed himself to be a handsome man, and despite originally being born a second son he was now heir, which gave him access to money and land. So what, then, could be the reason for her rejection?

"Because as I just told you, I'd likely have to accept your suit."

He frowned, his jaw tight. "And that would be so terrible?" Why wouldn't she accept his suit? It made no sense because, from his perspective, everything had been going so well between them.

"Milord, you are in need of a wife whereas, contrary to my mother's belief, I am in no need of a husband. I have lived out nine Seasons to realize that gentlemen such as yourself do not require a specific woman. All you need is a titled, connected woman who can beget you an heir and be your hostess. While I am likely capable of all those things, it is not something I want to be. Thus, yes, accepting your suit would be terrible to me because I would be filling a role any woman could fill."

"So by your estimation, I could have any woman I wanted?"

Lynette inclined her head. "Indeed."

"Then I want you," Aiden declared.

"Why?" she asked, finally turning to face him. Their eyes locked in a clash of wills, daring the other to yield. "You've already witnessed how my words get the better of me, and I'm not at all accomplished." She ticked off all the reasons only a handful of suitors had come calling over the years. "I disdain needlepoint and have no patience for the pianoforte. So, likewise, are my singing and watercolors. Truly, the only interest I possess is reading. So tell me, milord, one thing I can offer you that no other woman can."

"You intrigue me."

Lynette laughed. "You have found no other woman intriguing since returning to London?"

"Not in the same way you are."

"How endearing." She continued to smile. "To be so differently intriguing that I garner a marriage suit."

Aiden smiled despite himself. When put that way it did sound ludicrous. But what else was he supposed to say? There was no logical reason for him to set his cap on her and not some other young woman, except for the fact that she was somehow different from all the rest. "Most young ladies want to marry me based upon the title I so recently inherited. Those same young ladies, and their mothers, likely wouldn't be as interested in me if I was still the second son."

"Maybe you don't have it much different from me then," Lynette said, her tone much softer. Again, their eyes met, and Aiden had to resist the urge to place his lips upon hers. Then, as if sensing the heat burning between them, she turned away and fiddled with the lace on her glove. "I really should be returning home, milord."

He flicked his wrists, and the horses started off again. As they made their way through the streets, he thought of what words to use when parting. Too soon, they were back at the Keiths' residence, and Aiden passed the reins off to a footman so he could be the one to help Lynette down.

"Allow me to court you," he said, his eyebrows meeting in the middle of his forehead.

"Milord—"

"Please." He met her eye. "Allow me to show you that you are the one I seek."

Lynette wanted to refuse him at first, but then he added the last remark, and she couldn't anymore. If he wanted to prove that she was special and not just a means to an end, then she was powerless to stop him. "Yes, all right." She granted her permission with an incline of her head.

Aiden smiled and released a breath before walking her to the door, where he bowed and kissed her hand.

Chapter Six

Nine o'clock the next morning, Aiden knocked on the Keiths' door again, only this time to see Lord Keith. Aiden originally expected a marriage of convenience, but after their conversation in the park, he realized Lynette wanted a love match. Therefore, he had two choices: he could simply offer for her, and she'd likely be forced to accept, which would see them married well before the end of the Season and would put a smile on his granny's face, or he could give Lynette what she wanted and court her properly. He decided it didn't matter to him *when* he married as much as it mattered *whom* he married. Therefore, he was going to make her fall in love with him. He'd spend the time wooing her, seducing her, making her want him as much as he wanted her, and when the time was right, he'd propose to her, and she'd accept because she found the love she'd been searching for. The only thing he had to do was ensure she was still free to accept his proposal when he made it, and that involved gaining the permission of her father.

"Lord Elliot to see Lord Keith," Aiden told the butler when he opened the door.

"Certainly, milord." Mr. Williams bowed and took his

hat and walking stick. "If you'll just wait in the reception room while I determine if he's available."

Aiden did as the butler directed and returned to the same room he'd met Lynette the day before when he'd picked her up for their ride. A few minutes later, the butler returned and led him up the stairs and to Lord Keith's study.

"Milord." Lord Keith stood up and extended his hand. Aiden wanted to think of the man as a father figure since he was closer to his father's age than his, but Lord Keith looked much healthier than Seymour. Lord Keith was stout and fit, whereas Seymour still hadn't seemed to recover from the death of his firstborn son. "Williams, if you'll bring up some coffee?"

"Certainly," he said before leaving the men to their business.

"To what do I owe the pleasure of this visit?" Lord Keith asked while they waited for their coffee.

Aiden adjusted his coat. "I would like to discuss your elder daughter, milord."

"Yes, yes, I do believe I recall my wife telling me you called yesterday."

Aiden smiled, but before he could say anything else, Mr. Williams returned with the coffee, which he set out on the sideboard before taking his leave again. "I would believe it is quite obvious then that I would like to court her," he said after taking a sip of his coffee.

Lord Keith gestured for Aiden to take a seat. "Quite."

"What I hoped to gain was your permission to do so with a conclusion of marriage." He unbuttoned his coat and sat. "I hope you don't find me too forward, but I am in the market for a wife by the end of the Season, and I have decided to set my sights upon your daughter."

"Completely understandable given your situation." Lord Keith sat as well. "I would happily accept your suit of her. The two of you would make a fine match."

"I appreciate that." Aiden knew such approval rested on his wealth and title in relation to the beauty of Lynette. Those were the only two characteristics of a good match according to Society's standards. "Since we have only been acquainted for a few days, I would like a suitable amount of time to court Miss Elphinstone before I propose the notion of marriage to her. However, we will have an understanding . . ."

"You do not want me to inform her now?" Lord Keith asked with a furrowed brow.

Aiden nodded. "I would prefer to bring it up myself, at the right moment."

"But we will have an understanding?"

"Yes, I will direct my man of business to draw up a contract to be approved by yours," Aiden said.

"Then we will have an understanding." Lord Keith smiled. He was slightly confused by the arrangement but still happy his oldest daughter would finally be married off without much fuss. He extended his hand to the younger lord, and they shook in agreement. Once business was settled, they went on to casually talk about current events and sports while they finished their coffee, and by the end of their meeting, the gentlemen parted ways, both satisfied with the conclusion of it.

Lynette woke up at her usual time of nine thirty, even though she'd once again stayed up well past midnight to attend Mary Courtenay's come-out ball. Lord Elliot had been there and had requested another waltz. She smiled to herself and thought of how much she'd always enjoyed dancing but rarely had the chance to before Lord Elliot asked to court her. Interestingly enough, other gentlemen whom she thought had overlooked her before asked her to dance as well. Kathleen still received the majority of the attention, but Lynette was no less giddy at her change of circumstances. Sighing softly, she got out of bed and pulled the bell for Milly to come and help her dress. A few moments later, the maid arrived bearing a toothy grin.

"What has you so joyful this morning, Milly?" Lynette asked.

"The gentleman from yesterday, miss, he's speaking with your father."

Lynette appreciated the fact she was sitting at her dressing table since Milly's news would have knocked her off her feet otherwise. "Lord Elliot?"

"The one who took you to Hyde Park?"

"Yes." Lynette confirmed that they were one and the same.

"He arrived at nine," Milly said as she started brushing Lynette's hair. "Been speaking to your father ever since. He must be asking permission to marry you as he alluded to yesterday."

"He must," she said with a frown. She looked at herself in the mirror but couldn't focus on her reflection, her mind too busy trying to imagine a scenario where their blossoming courtship required a meeting with her father.

It only took Milly fifteen minutes to style Lynette's hair and help her dress before she was ready to go down to break her fast. She saw Mr. Williams in the morning room rearranging the flower arrangements and caught sight of a few new ones that must have just arrived. However, she decided against bothering the butler and went directly to the dining room where breakfast was being served.

Kathleen looked up as her older sister entered the room. "Are you engaged?"

Lynette paused in front of the sideboard with her plate in her hand. "Not that I'm aware of." Surely if she was, her father would inform her immediately.

"Mr. Williams told me that Lord Elliot came to see Father while I was looking at my flowers," Kathleen said.

Lynette sat down with her breakfast. "Yes, Milly told me the same, but I haven't spoken to Father about it yet."

"Did Lord Elliot propose to you?" Kathleen continued to question.

"He told me he intends to marry by the end of the Season," Lynette replied. It was only a slight lie. She didn't think her sister needed to know everything that happened in the park as it would only fuel her inquisitiveness. Furthermore, if anything were to come of it, Kathleen would know soon enough.

In any event, Kathleen seemed to be satisfied with what Lynette told her and returned to her breakfast without any more questions. For Lynette, her day continued much the same as it had since arriving in London. Her father never requested her presence in his office to talk about Lord Elliot's visit, but she was still a ball of nerves by the time the lunch gong sounded. Trying to control the turmoil of emotions that were flooding her, she entered the dining room for lunch with as much confidence as she could muster. Her father and mother were already seated and whispering to one another as she took her seat. Kathleen arrived shortly after and, upon taking in the scene, decided to break the tension.

"Papa, is Lynette engaged?" she asked with a sweet

smile.

"Kathleen!" Lady Keith narrowed her eyes. "That has nothing to do with you."

"But it's true Lord Elliot came to see you," Kathleen said, looking from Lynette to her father. "Mr. Williams told me, and Milly told Lynette."

Mr. Williams had the decency to blush as he served the luncheon, but the family was unconcerned with the servants' gossip.

"Lord Elliot did come to see me this morning." Lord Keith nodded. "He is truly a decent gentleman and asked my formal permission to court you." He looked at his eldest daughter with pride.

"That's all?" Lynette asked with a tilted head. So Lord Elliot hadn't reneged on their agreement. He still intended to court her by showing her how she was different to him. Her lips spread with a slow smile as the heaviness in her chest abated enough for her to take a deep breath.

"For right now yes, though I wouldn't be surprised if a proposal is forthcoming," Lord Keith said with a cough.

"Could you just imagine? My daughter, a countess and future duchess!" Lady Keith beamed.

"What about me, Mama?" Kathleen asked, not wanting to be left out. She didn't appreciate having to share her mother's attention with her older sister, especially since it wasn't Lynette's first Season. "I have earls courting me," she said, reminding herself as much as her family. But while the title of countess appealed to her, she thought the title of duchess would suit her better.

"Yes, I do not doubt that both my daughters will marry respectably now." Lady Keith continued to smile, unaware of the jealousy Kathleen felt for her sister. Lynette was unfazed by the emotion as well, still

My Duty To You

struggling to understand why Lord Elliot had found it necessary to receive formal permission to court her, and why the idea affected her as it did.

"I thought you told me I would be exempt from these functions once I chose my intended bride," Aiden said as he assisted his grandmother from their carriage so they could attend an *al fresco* luncheon held by Viscountess Beaumont.

"Were you entertaining your betrothed?" Rowena asked.

"No, I was trying to clear my desk before the Duchess of Richmond's ball this evening," he replied. He was still trying to come to grips with all the paperwork that went into maintaining a dukedom. There were constant invoices and payments to be made. Earnings from the property and its tenants, servants to be paid. He didn't relish the duty but refused to allow the dukedom's finances to suffer since he'd obtained power.

She tsked and shook her head. "Those papers should be attended to in the mornings, as the afternoons and evenings are for social engagements."

Aiden opened his mouth to say that his meeting with Lord Keith prevented him from completing his correspondence in the morning but then thought better of it in the end. She wouldn't understand his agreement with Lord Keith nor why he would want to take the time to court Lynette.

"You are to remember that even once you marry, social engagements are not to be ignored," Rowena said. "I know you aren't used to the demands of the Season, but you will need to become accustomed to them."

"Men do not attend these parties, Granny." He sighed as they entered the viscountess's garden and ignored his granny's barb regarding his social competence so as not to start an argument, but the words still stung. He might not have been familiar with the London Season, but he wasn't entirely out of his realm of expertise. Part of his job as a diplomat in Switzerland was to participate in Society and attend social gatherings. However, his grandmother overlooked his time spent on the Continent and anything he did there.

She looked at him pointedly. "They do when they are looking for a wife."

"I am no longer looking; I have found whom I intend to marry."

"Then marry her." She huffed. "Or short of that, escort her through the park, on a walk, call on her at home. Do anything bar sitting at your desk alone while other men vie for her attention."

Aiden almost reminded his granny that Miss Elphinstone was six and twenty with no other gentlemen currently vying for her attention, but then he decided it wouldn't make a difference. She wouldn't allow her mind to be changed, so he kept silent while escorting her around the party.

Aiden and Rowena had been mingling for some time when they came upon Lady Keith and her daughters, who were talking to Roderick Fitzroy and his mother. As soon as Rowena was done with her current conversation, Aiden started to lead her toward his intended bride. "Good day, Lady Keith." He smiled. "You remember my grandmother, the Dowager Duchess of Northumberland?"

"Yes, it is lovely to see you today, Your Grace." Lady Keith curtsied and then instructed her daughters to do the same.

"'Tis a lovely day to be out and about," Rowena said with a sidelong glance at her grandson.

My Duty To You

Lady Keith conducted the introductions between Rowena, Aiden, Lady Fitzroy, and Lord Fitzroy, who'd just inherited his father's viscountcy. The young lord couldn't have been more than twenty-one, with blond hair and blue eyes. He smiled broadly at the group, but Aiden could see his eyes continually flicking toward Miss Kathleen.

"Miss Elphinstone." Aiden turned to Lynette, who looked at him wide-eyed. "Would you and your sister care for a walk through the garden? I'm sure Lord Fitzroy would be agreeable to joining?" He arched a brow over Lynette's head.

Lord Fitzroy bobbed his head up and down. "Indeed, I'd be delighted to be an escort."

"If it is all right with you, Lady Keith?" Aiden turned to her for her permission.

She nodded. "Quite all right, milord."

Aiden held out his arm to Lynette, Fitzroy did the same to Kathleen, and the foursome began to meander through the garden, chaperoned by the matrons, who took up the rear.

"How has your day been so far, Miss Elphinstone?" Aiden asked after a moment or two of silence.

"Just fine, milord," she replied. "I must admit, I didn't expect to see you here."

"My granny insisted," Aiden explained. "She is under the belief that I could meet my future bride at one of these functions."

"I suppose that depends on whom you want as your future bride." She scanned the garden. "Are you in the market for a debutante?"

He scrunched his nose. "Certainly not."

Lynette laughed loudly, garnering a severe look from

her mother. "My apologies, milord. I didn't mean any offense."

"It is quite all right." Even though it wasn't proper, he truly enjoyed her ability to be so free with her words and actions. "It should be noted that I met you at a similar function."

"Indeed, milord, I am here for the same reasons as you. My mother has not given up hope that I may stumble upon my future husband at a garden party." She lowered her voice for fear she'd be overheard. "She obviously hasn't realized that the men here, you excluded, of course, are all at least two or three years my junior." Her lips parted in a silent laugh, and her brown eyes danced.

His eyebrows rose. "Truly?"

"Indeed." She nodded. "Then again, I also met you at such an event."

Aiden's blue eyes gleamed. "True, and I assure you I am not your junior."

"No you aren't." Lynette's smile slowly faltered. She looked away, trying to think of an appropriate way to continue their conversation. Not that their current conversation was appropriate in any way. With a sigh she turned back to him, her curiosity getting the best of her. "You saw my father this morning."

"I did." Aiden reeled back. "Did he tell you my reason for it?"

She nodded and pursed her lips. "He said that you requested formal permission to court me."

"You agreed to as much yesterday," he said with a tilt of his head.

"Yes, I just didn't expect you to go to my father." She exhaled, and her fists clenched at her sides. "Before knowing the nature of your visit, I thought maybe . . ."

"Maybe?"

"That maybe you decided to simply ask for my hand."

Aiden tried to control his breathing despite his racing heart. Lynette was smart and had figured out part of his plan. But just because he'd secured her father's permission didn't mean he'd act on it without her consent. Still, instinct told him that she would see his actions as a sort of betrayal, so he needed to spin it in a more appealing way.

"I asked your father's permission so that I could simplify things at a later date if it was agreeable to you," he explained. "Of course, I assumed he would have no reason to reject my courting you, but I wanted to make sure, to save us time in the future."

"A future we may not have," she reminded him. "By doing as much, you are likely forcing my hand with your suit. My father couldn't possibly say no now."

"And what could I do if I'd taken the time to court you and then for some reason your father objected? I do have a duty to my family that I must take into consideration. I can't have spent my time courting you if he would reject me out of hand." He framed his reasoning around his duty to marry since it was the easiest to explain, despite not being the main reason he'd taken pains to secure her hand.

You could simply choose another woman, Lynette wanted to suggest. How could he not see that she was replaceable by any lady of his station? Furthermore, it would be ludicrous to believe her father would reject a future duke out of hand. She wanted to argue, but instead she simply said, "I see."

"Do you?"

"Indeed."

"Miss Elphinstone," Aiden said, turning to face her,

"I would marry you tomorrow if you gave me your acceptance, but as I know you won't without a traditional courtship, then I will take the time to do that. If in the end you decide to reject my suit, I will accept that as well."

"You'd accept my refusal but needed to prematurely gain acceptance from my father?"

"Yes." He caught her eye. "Your father's mind I cannot change, but yours, I'm up for the challenge of." He grinned broadly, and Lynette found herself doing the same despite her irritation.

"You may be the most infuriating suitor, Lord Elliot," she said a moment later.

"Infuriating and intriguing, my what a pair we make, Miss Elphinstone." He smiled teasingly. "How does Lord Fitzroy fare with your sister?" he asked, changing the subject.

"I fear not well." She assessed the younger couple. Lord Fitzroy seemed like a nice young man who would dote on Kathleen, but with her continued talk of earls, Lynette worried her sister had no interest in Lord Fitzroy due to his lower title. "My sister . . . has a lot of maturing to do."

"She needn't make a match in her first Season, does she?" Aiden asked, unaware of the standards for young debutantes.

"There's no reason for her to make a match posthaste." Lynette shook her head. "If anything, your courting me makes it even less necessary."

Aiden nodded as they continued their stroll through Lady Beaumont's garden, then once they completed their promenade, he returned her to her mother. "Will you be attending the Duchess of Richmond's ball tonight?" he asked her before they parted.

"I daresay everyone will," she replied.

"I shall find you there then." Aiden took her hand and brushed his thumb over the back of it. "Make sure to save me a waltz."

Lynette agreed, and then she watched as he led his grandmother back through the party, her hand still tingling from his touch.

Chapter Seven

Just as Lynette had expected, the Duchess of Richmond's ball was an absolute crush. It had taken an age for the Keiths' carriage to make it to the front of the processional, and even once inside the Richmonds' ballroom, it was hard to walk around. Once it was clear Kathleen no longer needed her support, Lynette left her to her group of friends and admirers to find her own.

"I'm head over heels in love with Edward Ferrars," she said, eager to discuss *Sense and Sensibility*, when she finally found Teresa in the crowd. "I sincerely hope he loves Elinor. They are practically made for each other."

Teresa swallowed her lips. "I didn't go out last night, so I'm quite a bit ahead of you."

"Unfair!" Lynette pouted. "You better not spoil it for me."

"I would never." The two ladies linked arms and promenaded together. "How was your afternoon yesterday?"

Lynette's stomach fluttered. "It's just as you thought. He's not looking for love."

Teresa patted her friend's hand. "We can be spinsters together. Maybe when my brother inherits the earldom, he'll settle some money on me, and we can find a nice cottage to live in together."

Lynette smiled but didn't find the idea as appealing as her friend did. "I'm going to allow him to court me, though."

Teresa stiffened. "Are you sure that's wise?"

"Just because he's not looking for love doesn't mean he won't fall in love with me," Lynette replied.

"Have you already decided to love him then?"

"No." Lynette's mouth moved from side to side. "But he's kind, and he makes me laugh."

"But what happens when he offers for you, and you can't refuse?"

"He said he'll respect my rejection should it come to that."

Teresa frowned. "You seem to have put a lot of faith in a man you've only recently met."

"I—"

Lord Bath appeared before them. "Miss Elphinstone, I hope you have been well through the winter."

Thomas Thornburn was the new Marquess of Bath and was a respectable gentleman of approximately the same age as Lord Elliot and still unmarried. He and Lynette had been introduced during her debutante year, and since then, he would always ask her to dance when they met at a ball, even though nothing more had ever come from their long acquaintance.

"Excuse me." Teresa pulled away from Lynette. "I must go pay my respects to my aunts."

Lynette watched her friend go, then turned back to Lord Bath with a sigh. "I have, milord, but I must admit it was a very wet winter indeed."

"That it was." He nodded. "I sincerely hope it will not

affect my crops this year."

They continued their easy conversation about the weather, agriculture, and what they'd done during their time away from the capital. Then as usual, Lord Bath requested a dance from her before releasing her to promenade the ballroom again.

Having been caught in the traffic coming to the Duchess of Richmond's ball, Aiden arrived fashionably late with his mother and grandmother, his father having elected to stay home. After excusing himself from his family, he began looking for Lynette in the crush of bodies and caught sight of her just as Lord Bath was stepping away. He remembered Thornburn from his Eton days and recalled they might have been separated by a year. However, since Aiden had been away for so long, he wasn't sure if Thornburn remained unmarried. A twinge of jealousy flared at the sight of Lynette and Thornburn together, but he tried to ease it by reminding himself that she'd been out for nine Seasons. Surely if Thornburn wasn't married and was seriously interested in her, he would have offered for her already.

All rational thought escaped him, though, when he reached Lynette and went to add his name to her dance card. Lord Bath had secured a waltz with her in the course of their meeting. *At least it isn't the before-supper waltz*, Aiden tried to reason but remained irked by the interaction. He released the dance card and replaced it with Lynette's hand, hoping it would have a soothing effect on him. If nothing else, with her by his side, mothers were less likely to approach him with their daughters.

"Even though you are courting me, milord, you have the freedom to dance with other ladies if you so choose."

Lynette wasn't exactly complaining about being on the arm of one of the most eligible bachelors in Britain, but she felt it necessary to remind him there were others he could give attention to.

"There are more than enough gentlemen at this event, so no one will be in want of me as a partner," he replied, having no intention of leaving her side unless he had to. But unfortunately, the time did come when he needed to relinquish her hand. His jaw clenched as Thornburn approached to claim his waltz. Face to face, the gentlemen assessed one another and then exchanged pleasantries about the various ways they'd spent their time since attending Eton. Once they adhered to social strictures, Thornburn led Lynette away.

Aiden watched from his spot at the dance floor's edge as Thornburn pulled Lynette close and only tore his eyes away when his teeth began to hurt. He shook his head and then sought out a footman to bring him a glass of wine. With it in hand, he took a sip and let the liquid slide down his throat.

"So, you did find a diamond in the rough?" his friend Dominic asked on his approach, referring to Miss Elphinstone.

Aiden took another sip of wine. "Aye."

"Then why are you allowing Thornburn to dance with her?" Dominic asked, his brow arched quizzically. "His father passed away roughly the same time your brother did, so he is searching in earnest for a wife."

"Much like myself." Aiden nodded. "I was planning to lengthen our courtship; let her enjoy a final Season since my deadline is not till the end of it."

"Posh! Wed her and bed her, I say," Dominic replied, thinking his friend's plan was a waste of time.

"I'm considering it," Aiden said gruffly, his throat still sore from the lump that had settled in it. He turned his attention to his friend. "And you're one to talk."

"I haven't found my diamond yet." Dominic shrugged, and then a devilish smile pulled at his lips. "Until then, I am only too happy to keep bedding without the wedding."

Aiden groaned when he realized it had been months since he'd last taken a woman to bed. The last mistress he'd kept was in Switzerland since it hadn't felt right to keep one while he was mourning his brother's death. He'd intended to take one up in London, at least until the end of the Season when he had to be wed, but then he'd met Lynette within a few days of arriving and hadn't felt the need for a mistress. He downed the rest of the wine in a single gulp, praying for the temperance to get through the evening.

Temperance, patience, and any other virtue eluded Aiden that night. Thornburn had seen fit to continue to occupy Lynette's time after their waltz, much like he'd occupied her time prior to it. Without Lynette by his side, he had to interact with the other ladies in attendance by conversing and dancing with them. Some weren't entirely horrible, while others were extremely obnoxious in their pursuit of him. By the time the before-supper waltz began to play, Aiden was more than happy to pull Lynette back into his arms, and against her better judgment, Lynette decided she was happy to be there.

It wasn't that Lynette was unhappy in Lord Bath's company; she just wasn't *as* comfortable with him as she was with Lord Elliot. In addition to that, the whole encounter had been entirely unexpected. She'd assumed Lord Bath would collect his dance and then bid her adieu as he had at every other event where they'd met in the previous nine years. At the end of their waltz, though, instead of leaving her at the edge of the dance floor, or even returning her to her mother as was the custom for younger ladies, he tucked her arm in his and promenaded through the ballroom with her by his side. As a result, she needed to engage him in the longest conversation they'd ever had in the course of their acquaintance. Naturally, she didn't want to consider the actions as anything other than friendly, but when she dwelt on it, she came to the conclusion Lord Bath might intend to court her as well! The idea that not one but two gentlemen were courting her in her final Season baffled her to no end.

"Are you all right, milord?" Lynette asked Lord Elliot as they danced. She'd been so focused on her own thoughts and feelings she hadn't registered his demeanor. She could tell by the way he clenched his jaw and held her quite stiffly that he wasn't at ease. While they'd only danced twice before, she was sure his present disposition wasn't his usual.

"Quite fine," Aiden said, trying to shake off his frustration. "I hadn't realized how heavily attended an affair it would be." *Or that I'd have to compete for your attention*, he added silently to himself.

"The amount of people here does make it quite warm. If you plan to stay for any longer, milord, you might want to take a breath of fresh air."

Fresh air . . . his lips parted as an idea formed in his head. When the waltz ended, he kept hold of her arm as he asked, "Would you enjoy taking some air with me?"

Lynette hesitated, not knowing whether to accept or not. She couldn't deny she wanted to, since a gentleman hadn't ever tried to entice her out of a crowded ballroom before, but she also accepted that it wasn't at all proper.

Sensing her inner conflict, Aiden tried to reassure her. "We'll simply step out onto the balcony, in full view of everyone."

"All right." She released a shaky breath. Surely nothing illicit could happen on a balcony in front of a party.

Aiden led her through the ballroom and out the French doors onto a large balcony. They breathed the cool spring air while admiring the clear starlit sky. After a few minutes, Lynette was thoroughly refreshed and turned toward Lord Elliot to see if he thought the same. But when she turned, she caught him staring at her, his eyes unblinking. He stepped toward her, close enough to be almost nose to nose; their eyes met, and they gazed upon each other.

"Milord," Lynette whispered, the heat of his body warming her.

"Aiden," he supplied, wanting to hear his name on her lips.

"Aiden," she repeated, and it was enough for him.

He leaned in and kissed her gently to start so as not to overwhelm her. He wrapped his arms around her, pressing her body against his, and then placed one hand on her cheek, the other on her neck. She didn't know quite what to do with her hands but decided it felt good how he was holding her, so she attempted to mimic him by wrapping her arms around his neck and then running her fingers through his hair. He took it as a sign to deepen the kiss and coaxed her mouth open so he could taste her. A moan escaped her lips, which was a surprise, but the sound only made him want to double down in his assault on her mouth. Reluctantly though, he stopped after just a few short minutes because he knew if they continued, they would risk her being ruined. It wasn't an unappealing prospect, since he would only be ruining her for himself, but he accepted it wasn't what she would want.

"It's time to go back," he whispered in her ear.

"What? Oh." She blinked quickly, trying to regain her mental faculties. The man had stolen her wits as soon as he kissed her, and heaven help her, she thought she might never be the same.

Somehow, Aiden led the dazed Lynette back into the ballroom and integrated them with the other guests who hadn't left for supper yet. He made sure they were among the last to enter the dining room as if they'd just been caught up in the crush of bodies. In his assessment, Lady Keith seemed none the wiser, and he wished Lynette farewell for the evening. He collected his mother and grandmother and couldn't help but think just what an evening it had been.

Chapter Eight

After a weekend full of entertainment, Lynette was happy to have the time to sit down and read. Despite yet another late night, she got up early and after breaking her fast, took her novel out to the garden to read until the lunch gong rang. Once she finished her lunch, she returned to her reading, only this time in the drawing room. The sun warmed the room nicely as she became consumed with the tale of Marianne's suitors. At first, she had her heart set on Marianne and Mr. Willoughby as a couple, but as the chapter went on, Lynette found herself feeling much like Elinor, grievous that poor Colonel Brandon was being overlooked due to his age and good sense. She wanted to relate to Elinor, since she also had a younger sister who seemed to be the object of everyone's affection. But considering she had nearly two suitors herself, the similarities between her and the character didn't stretch to all aspects of her life.

Lynette was so immersed in *Sense and Sensibility* and her own suitor troubles she didn't hear her mother enter the room.

"Lynette Elphinstone," her mother said with narrowed eyes.

"Yes? Sorry." She saved her page and put her book down.

Lady Keith considered scolding her daughter even more but ultimately decided there wasn't time. "There is a gentleman here to see you."

"For me?" Lynette knew Kathleen was entertaining suitors, but she hadn't expected anyone to call upon her.

"Yes, now come along." Her mother urged her down the hall.

Lynette clutched her stomach as she walked, hoping Lord Elliot was calling upon her again. She knew she was becoming dangerously attached, but there was just something about the man that made her want to see him more and more. It didn't help he'd kissed her the night before, and if anything, it only made the butterflies in her stomach worse.

But when she entered the reception room and saw Lord Bath, her shoulders sagged. In all the years of their acquaintance, Lord Bath had never once called upon her, which further confirmed that he was attempting to court her now.

"Sorry to keep you waiting, Lord Bath. My daughter was just practicing her pianoforte," Lady Keith said.

Lynette wanted to roll her eyes, but she knew it would be even less ladylike than being caught reading instead of playing the piano.

Lord Bath bowed over her hand. "I must hear you play one day, Miss Elphinstone."

She stared at her hand in his, but her pulse remained stable. When her mother cleared her throat, Lynette dropped into a curtsy. "It'd be my pleasure to play for you, milord."

"Mr. Williams, will you please bring us some more

refreshments?" Lady Keith asked the butler, who still stood at the door. Then with an eerily sweet smile, she encouraged her elder daughter toward Lord Bath. Lynette did as her mother expected and engaged him in conversation as she took in the scene. Three suitors had called on Kathleen: Lord Fitzroy, whom she'd met a few days prior; Lord Fowler, the Earl of Aylesford; and Lord Waldroup, the Earl of Portsmouth. Within the first few minutes of being in the room, Lynette realized Kathleen had no intention of entertaining Lord Fitzroy while the other lords were present. And even they couldn't seem to hold Kathleen's attention while Lord Bath was in the room, even though he wasn't there to call on her.

If anybody would be happy with a marriage of convenience, it would be Kathleen, Lynette thought as her sister tried to include Lord Bath in her conversation. Kathleen seemed to be disinterested in the romanticism of courtship, and she simply wanted a wealthy man in possession of the highest title. Thus it had become increasingly clear to Lynette that Kathleen was jealous of her for being courted by a future duke. Add a marquess to the mix, and Kathleen was practically foaming at the mouth. Deciding it was best to allow her sister to entertain Lord Bath as she wanted, Lynette did what any other sensible person would do and conversed with the other gentlemen so they wouldn't feel left out.

Aiden stopped his curricle in front of the Keiths' residence and was slightly ruffled at the sight of the other curricles waiting outside the town house. He bounded up the steps, and the butler opened the door before he could even knock.

"For Miss Elphinstone, I presume?" Mr. Williams

asked.

"That's right," Aiden replied roughly, his northern burr making an appearance. The butler led him directly to the reception room, where Lady Keith, Lynette, and Kathleen were entertaining the four gentlemen. At first, Aiden assumed Thornburn had called on Lynette, but after taking in the room, he decided he was mistaken. Instead, Thornburn seemed to be conversing with Kathleen, leaving the other three gentlemen with Lynette. Aiden couldn't believe that young Fitzroy would seriously be entertaining Lynette, but Lord Fowler and Lord Waldroup were of a similar age to her, which made them calling on her more likely.

"Lord Elliot for the Honorable Miss Lynette Elphinstone," Mr. Williams announced Aiden's presence, then escaped back to the hall.

"Lord Elliot, it's a pleasure to see you again and so soon." Lady Keith's high-pitched voice gave away her excitement.

In her eyes, Aiden knew he was the front-runner, if only for his title and connections. "Lady Keith, it is a pleasure as always." He bowed over her outstretched hand, happy to have the opportunity to use such things to his advantage. He then turned to Lynette, who stood by the window with an expression on her face he couldn't quite read. Was she happy to see him? Or was she happier in the presence of the other men? "Miss Elphinstone, you're looking lovely today." He smiled and bowed over her hand but lingered just a trifle longer than necessary. "I was thinking that it was such a fine day that you'd maybe like to go for a walk."

"That sounds like a fine idea," Lady Keith said. "Why don't we all go for a walk? If you gentlemen are in agreement?" She extended the invitation to the rest of the party. Not wishing to be left out, everyone made a sound of agreement, which saw the matter settled. Lady Keith excused herself and her daughters to get ready for the walk, leaving the five gentlemen alone.

"Be careful, Elliot," Fowler warned him with a smirk. "Or the younger one will capture you like she did old Thornburn."

Aiden turned to Thornburn. "You're not here for Miss Kathleen?"

"I called on Miss Elphinstone," he said. "But Miss Kathleen drew me into her conversation."

"And then left us to our own devices," Fitzroy quipped, not looking entirely thrilled with the occurrence.

"I won't complain." Waldroup waggled his eyebrows. "I find Miss Elphinstone much more to my taste now." This was a sentiment Fowler agreed to, whereas Fitzroy continued to look displaced.

Thankfully, Lady Keith, Lynette, and Kathleen returned, changed and ready for their walk before any more conversation was necessary.

"Miss Elphinstone, if you'll do me the honor." Aiden stepped forward and offered his arm before another gentleman could. Even though his idea of an intimate walk had been ruined, he wasn't going to share her any more than he had to.

Chapter Nine

Lynette sat in front of her mirror as Milly pinned her curls in preparation for the Countess of Pembroke's ball. She'd picked out a pale-blue gown, which reminded her of Lord Elliot's eyes, and had decided on a pearl necklace and earrings to complement it. A soft knock sounded at the door before Lady Keith stepped into the room, ready in her evening finery. "Are you almost done, Milly?" she asked.

"Yes, milady," the maid said before placing the final few pins. Lynette had started to hand Milly her necklace to have her help fasten it when Lady Keith moved to take her place.

"It's all right, Milly. I can take it from here." Lady Keith dismissed the maid and took the necklace from her daughter's hand.

"Is there something wrong, Mama?" Lynette asked as she shifted in her chair. Since coming of age, she'd had Milly to help her dress, pin her hair, and fasten her jewelry, making her mother's undertaking of it quite rare.

"I did not appreciate your behavior this afternoon," Lady Keith said, meeting her daughter's eye in the mirror. "You had two gentlemen call on you today, and you only entertained Lord Elliot during our walk."

"You said that I should allow him to court me." Lynette had half a mind to remind her mother that Kathleen had three gentlemen call on her, and she ignored them all in favor of the higher-ranked Marquess of Bath.

"Yes, but I don't want you to show him any favoritism. You must treat each gentleman equally until you have a formal understanding with one," Lady Keith said. "I don't want you to set your cap on Lord Elliot and then have him not offer for you. You'd then be ostracized by Lord Bath or any other gentlemen like him whom you snubbed while Lord Elliot was giving you attention. You must play your hand very carefully this Season since it may be your last chance to make a match. The next time you have a situation like the one you experienced today, you must walk beside each gentleman who comes calling to give them an equal chance to express an interest in you. Am I understood?"

Lynette nodded and bit her tongue.

"Right, then let's be off." Lady Keith clapped her hands and ushered her daughter out of her bedroom. They collected Kathleen, who stood waiting in the foyer, and then all three women were off to the ball.

Lynette silently seethed the entire carriage ride to Pembroke House. She just couldn't understand where her mother got her ideas. Did Lady Keith think so poorly of her daughter that she believed Lord Elliot would cease his courtship and relegate her to accepting someone like Lord Bath? And what did that say of Lady Keith's opinion of Lord Bath? Did she believe he was any less of a man than Lord Elliot? It was true Lynette didn't like Lord Bath in the same way she did Lord Elliot, but that didn't make one man lesser than the other. If love wasn't the goal, Lynette was certain she would be happy marrying either gentleman. But love was the goal, which was why she paid Lord Elliot more attention during their walk. Despite her better judgment, she felt herself falling in love with him. But unfortunately, to the likes of Lady Keith and Kathleen, love was inconsequential.

After what felt like an age, the carriage pulled up in front of the Earl of Pembroke's residence. Once inside the ballroom, Lynette decided to stay with Kathleen near their mother for no other reason than to spite them both. It wasn't long before Kathleen's suitors began descending, Lord Fitzroy being the first, followed by Lord Fenn. To Lynette's irritation, Kathleen paid the gentlemen little mind as she continually scanned the ballroom for someone better, but their mother never said a word. Disgusted with her family, Lynette was turning away when Lord Waldroup appeared at her side.

"Good evening, Miss Elphinstone." He reached for her hand. "I'm happy to have found you here as I had such a lovely afternoon with you."

"It was my pleasure." She smiled. "I'm sure my sister also enjoyed your company," she said, hoping to involve Kathleen since Lord Waldroup had originally been her caller.

Shifting away from Lord Fitzroy and Lord Fenn, Kathleen stepped closer to Lord Waldroup to greet him, but it was his turn to pay her no mind. "Miss Elphinstone, would you honor me with a dance this evening?" he asked, reaching for her card.

The blood drained from Kathleen's face, and Lynette wished she could refuse, but she knew it would be rude to cut the gentleman down. It wasn't her fault Kathleen had offended Lord Waldroup earlier in the day, and she sincerely hoped that accepting the dance would teach Kathleen a valuable lesson.

Regrettably, Lord Waldroup wasn't the last of Kathleen's suitors who had decided to approach Lynette. Lord Fowler appeared after Lord Bath secured a waltz to remark on how much he'd enjoyed their conversation and to request a dance. Even Lord Fitzroy and Lord Fenn solicited a dance from her, much to Kathleen's dismay. Lynette felt for her sister, who she thought was too young to know how much of a faux pas she'd made with her suitors, but Lynette still enjoyed the attention being showered upon her. She'd never been so popular in all her nine Seasons!

Aiden started scanning the crowd for Lynette as soon as he and his grandmother stepped into the ballroom. His patience was wearing thin after the events of the afternoon when he had to pretend he was in competition for her hand with other gentlemen. He wanted to believe she'd paid more attention to him than to the others because that would mean she was softening to his advances. But despite making such excellent progress, he still wasn't sure she'd accept his proposal. Thus he wanted to use the Countess of Pembroke's ball to further his courtship of her; anything to get him across the finish line, he reminded himself.

"Now then, what are your plans for this evening?" Rowena asked her grandson after they had found a place for her to sit with the other *grandes dames*.

He sighed. "To find Miss Elphinstone and ask her to dance."

"Ask some other ladies to dance while you're at it."

"I have no interest—"

My Duty To You

Rowena shook a finger at him. "If you're not ready to offer for her, then you shouldn't be ready to dance with her alone."

Aiden's lips thinned. "If you detain me any longer, no ladies will have any dances on their cards left."

"Very well then, off you go." She dismissed him with a nod.

He turned on his heel and searched in earnest for his soon-to-be fiancée. In the end, it didn't take him long to find her, standing with a distressed-looking Kathleen and a handful of gentlemen. Frustration rising, he quickly made his way through the crush of people, trying to calculate how many dances Lynette's group of admirers took up.

"Good evening, Miss Elphinstone. You look simply enchanting. The blue of your dress suits you." He disturbed the group as if it was his right, took her gloved hand, and brought it to his lips. After greeting the rest of the group and partaking in the prerequisite chatter, he turned back to her and picked up her dance card only to find it was just as he'd feared; there were no waltz spaces left open. In an attempt to make the best out of a poor situation, he tried to decide whether he'd prefer a cotillion or a country dance when she spoke up.

"Which dance would you prefer, milord?"

"I'd prefer a waltz," Aiden whispered, so none of the other members of their group could hear, and he was rewarded with a secret smile. "But I shall be content with a cotillion."

Lynette nodded, and they turned back to the group. From the looks he received, it was obvious to Aiden that their brief interlude did not escape the other gentlemen's notice, which was fine by him. He was ready to do anything to halt their advances, within the realm of reason.

As the night wore on, Aiden continuously watched Lynette as she danced each dance with a different man. He waited for his turn at the side of the dance floor, internally brooding, when Thornburn came to stand beside him.

"Things seem to be faring well for you with Miss Elphinstone," he said after a moment of silence. "Do you have an understanding with her yet?"

Aiden sucked in his lips. "Not yet, but soon."

Thornburn took a long sip of his wine. "We have known each other since the year she made her debut, and I have to admit I have always found her quite pleasing."

"Then why didn't you offer for her before this Season?" Aiden arched an eyebrow. If he'd known Lynette for so long, she wouldn't have remained unmarried.

"I never felt any urgency to marry until now," Thornburn replied. "I thought it would be easy, with it likely being her last Season. But of course, I have competition."

"I'm happy to allow the best man to win." Aiden offered his glass, a gesture Thornburn accepted by clinking it with his. It was another lie of course; he knew the marquess stood no chance for the simple fact that he'd already secured Lord Keith's blessing. Additionally, he no longer believed he imagined Lynette's preference for him, so he hoped it was only a matter of time before she accepted his suit.

Lynette tried to catch her breath while sipping some wine. She'd danced every dance of the night, each with a different gentleman. Her feet were aching, and she was simply tired. She was tired of making small talk and leading conversations while repressing her unladylike qualities. Her tongue hurt from having to bite it so much. She'd been asked about the weather far too many times to count, in addition to her ideas about the current Season. Exhausted, she decided a ball was simply not the place to try to get to know a gentleman. Sure, each one she'd become acquainted with seemed nice enough, but none of them made her yearn to lengthen the conversation as she did when talking with Lord Elliot.

Speaking of the gentleman, she watched as he approached her for the second time that night. His evening wear fit his body in all the right places. His cravat was expertly tied; his hair styled to go along with the current fashions. She was instantly heated under his gaze, recalling how he referred to her as enchanting. He was making it evident to everyone that he was singling her out, and she couldn't help but feel uniquely special. While it had been a mere few days, Lynette wondered how long he'd hold out before he proposed. She just hoped it would be long enough for her to decide whether to accept him or not.

"Miss Elphinstone, my dance, I believe?" Aiden offered her his arm.

"Oh." She exhaled and set down her glass of wine. She'd been looking forward to dancing with him all night, but now her feet ached so much she couldn't muster the enthusiasm.

"Something wrong?" he asked, looking over her face carefully.

"Nothing." She forced a smile and placed her arm on his.

"Lynette," Aiden said softly, using her Christian name without being given leave to do so.

Her eyes widened, and her lips parted. No gentleman

had used her given name before. She liked the way it sounded, though; his pronunciation was by far the best.

"Tell me what's wrong."

"It's nothing. I'm just tired of dancing," she said. "But 'tis your dance, so we shall dance." She forced her shoulders back and lifted her head high.

"We do not have to dance." He didn't want to force her into something she was too tired to do, as she had been dancing the entire night without much time to rest. Dancing with her wasn't of the utmost importance, since it was mostly just a show for Society. There were other ways—better ways—they could get to know each other instead. "Where is your mother?" he asked.

"Just there." She motioned with her chin to a position behind him.

"And is she watching you?"

"She stopped watching as soon as you came up to me."

Aiden released a breath. For whatever reason, Lady Keith did not view him as a threat. Or if she did, she didn't care if he ruined her daughter because then they would be forced to marry. "Let's go this way." He led Lynette by placing his hand on the small of her back. The heat of it seared her, shooting tingles up and down her spine. She looked at him, wanting to know if he felt it too, but he continued as if nothing had occurred, and soon they were in the corridor. "Follow me," he said as he opened the door to a drawing room.

"Is this proper?" Lynette asked, her eyes darting from left to right.

"The only person who might notice is your mother, and you said she wasn't watching you. There are so many people here tonight, they won't notice if you're gone for one cotillion. Here, take a seat." He offered her a chair, and after another moment's hesitation, she sat.

He was making this interlude up as he went along and estimated they had at least ten minutes before Lady Keith might go looking for her daughter. He sat across from Lynette and watched as she leaned forward to partly remove her shoe and rub her heel.

"Allow me?" he asked her softly, making his first move.

"Lord Elliot—" she sighed in pleasure as he took her foot in his hand and began to massage it.

"It's Aiden." He met her eye and smirked. He'd enticed her to use his Christian name the night before, so there was no reason for her not to continue using it. He massaged one foot for a couple of minutes before reaching for the other. Lynette relaxed into his touch, and her body melted into the chair. For her, it was such an intimate thing to be touched in such a way by someone else, whereas for him it was not nearly intimate enough. "Feeling better?" he asked once he'd finished with both of her feet.

"Mmm, yes." Her eyes were closed in ecstasy. "I'm not used to dancing so much."

"It is something you might have to get used to."

"Perhaps." She sat up and put her shoes back on. "Should we be getting back?"

"Soon," Aiden replied, offering her a hand to stand.

Lynette expected him to place her arm on his and lead her back to the ballroom, but instead, he lifted her chin, and their eyes met. "I wore this dress for you," she whispered, recalling his earlier compliment of it.

Aiden's lips parted as he tilted his head to the side.

"It's the color of your eyes." A blush heated her face.

The dress might have been blue, but all Aiden could see was red. His lips captured hers roughly, releasing all the frustration he'd been feeling with his kiss.

She immediately matched his pressure and speed, hands tangling in his hair. Her lips parted, and she welcomed his deepening of it, feeling as though she needed it for survival. Then her bosom, which she'd never paid much attention to before, grew heavy, and she felt as though she couldn't get close enough to him.

He relished her enthusiasm, her soft moans, and the way her nails scratched his scalp, but when she pressed her chest into his, it nearly broke him. Knowing what she wanted more than she did, he let his hand fall from her face to her breast. He molded his hand to it and kneaded gently. She broke the kiss on a sigh, and he ran kisses around her jaw and down her neck. The swell of her bosom called to him, and he wanted nothing more than to release them from their confinement, but they simply did not have enough time.

"We must get back," Aiden said reluctantly, pulling away from her. He watched as she slowly regained her senses. *To think what I can do when we have unlimited time*, he thought smugly. "We can't be seen returning together. The withdrawing room is just two doors down on this side. Go there and wet your lips with cold water before returning to the ballroom, and I'll see you there."

Lynette only had the capacity to nod dumbly and follow his instructions. After a longing look at him, she hurried to the withdrawing room. There, she studied herself in the mirror to find her lips red and swollen and her cheeks flushed. Otherwise, she looked as she always did but knew if someone noticed the subtle differences, she'd likely be ruined. She requested some water and linen from the maid and then used both to bring the swelling and redness down. Once she thought she was presentable again, she left the withdrawing room to return to the ballroom but ran into her mother and sister on the way.

"Are you all right?" Lady Keith asked her daughter, genuine concern coloring her face. It was almost enough to make Lynette feel guilty for sneaking out from underneath her watchful eye, but then she thought of the moment she was able to share with Aiden, and she couldn't feel anything but happiness regarding that.

"My feet, they hurt," Lynette said. "I was also very warm and needed a moment in the withdrawing room."

"I see." Lady Keith studied her daughter. "You may be six and twenty, but you still need to inform me when you decide to leave the ballroom. When I didn't see you on the dance floor any longer, I became worried."

"Of course, I'm sorry." She hung her head slightly.

"Perhaps if you're tired, we should make a start for home," Lady Keith said.

Lynette wanted to argue simply because she wished for more time with Aiden, but then thought better of it since it was likely she'd already lost him in the crush and she didn't want to chance an encounter with another gentleman whom she had no interest in talking with.

"I'm tired as well," said a dejected Kathleen.

"Let's see a footman about our cloaks then." Lady Keith ushered her daughters toward the front door.

Lynette was trudging behind her mother and sister when she heard someone groan, "It's too late for me." She turned toward the voice as her mother spoke with a footman about bringing their cloaks and carriage around and saw Aiden escorting his grandmother down the hall. He smiled when he saw her and then turned to a footman to request the Elliot carriage to be brought around as well.

Leaving her grandson to see to the carriage, Rowena

approached Lynette. "Did you enjoy the ball, dear?"

Aiden shook his head and smirked. When he returned to the ballroom, Lynette was nowhere to be found, but his grandmother insisted they leave directly. Now he realized it was her ploy to meet Lynette in the corridor.

"It was wonderful, Your Grace. I must get used to all the dancing," Lynette replied with a smile.

"You were very popular tonight, from what I could tell, my dear." Rowena tapped the young lady's hand. "You must be very proud, Lady Keith, since you have two diamonds of the first water on your hands."

"Oh, Your Grace, it pleases me to hear you say that." Lady Keith beamed.

Both families then departed. Since the Keiths' carriage arrived first, Aiden took the opportunity to help Lynette and her family in, rubbing his thumb over the back of Lynette's hand as he did so. They said their goodbyes and watched the carriage drive away before their own carriage appeared. Aiden helped his granny step up before climbing in behind her and closing the door.

"She was wildly popular tonight," Rowena said.

He looked out of the window. "I have it all in hand, Granny."

"You'd better because if you let her get away, you will only have yourself to blame," Rowena warned, and Aiden silently agreed that losing Lynette would be the single greatest mistake of his life.

"Lynette has stolen all my suitors, Mama!" Kathleen moaned as soon as the carriage started to roll. "This was supposed to be my year! She has been out nine Seasons and yet waited until my debut to make a match!"

Lynette scoffed. "As if I have any control over Lord

Elliot courting me this Season."

"What about the other gentlemen, Lord Fowler and Lord Waldroup? You have a duke courting you, so there's no need to steal my earls." Kathleen crossed her arms over her chest.

"I merely entertained them since you'd ignored them in favor of Lord Bath, who may I remind you, called on me and not you today!" Lynette defended herself.

"Girls—" Lady Keith tried to interrupt for the sake of her eardrums.

"So you need both a duke and a marquess courting you?" Kathleen goaded her sister.

"No, I do not!" Lynette proclaimed. "You can have every last gentleman of the *ton*, save one, but you surely need to learn how to treat them if you expect any to offer for you!"

"That is enough!" Lady Keith roared, garnering the attention of both girls. "I will not stand for this bickering between the two of you."

"Lynette started it—" Kathleen tried, but a look from her mother silenced her.

"Your sister did nothing wrong by dancing with the gentlemen who asked her, even if they had been courting you," Lady Keith said to her younger daughter, to Lynette's surprise. "I told you this afternoon not to snub any gentlemen, even those who possess a title that doesn't appeal to you."

Kathleen huffed at her mother's admonishment but stayed silent. Once they arrived home, she stepped out of the carriage first and made a beeline for her room. Lynette and her mother, in contrast, walked peaceably into the foyer.

"Which gentleman were you referring to earlier?"

Lady Keith asked her eldest daughter as she removed her cloak. Lynette narrowed her eyes, not recalling a reference to any gentleman. "When you told your sister she could have all the gentlemen save one?"

Lynette's eyes widened. The statement had been said in a state of exasperation, and she regretted saying such a thing out loud. Of course, she'd been referring to Aiden because he was the only gentleman she'd come to care for. He wasn't just a gentleman with a lofty title; he was a respectable and handsome gentleman whose touch made her weak. She didn't particularly care if he possessed a title at all. But she wasn't ready to admit such a thing to her mother because voicing her growing feelings for him would only make them more real; instead she shrugged and continued to feign ignorance.

"Whoever it is, I truly hope he offers for you," Lady Keith said, not wishing to pry anymore. "If he is your heart's desire." She caressed Lynette's cheek affectionately before bidding her good night.

Chapter Ten

Aiden woke up the morning following the Pembroke ball with new intent. His grandmother had been right: Lynette had been very popular, and therefore she had a whole new range of gentlemen who were vying for her attention and hand in marriage. He would have liked to believe that by proactively making an agreement with Lord Keith, her other suitors stood no chance, but he resignedly accepted that he was naïve in thinking so. The point of completing a formal courtship was to have her pick him at the end, not be forced into a marriage. Thus, Aiden needed to be out in front of the rest of her suitors.

He felt as though he'd made progress to that end over the last few nights. There was no doubt his kisses affected her, but what more could he do to advance his cause? Aiden sighed and finished his breakfast. Only one person could help him in his current situation, and she usually ate her breakfast in her room. He would just have to wait until his granny was up and about to ask for her assistance.

Aiden attended to some estate work while he waited to meet with his grandmother. Her schedule rarely varied, so he kept an eye on the window, which looked out into the back garden where he knew his grandmother liked to take the morning air after breaking her fast. When he heard the telltale signs of her ambling through the garden, he quit his work and went out to meet her.

Rowena was sitting on the bench admiring the flowers when her grandson appeared. "Good morning, Granny." He greeted her with a peck on the cheek.

"Don't you have estate work that needs tending?" she asked.

"I've come to ask you for advice regarding Miss Elphinstone," Aiden replied with a sigh.

"It's about time, my boy." Rowena squinted up at him. "Do sit down, will you? I won't crane my neck in order to look at you while we converse."

Aiden did as requested and sat down next to his grandmother before posing his questions. "What sort of entertainments should I engage in with her to further my suit?"

"You mean besides the ones you have already participated in?" she asked, to which he nodded. "You could invite her to the theater. Invite the whole family while you're at it, and we can open up our box."

His eyebrows rose. "That's a good idea."

"I do still have some of those, my boy," Rowena said, bewildered that her grandson would think any differently. With another kiss and a thank-you, Aiden bid her adieu to finish his estate business before calling on Lynette in the afternoon.

Aiden guided his horses into Hyde Park later in the day. When he'd arrived at the Keiths' residence, he'd been informed that Lady Keith had taken her daughters to Rotten Row, the place to see and be seen. Once he'd parked his curricle, he grabbed the bouquet he'd bought

My Duty To You

and went to find Lynette. When he found her, she was promenading along the Serpentine with her mother, sister, and Lord Waldroup. Lady Keith walked behind her daughters, acting as chaperone, while Lynette walked on Waldroup's arm. Kathleen, who was without an escort, looked forlornly at the couple.

"Miss Elphinstone," Aiden called out to her once he became close. She stopped as soon as she heard his voice, and the entire party looked at him as he approached.

"Good afternoon, Lord Elliot." Lynette smiled, happy to see him. She knew her mother didn't want her to favor him, but she couldn't stop her stomach from fluttering.

"I came to call upon you and was told to find you here." Aiden offered her the flowers.

"Thank you. They're beautiful." Lynette released Waldroup's hand to accept them. "Would you care to join us on our walk?"

"If it's not an intrusion," Aiden said politely, even though he had no intention of leaving her while she was on another gentleman's arm.

"Nonsense." Lynette waved her hand dismissively. "Lord Waldroup was just telling me about the art on display at the Royal Academy. Have you seen it?" she asked, allowing Aiden to fall into step with them.

Aiden answered negatively but encouraged Waldroup to tell them both about the exhibition, much to the lord's displeasure. He could tell that the other gentleman did not appreciate his interference, but it was just as well; if Aiden had to compete, so did Waldroup. Thornburn appeared not long after Aiden, having also been directed by Mr. Williams to the park, and joined in their discussion of the finer arts. Lynette became animated when the conversation turned to poetry since it was a topic she was knowledgeable about and enjoyed.

Despite the presence of the other two men, Aiden enjoyed his afternoon listening to Lynette talk until Lady Keith insisted they return home to prepare for their evening events. Aiden hung back, allowing Waldroup and Thornburn to say their goodbyes before him so that he might offer to walk Lynette back to her carriage, where he could extend his invitation to the theater in relative privateness. A silent struggle erupted as the other gentlemen seemed to have roughly the same idea, but as politely as Lynette could, she manipulated the other gentlemen into leaving first.

Private interview secured, Aiden offered Lynette his arm, and they strolled with her mother and sister to their carriage. "I had an ulterior motive in seeking you out today," he said. "I would like to invite you and your family to the King's Theater for its presentation of *Die Zauberflöte* this Friday."

"That is very kind of you, milord." Lady Keith smiled.

"I would like that very much." Lynette met his eye. As they got closer to their carriage, Kathleen hastened her steps, and Lady Keith had more of a mind to keep up with her younger daughter than her elder one.

"I can extend an invitation to a gentleman of your sister's choosing," Aiden said as they continued to amble along the path.

"You wouldn't happen to know a duke you could introduce her to?" Lynette asked with a wry smile. "My sister has become very jealous of your courting me."

"I'll see what I can do." Aiden chuckled as they reached the carriage. He wished her goodbye with a squeeze of her hand and then returned to his own curricle.

The next two days continued similarly to the previous ones. Lynette was being courted in earnest by four gentlemen: Lord Waldroup, Lord Fowler, Lord Bath, and of course, Lord Elliot. Thus, she was never in want of a partner, whether for a stroll in the afternoon or a dance in the evening. By Friday evening, she was drained but delighted to be attending the theater, where she could relax in Aiden's presence instead of constantly needing to be active in it. Who knew being courted was such hard work!

Dressed in a jewel-green gown and accented by gold jewelry, Lynette made her way to the foyer in anticipation of Aiden's arrival. Kathleen descended the stairs shortly after, dressed in a blush-colored frock, with a depressed look still clouding her features. Lynette felt for her sister and sincerely hoped that Aiden had arranged for some gentleman to escort Kathleen to the theater, wishing for something to lift her spirits.

Lord and Lady Keith joined their daughters shortly before Aiden arrived, his carriage pulling up in front of the town house. Aiden stepped down in front of his friend Lord Wiltshire, whom he'd persuaded to join them the night before.

"I have no interest in the theater," Dominic had insisted when Aiden broached the topic. They'd been sitting at White's, the exclusive gentlemen's club to which they were both members, playing a round of cards. "Nor do I have any interest in the younger Elphinstone chit." He motioned to the dealer to grant him another card.

"I'm not asking you to court the girl. I'm simply asking you to escort her to the theater for one night," Aiden said. He'd already tried to invite the young Lord Fitzroy to be Kathleen's escort, but it seemed the young debutante had cut down her suitors quite severely, thus encouraging them to direct their attention elsewhere. "See it as a favor to me."

Dominic slapped the table in disgust when it was clear he'd lost the hand. He stood, having decided to cut his losses. Aiden, not at all interested in the game, folded and followed Dominic away from the table.

"And what can I expect in return?" Dominic asked, sipping his brandy.

"I shall owe you a favor that you may call in at any time," Aiden replied, willing to give his friend anything he wanted if it meant he could make Kathleen and, by extension, Lynette happy.

In the end, Dominic reluctantly agreed and therefore stood beside Aiden as he greeted the Keiths. "I hope you all remember my friend, Lord Wiltshire?" He conducted the reintroductions before they all stepped back into the carriage and rode to the theater.

They joined the crush of people promenading in the lobby when they arrived. Aiden and Lynette were met with curious stares, whispers trailing behind them. Her stomach rolled as they ambled through the crowd, unused to being the center of attention while he was too focused on her to care. They stopped and chatted here and there, and then when the candles started to be snuffed, he led the group to the Duke of Northumberland's box, where they met his family. After everyone had taken their seats, he noticed Kathleen talking animatedly to Dominic and desperately hoped his friend wasn't regretting his decision to escort her.

"Thank you," Lynette whispered in Aiden's ear. "I know that Lord Wiltshire isn't the type to escort young ladies to the theater, so you must have used your friendship to persuade him."

His eyes found hers, and his heart began to race. "You know Dominic?"

"I know of him," she replied. "We've only met a few times over the years, but his reputation precedes him."

He nodded as his heart returned to its natural rhythm. He'd been away from London for so long, it shouldn't have surprised him that she knew his friend better than him. "My apologies. He is merely the heir to a marquess. I couldn't find a duke available."

"My sister will simply have to endure the trial," she said, biting back a snicker. In truth, she was grateful to him for taking the pains to arrange an escort for her sister and hoped that in doing so, he was showing a growing attachment between them.

The thought captured Lynette as the opera began, and as much as she wanted to enjoy the production, she found her mind straying away. It had been a week since they'd met and started courting. She was the only woman he was entertaining, which was a clear sign of his intentions. She'd even begun to hear the whispers speculating when a formal engagement would be announced. All of it made her aware that the time was nigh, and she would need to make a decision forthwith. Did she want to marry Aiden?

The answer to that question still hinged on their ability to love each other. Lynette's feelings had definitely softened toward Aiden. He'd succeeded in making her feel irrationally special by calling on her every afternoon, doting on her at every ball, taking her to the theater, and arranging an escort for her sister. Not to mention his touch and kisses! She was alive in his arms and yearned for the day she would be in them again. Even sitting next to him in the box was enough to make her heated. Their elbows touched as they rested on the arms of the chair, the distance between their legs so small that she could feel the heat radiate off him. Did all of it mean that she should accept him as her husband? Lynette remained unsure.

Despite her wandering mind, she thoroughly enjoyed the production of *Die Zauberflöte*, enthralled by the story of love and magic. At its completion, Aiden led her back through the lobby, where they discussed the opera in great detail before calling for their carriage to take them home.

"Did you girls enjoy the theater?" Lady Keith asked her daughters as she removed her cloak.

Still walking on air from her time spent in Aiden's company, Lynette answered in the affirmative and then excused herself to her room.

"Lynette," Kathleen called to her sister just as she reached the first floor. Lynette turned to see Kathleen trot up the stairs to catch up with her. "I wanted to thank you," she said when she gained her sister's side. "I know you must have had a hand in Lord Wiltshire escorting me tonight."

"It is Lord Elliot you should be thanking, but you are right, I requested his help in the matter." Lynette accepted her sister's gratitude but decided to issue a warning as well. "I wouldn't get my hopes up that Lord Wiltshire will court you now."

"Oh, I know," Kathleen said quickly. "I'm simply hoping that by being seen by his side tonight, others' opinions will soften toward me." She paused and looked away. "I really made a muck of my first Season, didn't I?"

"Oh, Kathleen!" Lynette reached for her sister and pulled her into a hug. "You are still so young, and while that isn't an excuse, it did play a role in your behavior."

Tears pooled in her eyes. "I'm worried I will not make a match now."

"Just enjoy this Season, Kathleen, since there will be others. I'm proof of that!" Lynette said in an attempt to console her sister, which at least garnered a small laugh. "Truly, Kathleen, when the time is right, you will meet your match."

While not wholly convinced, Kathleen still agreed, and the two sisters, friends once more, went to sleep.

"Elliot."

Aiden looked up at the sound of his name and saw Thornburn striding toward him. After the theater, he and Dominic had decided to retire to White's for a few drinks and some cards. In his estimation, the evening had gone quite well, if rather dull, but still hopefully bringing him one step closer to Lynette accepting his proposal.

"Thornburn," Aiden greeted with a congenial nod.

His eyes narrowed as he joined the gentlemen at the table. "You told me less than a week ago that you did not have an agreement with Miss Elphinstone."

"That is correct," Aiden said but wondered where their conversation was going.

"Then tell me why Lord Keith told me that his eldest daughter was spoken for this afternoon?" Thornburn asked. "And then offered me her younger sister?"

Aiden shrugged. "Miss Kathleen is quite beautiful."

"I do not want the title-hungry doe-eyed debutante," Thornburn said, his tone short and clipped. "I want the mature, more refined sister."

"Then why haven't you offered for her?"

"I just tried!"

"No, I mean before," Aiden clarified. "She's been out for nine Seasons, so what stopped you from marrying her at any point up until now?" He arched a brow. "From my understanding, you would have met with no resistance since you have always been a first son, an heir. You're just angry that now I have taken pains to secure what you have until so recently overlooked."

"You're an insufferable bastard," Thornburn growled, having no other retort, and then took his leave as quickly as he came.

"What has him all riled up?" Dominic asked after witnessing the confrontation.

"Marriage," Aiden replied simply. As if it was simple at all. Now that Thornburn knew of his agreement with Lord Keith, it wouldn't be long before the rest of Society became aware. At that point, it would be impossible to keep Lynette in the dark, but he was still afraid he needed more time to woo her. While he had indeed made great strides, he didn't think she was quite ready to accept his suit yet.

But he was also getting tired of waiting. Even though it was true it had been no more than a week since they'd met, he was still feeling increasingly unsatisfied with their arrangement. The harsh reality was that there was only so much that stolen kisses could provide. He wanted Lynette sprawled underneath him without a stitch on her.

"I don't envy you gentlemen," Dominic said. "The pains you must go through to secure a bride . . . there will be no courtship of my future bride; I'll simply select her and make the arrangements with her father."

"It is becoming increasingly hard to do that these days." Aiden shook his head. "Ladies fancy themselves a love match."

"Love is a useless emotion." Dominic's lip curled. "Passion I can understand, since it makes it all that much easier to take a woman to bed, but love . . . I don't see the need."

Aiden had no cause but to agree. Lynette's desire for a love match was what had him in his present situation, unfulfilled by either passion or duty. While he'd already made the arrangements with Lord Keith and could act on them whenever he wanted, he had an irrational inclination to protect her tender sensibilities. Torn between conflicting emotions, he couldn't advance in either direction. But despite his inner turmoil, Aiden remained certain that one way or another, he was marrying Lynette.

Chapter Eleven

"How are you feeling?" Lynette asked her sister as they walked into Lady Paxton's ball the following evening.

Kathleen gently bit her lip. "Better."

Lynette studied her sister and truly hoped she intended to turn over a new leaf, but only time would tell. Once in the ballroom, she caught sight of Lord Bath, but for whatever reason, he didn't solicit a dance from her. It was just as well since rumors were flying about her and Aiden. Apparently, their evening at the theater had caused an uproar because there was speculation that they already had an agreement. She stepped away from the crowd and sighed. The sands in the hourglass were falling, and it was unlikely Aiden or Society would wait much longer.

"How would you feel about dancing twice with me this evening?" Aiden asked when he found her. His chest tightened, and he hoped she couldn't feel the clamminess of his hand through her glove.

Lynette's lips parted, and her pulse quickened. Two dances were the maximum allowed for an unengaged couple. "You want to dance with me twice?"

"You're the only one I want to dance with."

She chewed on her cheek, his intentions perfectly

clear. By dancing only with her, Society would assume he intended to offer for her. Likewise, if she danced with nobody but him, she'd be signaling her willingness to accept. But did it really matter if everyone already believed they had a connection? Furthermore, she didn't particularly want to dance with anyone else either, albeit for different reasons. So Lynette simply nodded, and Aiden exhaled beside her. They promenaded the ballroom, each lost in their own thoughts.

When the first waltz began to play, he pulled her into his arms. His eyes strayed to her necklace and then fell lower. He cleared his throat. "Do you think Lady Paxton has any ripe peaches this evening?"

Her eyelashes fluttered, and her cheeks turned pink. "If she doesn't, it can't be blamed upon me, as I haven't stolen any in a week."

Aiden's eyes were filled with heat. "Would you like to join me in finding out?"

He was enticing her to join him for a tryst! Lynette knew she should be scandalized, but she simply couldn't deny that she wanted to partake in whatever he had planned. It wasn't like dancing together. As long as they were careful, there would be no societal repercussions. "How?" She swallowed hard.

"I shall trip on your flounce," he explained. "And you will tell your mother you are going to the withdrawing room to fix it but will meet me in the orangery instead."

"And what if my mother insists on accompanying me to the withdrawing room?"

He smirked. "I trust you to convince her otherwise."

In the end, Lady Keith seemed none the wiser. Aiden made a show of stepping on Lynette's flounce and apologized profusely. Lynette assured him it was nothing she couldn't fix and then excused herself to do so. Her mother believed her story without much convincing, and Lynette left the ballroom to meet Aiden in the orangery as they had planned.

When she entered the glasshouse, he stood by the peach tree waiting for her. Her body tingled in anticipation of what might happen while they were alone together. She began to say something, wanting to break the tension she felt building between them, but he silenced her with a forceful kiss.

"We won't have much time," he said between kisses, his hand massaging the nape of her neck without disrupting her curls. He thought two waltzes would be enough, but then his fantasies got the better of him, hence the trampled flounce charade. It had all gone well but still did not afford him as much time as he would have liked. Nonetheless, he planned to make great use of the time he did have.

Aiden kissed Lynette fervently, cupping her face in his hands. She grasped his lapels and then ran her arms around his neck. Taking it a step further, his hand found her bosom and stroked her through her dress. Cursing the fabric that lay between him and her sweet bounty, he reached for her laces and loosened them enough so he could free the object of his fantasy. He kissed a line down her neck, straight to the gentle swell of her bosom.

She sighed at the contact between his lips and her skin, and her fingernails scratched at his skull. There was a rush of air when he pulled the neckline of her dress down, but she was simply too heated to care. His hands felt too good, and his kisses were even better. Her head fell back of its own volition when his fingers dipped even lower and rolled her runched nipple in between his thumb and forefinger. She groaned in delight, her back arching to push her breast even further into his hand. Unable to look at him as he continued the exercise, she lost herself in the sensations.

Aiden lifted a breast to his mouth, suckling the stiff peak of her nipple and teasing it with his tongue. He let his hand continue its ministrations on the other breast while Lynette held his head to her chest. The sounds she made only spurred him on, making him want nothing more than to bring her to completion by reaching his hand up her skirts and finding out just how hot and wet he'd made her. Sadly, that wasn't in the cards for the night, and he slowly tapered off his caresses and brought his lips back to meet hers. He kissed her for a moment longer, until her breathing became even again, and then pulled back enough to look into her honey-colored eyes.

"We must go back before we're missed," he said with a heavy voice.

She nodded in agreement, and he helped set her dress right. He thought to broach the topic of a marriage proposal but ultimately decided against it. She'd been hesitant to accept two dances with him, so talk of marriage was still premature.

"Return by way of the withdrawing room again, and I'll see you back in the ballroom." He kissed her once they got to the doors.

Their eyes met when he pulled back, and Lynette's heart burst with emotion. But she was struck speechless for the first time in her life, so she did as instructed and left Aiden to make his own way back to the ballroom.

She tried to feel scandalized by their tryst but ultimately couldn't muster any shame. It was common knowledge that couples partook in assignations at nearly every ball.

She just hadn't expected to engage in such an activity herself. Before Aiden, she'd just been another woman at a ball, more or less in search of a husband. Since him, she felt as though she'd gone through a metamorphosis and was now the type of woman to meet a man for an illicit encounter. Therefore, she wasn't the same woman she'd been when he'd found her in Lady Paxton's orangery a week before. His attention had changed her. Aiden had achieved his aim; Lynette had fallen in love with him.

But what did that say about him? Instead of answering her questions, it only created more. A marriage of convenience might have been horrid for her, but the prospect of one that contained unrequited love felt even worse. At least in a marriage of convenience, she could know what to expect. In one where she loved but felt none in return, her feelings could be hurt. Lynette paused to collect herself before reentering the ballroom and wondered if Aiden could love her. And if he did, how would she know?

Chapter Twelve

Aiden woke late the morning following Lady Paxton's ball. After returning to the ballroom, he spent the remainder of the evening at Lynette's side but noticed a shift in her demeanor. She held herself very stiff and didn't melt into his touch as she usually did. Did she regret their encounter in the orangery? Was she embarrassed? And what did it mean in regard to his courtship of her? He was unsure of himself, which was a rarity, given how confident he typically was with women. In any case, he couldn't bring himself to regret their encounter and decided his only genuine regret was their inability to finish what they'd started.

After going through his morning ablutions, Aiden went to break his fast. He'd been enjoying his selection of meats while reading the paper when suddenly, there was a loud thud and crash from upstairs.

"Seymour!" Eleanor screamed.

Aiden dropped what he was doing and ran up the steps to his parents' bedroom. Inside, he saw his father on the floor with his concerned mother beside him. "What happened?"

"It's nothing." Seymour waved him away and attempted to stand, but he couldn't steady his legs underneath himself and fell again.

Aiden turned toward the door. "I'm calling for a doctor."

"No." Seymour shook his head. "I am fine. I just need some time." He tried to sound strong and in charge, but from his wife's face, all was not what it seemed.

Carson, the Elliots' London butler, stood behind Aiden at the door. "Milord, I can fetch the footmen for you."

"Yes, please," Eleanor replied with a forced smile.

Two of the larger footmen appeared in the bedchamber, essentially picked Seymour up off the floor, and helped him into a chair. Once the servants had been dismissed with the order to bring the duke's and duchess's breakfasts to their room, Aiden turned back to his parents.

"This isn't the first time this has occurred, is it?" he asked them softly.

Seymour gave his son a small nod, whereas Eleanor averted her gaze, unable to look her son in the eye.

Aiden's jaw clenched. "For how long?"

"A little more than two years," Seymour replied resignedly. "I am very weak in the mornings especially, and the doctors have tried to treat it to no avail. Unfortunately, it's gotten increasingly worse over the last six months or so."

Aiden struggled to breathe. "And you didn't think to inform me?"

"We thought you had enough responsibilities." Eleanor finally brought herself to look at her son and speak.

"My responsibilities are to this family and the dukedom," Aiden spat, and his arm slashed through the air between them. "Does Granny know? Did Ferdy?"

"Of course I know." Rowena stood at the door in nothing but her dressing gown. "Why do you think

I'm so insistent for you to marry? The Northumberland Dukedom was created for the Elliots, and I am not about to see it dormant or, worse, extinct."

"What about Ferdy?" Aiden asked again.

"I had told Ferdy—" Seymour began before being cut off by a cough.

"We had told Ferdy the day of his accident," Eleanor finished for her husband.

Immediately, it all began to make sense. Aiden had struggled with his brother's death for so long, obsessing over why Ferdy was in his curricle when he should have been with his wife and daughter. He wiped a hand through his hair. "I can understand why you didn't, but I should have been informed when I became heir."

"Would it have truly changed anything?" Rowena narrowed her eyes. "What will you do differently now that you know? Marry quicker? Sire an heir?"

"It does not matter what I would have done or will do. If I am to be head of this family, then no secrets should be kept from me, especially those regarding my father's health!" Aiden whirled around and roared.

Rowena stared at him with pursed lips but did not reply. His chest heaved, his heart beating so loud he could hear it. He turned back to his parents, who were also silent where they sat. Unable to remain in their presence any longer, he turned on his heel and strode to the door.

"Aiden," his mother called to him, and his heart contracted when he heard the fear in her voice.

"I am simply going for a walk," he said without turning back and then left the room.

Aiden found himself at White's an hour later, sipping on a brandy. He swirled the amber liquid in the glass and contemplated the morning's discoveries. With his new insight, he couldn't believe he hadn't seen the signs earlier. Since his return from the Continent, his father had looked poorly, with pale skin and dullness in his eyes, but Aiden had attributed it to grief as it was not uncommon for it to affect a person's health. Now he rued his naïveté! His grandmother's questions plagued him. What would he do with his newfound knowledge?

When he thought that his father was the picture of health, marrying by the end of the Season seemed like an acceptable time frame. But now with his father's ailing health out in the open, he didn't feel so sure. He understood the importance of keeping the Northumberland Dukedom within the Elliot family since he'd been raised with the knowledge that he could trace his ancestry back to not only the first Duke of Northumberland, but to the Scottish laird and Norman conqueror that duke descended from. They were one of the oldest families in all of Britain, which was not something that anyone, including Aiden, could put aside. Therefore, he would make the straightforward decision of marrying for duty.

"A little early, don't you think?" Dominic appeared and gestured to the glass in Aiden's hand.

"There's a Scottish branch in my family tree, if you recall, so it's never too early." He took a large gulp from his glass.

"What troubles you?" Dominic asked bluntly, sitting in the chair across from his friend.

"Family," Aiden replied, but he wasn't willing to reveal his family's secrets, not even to a close friend. "Women." He sighed.

Dominic arched a brow and smirked. "I thought you only had one of those."

"That I do." He nodded and swirled the brandy some more. One singular, intriguing woman who would likely refuse him her hand in marriage since he was now duty bound to marry quickly. Lynette had told him she wouldn't marry him for duty, but duty had just slapped him in the face. His father was ill, likely dying a slow death. It simply felt wrong to wait when faced with his father's impending mortality, but he still wanted to marry Lynette. No other woman would do.

After their tryst in Lady Paxton's orangery, Aiden didn't know where he stood with her. He'd enjoyed the rendezvous immensely but was still concerned she hadn't. He just couldn't fathom her reaction to him when they reunited in the ballroom. Had he offended her? And would it influence her response to his marriage proposal?

"You are definitely in a predicament, my friend," Dominic said pointedly.

"Don't wait too long on yours or you might be in the same." Aiden sat back and sighed. "How does one propose marriage?"

"Well, not that I'm experienced in such things, but I think you must first gain permission from the chit's father."

Aiden nodded. "Aye, but I mean to the woman."

"It's not as simple as asking, will you marry me?" Dominic asked with a furrowed brow.

Aiden shrugged. "I believe women appreciate some flowery language, but I'm not sure as I've never done it before."

"Well, neither have I." Dominic laughed.

"I shall let you know, for future reference." Then with nothing left to contemplate, Aiden downed his brandy, stood up, and exited White's, intent on securing Lynette's hand in marriage before lunch.

Aiden took a hackney from White's to the Keiths' town house and paid the driver once he pulled up. Exiting the hackney, he jogged up the stairs and rapped on the door, which Mr. Williams opened with alarming speed. "Is Miss Elphinstone available?"

"Please, wait in the reception room, and I'll see for you." Mr. Williams led him there before going in search of his mistress. Left alone, Aiden paced the room, the palms of his hands becoming sweaty.

"Lord Elliot, we are very sorry to keep you waiting." Lady Keith appeared at the door with Lynette by her side. "My daughter was just so immersed with her watercolors."

"It is quite all right." He smiled at the matron. "I wondered if I could possibly have a private audience with Miss Elphinstone."

Recognition flashed across Lady Keith's face, and a broad smile spanned ear to ear. "Of course!" she screeched with excitement. "I will be just in the hall if you should need me." She tapped her daughter on her shoulders and then bounced away.

Lynette rubbed her hands over her skirt and stepped farther into the room. Aiden met her halfway, and once they were close, he reached for her hand and held it up to his face. "You weren't really painting, were you?"

Lynette cast a sidelong glance at the door. "No, I was reading a novel."

"Will your mother be listening?" Aiden whispered.

"I would imagine so." She nodded, her hand still held in his.

"I came here . . ." he started and then stopped. He

looked deeply into her light brown eyes and marveled at their gold specks while he tried to determine what to say. "Firstly, I want to apologize."

"Apologize?" Lynette asked, squinting up at him. Did he intend to apologize for their tryst in Lady Paxton's orangery? Despite being conflicted by the encounter, it had been an eye-opening experience for her since it made her realize she'd fallen in love with him. But she didn't know what her realization meant for them in terms of marriage and continued to wonder if they could happily marry with only her loving him. And now he was standing before her, looking contrite. Did he intend to withdraw his courtship? Had he found a woman more capable? She could already feel her heart breaking!

"This is not the way I wanted to do it. But circumstances have necessitated an increased urgency," Aiden said. "I know you are the type of woman to wish for a love match, and I had intended to give you a traditional courtship, but my father . . ." He sucked in his lips, unsure if he was willing to speak the truth of his father's health out loud, even to the woman who he hoped would be his wife. "Circumstances have changed." He tightened his grip on her hand. "There is increased pressure for me to marry with all possible haste. So I am here to offer for you now."

Lynette gasped loudly and almost reeled backward, but Aiden steadied her.

"All I can truly offer you is a marriage of convenience. You will never want for anything as my wife, and there would be an entire library at your disposal at Eldridge Castle! We can have any book shipped there, or if you would prefer, we can come to London, and you can browse the bookshops to your heart's content." He offered her the only thing he thought he could give her. "You may give me a truthful answer." His tone grew serious. "Tell me if my offer is acceptable to you or not. I will not push you into an unwilling marriage, no matter what your parents may decree." He lifted a hand to her face and stroked her cheek with the back of his finger. Her eyes gave nothing away, but the silence felt deafening. "You may either accept or deny me now," he whispered, not wanting to imagine what her refusal would mean to him. He would have to let her go and find another woman to marry. Not the greatest hardship he'd ever faced since there were countless other women in London that would jump at the chance of being the future Duchess of Northumberland. But Aiden didn't want just any woman; he wanted Lynette. From the moment he'd met her, she was the only woman he'd wanted. But he couldn't tell her that since she would surely ask why and his reasoning was indescribable, not to mention she'd already questioned his judgment once before. Thus it was better to offer her a sound marriage of convenience, which was something they could both understand.

Lynette took a step back and was thankful Aiden let her go. She averted her gaze, thinking, trying to organize her thoughts and feelings. He offered her a marriage of convenience, not the love match she'd dreamt about. At least one thing was clear for her now: he didn't love her. If he had, he would have given her a declaration of love, not a speech about his duty to his family and his ensuing responsibility to marry. A small, foolish thought made her cling to the idea that he might, just maybe, have some tender feelings for her that he was unwilling to speak on. Surely one did not look at another or touch someone as gently as he touched her without feeling something more than duty. But it was an errant thought, and after a moment, she decided that if she were sensible, she would take him at his word.

Where did that leave them then? Would it be better to refuse or accept his proposal? Lynette would love Aiden whether they married or not, but could she live with him knowing he did not love her in return?

"Lynette?" His blue eyes widened while he waited to hear his fate.

"I am thinking, milord," she said with a huff.

"If you would like to take some time..." Unfortunately, he couldn't afford much time, but he was willing to grant her what he could if it would mean a more favorable response.

She pursed her lips. "No, I can decide." But what to decide? Was it better to love or to be loved? She didn't know. What she did know, however, was that her heart ached at the thought of him marrying another, of never touching or kissing him again. Whether she married him or not, they would still move within the same circles, and she'd likely attend balls thrown by his wife. Could she really see him from across a ballroom and not yearn to be with him?

She placed a trembling hand over her stomach and took a deep breath. "I shall accept."

"Truly?" he asked, his mouth agape. He couldn't fathom what he'd said to convince her but was happy it had worked.

"Yes." She nodded, and a slow smile spread across her face.

Without thinking of the impropriety of it, he hauled her back into his arms and kissed her until he remembered their place. "Shall we tell your mother now?"

"She'll surely need to find out somehow," Lynette replied, ruing the need to break their embrace. They stepped away from each other, and then she opened the door to reveal the audience that stood waiting expectantly in the hall. Her mama was there, along with her sister, who glowered with what only could be described as jealous excitement. Her father also stood waiting, in addition to Milly and Mr. Williams, their hopeful eyes staring at her. A lump formed in her throat, which she struggled to swallow. She'd expected her mama to eavesdrop, but her entire family, including the servants? She was so annoyed she couldn't speak.

Thankfully, Aiden came to her rescue and made the announcement everyone was waiting for. "Miss Elphinstone has just done me the great pleasure of accepting my marriage proposal." Immediately, squeals erupted. Lady Keith stepped forward to embrace her daughter, and Lord Keith offered Aiden his hand to shake.

"We'll have to start planning right away!" Lady Keith exclaimed. "Do you have any date in particular in mind?" she turned to Aiden to ask.

"I'm sure I'll be able to secure a special license, so I would say with all possible haste."

Lady Keith scowled slightly, and her shoulders sagged. "A special license?"

"Yes, I'm afraid time is of the essence." Aiden inclined his head. "I suggest you all join my family and me this evening for dinner, after which we can discuss the logistics."

His offer was accepted by the entire family. And then after a final few congratulations, Aiden bid goodbye to his future wife, with the foolhardy intention of wedding and bedding her within the week.

Chapter Thirteen

Aiden returned home the happiest he'd been since returning from the Continent, a weight having been lifted from his shoulders. Lynette had agreed to marry him! He hadn't realized how much of his contentment rode on her acceptance until he had to wait for an answer. It felt as if his heart had stopped beating and fallen into his stomach. And then she agreed, and everything was right again. The sun seemed brighter, streaming into the reception room, and the air was fresher when he left the Keiths' residence.

The only thing left for Aiden to do was to inform his family. It was nearly luncheon by the time he made it home. Upon walking through the door, he told Carson to expect guests for dinner and then went to the dining room in anticipation of lunch being served. Seymour and Eleanor joined him shortly after the lunch bell rang, followed by Rowena. It was a silent affair since the tension from the morning was still present, but Aiden refused to let it sour his mood.

Once the sandwiches had been eaten and Carson had begun to clear the empty plates, Aiden decided to make his announcement. "Before you go, I would like to inform you all that I have asked Miss Elphinstone to be my wife, and she has accepted." He paused to allow his announcement to take effect. Glancing around the table, he noted a varying array of emotions: his father looked relieved, his mother close to tears, and his grandmother, dare he say it, proud. "I assume a special license can be procured under current constraints, and we can plan for me to be wed in a week?" He looked to the women of his family for confirmation.

"Absolutely not," Rowena bit off, her disposition changing in the blink of an eye.

Aiden stared at her. "I'm sorry, but I thought the idea was for me to be wed and sire an heir with all possible haste."

"It is, and congratulations on your engagement, my dear, but we mustn't act too hastily," Rowena said.

Aiden touched his fingers to his temple, his good mood thoroughly halted and a migraine teasing its beginning. "You'll have to explain your reasoning, Granny, because I am far from understanding."

"No one outside this family knows of your father's ailment; thus, if we act too quickly, Society may suppose we are covering up a greater malady than just Ferdy's death."

Aiden bit his tongue so that he didn't point out they were indeed doing just that.

"As such, we need to move quickly, but not so much so as to arouse any further suspicions," Rowena said as if it was the most logical thing in the world.

Damn Society, Aiden thought with disgust, and he was just about to say as much when his mother interjected.

"The traditional three weeks for the banns to be called will suffice, won't it, Rowena?" Eleanor asked.

"It'll be a highly sought-after affair." She rubbed her

chin. "But given current constraints, I would say three weeks would be quick enough for our needs while still being an acceptable timeframe for the *ton*. It'll be a rush to plan such an event." She sighed, acknowledging the trials and tribulations of planning a wedding. "We'll need to start immediately."

Aiden scrubbed a hand down his face. "I invited the Keiths over for dinner this evening to begin preparations."

"Well thought of you, my dear." Rowena beamed, once again seemingly pleased. "We shall announce it in the papers tomorrow, so you'll need to write up something for the *Gazette* and get that sent off promptly." She started listing off things she thought needed to be done. "Oh, it's Sunday today, so the first reading of the banns won't be until a week from today anyway." She smacked her forehead lightly. "Which means we're planning for four weeks—"

Aiden looked upward. "Four weeks?"

Rowena shook her finger at him. "Don't give me that look, my boy. It can't be helped that you decided to propose to her on a Sunday!"

He shook his head but remained silent.

"We should arrange the engagement ball to be held two weeks from today." Rowena turned to her daughter-in-law. "Eleanor, you and I will need to plan that. And then two weeks after the engagement ball, the banns will be completed and you can be wed."

Having already had his fill of wedding discussion, Aiden quit the dining room to allow his mother and grandmother to get on with their planning. He couldn't believe he would need to wait a month to wed Lynette. It felt like an eternity now that he'd garnered her acceptance. But he had little choice but to do what was being asked of him.

It was either that or commandeer his family's ship and sail Lynette to Gretna Green. The thought was tempting, he admitted to himself, but ultimately, he didn't wish to cause any more rifts within his family. He remembered the tears of joy his mother shed when he announced his engagement and decided they were worth more than the four weeks he needed to wait to make Lynette his.

Lynette's pulse raced as her carriage pulled up in front of Elliot House later in the evening. She'd visited multiple times over the years as ball guests of Aiden's brother- and sister-in-law, but something felt different now. Her eyes rose to the lion statue atop the central façade, and she rubbed her palms over her skirt.

"Lynette?"

She blinked. Her father stood waiting to help her down. "Sorry."

Lady Keith followed behind her. "You better not be woolgathering all evening. This is a very important dinner."

Upon entering, the butler divested the family of their cloaks and then led them to the reception room, where the Elliot family waited to receive them. Lynette smiled when she saw Aiden standing imposingly by the fireplace. He looked relaxed in the ornately decorated room, which shouldn't have surprised her, given that it was his home. He stepped forward to greet her, drew her gloved hand to his lips, and kissed her fingertips.

Aiden cleared his throat and turned to the rest of the Keith family. "Welcome. I'm happy that you could join us this evening."

"We wouldn't dare miss it." Lady Keith pursed her lips. "What with a wedding needing to be planned swiftly."

Lynette resisted the urge to roll her eyes. Her mother had been moaning about the need for a special license since Aiden had left earlier in the day. All of Lady Keith's dreams of an extravagant wedding were apparently being shattered, as if it was her wedding and not Lynette's being planned. Lynette didn't mind the prospect of a special license. In her sensible opinion, she and Aiden would be married no matter if it was a grand affair or not. Nevertheless, Lady Keith believed it was her daughter's right, given that she would be a future duchess.

"Have no fear, Lady Keith," Rowena said from her chair. "We shall have four weeks to prepare!"

"Four weeks?" she asked, eyebrows raised.

Lynette looked to Aiden, who nodded resignedly.

"Yes, indeed, it was decided this afternoon," Rowena said. "I'm sorry my grandson scared you with talk of a special license." She looked pointedly at Aiden. "Men will drag their feet while deciding *when* to marry, but once they reach their decision, it's a race to the altar!"

"This is wonderful news!" Lady Keith's delight was unmistakable.

"We were under the impression that time was of the essence," Lord Keith said, confused by the sudden change of plans.

Aiden swallowed and flattened his lips. "Family matters did increase my urgency."

Rowena glared at her grandson. "Be that as it may, we determined that four weeks would be entirely soon enough."

Since the Dowager's word was as good as law, everyone agreed the wedding would be four weeks hence. Lynette suspected that Aiden wasn't as at peace with the decision as he let on, but he didn't raise any concerns, so she didn't either. Instead, the butler appeared to usher the Elliots and their guests into the dining room for dinner, where the wedding talk began in earnest.

"We shall host all the wedding festivities here," Rowena said as soon as everyone was seated. "Including the engagement ball."

"Of course." Lady Keith offered no objection since the prominence of Elliot House appealed to her. "I think we should discuss flowers first since they will determine our color palette."

"What do you think, Miss Elphinstone?" Eleanor asked. "Do you have a color preference?"

"I quite like the color blue," Lynette replied, her eyes shifting to Aiden.

"Blue?" Lady Keith wrinkled her nose. "Why not a more romantic color, like pink or rose?"

Lynette refocused on her soup, unable to disagree with her mother while in the company of others. So, plastering a tight-lipped smile on her face, she was about to agree when Aiden spoke up.

"I think blue is a very romantic color," he said, meeting Lynette's eye. Her mouth fell open as her jaw unclenched. She swallowed and then smiled at him.

"Perhaps white flowers then to go with the blue?" Rowena asked, and outnumbered, Lady Keith was forced to agree.

Every new topic saw a similar discussion unfold. Lynette didn't have an opinion on many things, but she was still grateful that Eleanor continued to include her in the conversation. It was her wedding, after all, and even if she would have preferred a smaller, more intimate affair, the most important thing was that she was marrying someone she loved.

Once dinner was complete, the women left the men to their port while they retired to the drawing room. There, the wedding planning continued with talk of guest lists and invitations. Quills and paper were called for as the matrons created lists of family and connections they sought to invite. Then once the ink was dry, the lists were folded and put away just in time for the gentlemen to rejoin them for tea.

By the time the port was finished, Aiden had had his fill of lies. Since the start of dinner, he had been aware of his father's frailty. It was so apparent to him now that he had a hard time believing he hadn't seen it before. Seymour picked at his food and rarely engaged in conversation but requested the port nonetheless, which perpetuated the need for Aiden to converse with Lord Keith in the vain hope he wouldn't notice Seymour staring off into space.

While entering the drawing room, though, Aiden decided that maybe his lot hadn't been so bad. The ladies had continued wedding planning and barely acknowledged the gentlemen as they rejoined them. In the end, Seymour didn't stay long, excusing himself from the party, much to Aiden's relief. He could see his mother was torn between wanting to join her husband and needing to save face with their guests. But in the end, she reluctantly decided to stay where she sat.

For Aiden, it was the final straw, and he needed to step away from his family and their lies before he revealed their secrets in anger. He looked at Lynette sitting on the sofa between her mother and sister. "Lady Keith, would it be appropriate if I took Miss Elphinstone for a tour of the house?" he asked charmingly.

"But of course!" She smiled widely and then turned

back to Eleanor and Rowena.

Not wasting another second, Aiden extended his hand to Lynette and guided her through the house.

"We're allowed to be alone?" Lynette asked as she fell into step beside him.

"Since we are engaged, you can no longer be ruined by me," Aiden replied with a smirk. He thought they had twenty minutes, perhaps thirty maximum, before anyone questioned their whereabouts. He attempted to point out the different rooms as they walked through the corridors, such as the state dining room and the ballroom, which Lynette said she'd seen before. They also walked through the galleries, which contained the Elliots' art collections, but despite his best intentions, he rushed through his tour in order to get as much time alone with her as possible.

When they reached the library, Lynette's mouth dropped open. "It's so big," she said as she ran her hand along the shelves.

He followed her around the room. "The library at Eldridge Castle is much bigger."

"Truly?" Her eyes widened even more. "What I wouldn't give for a library even this size."

"It's yours," he said. "Essentially."

"Not quite yet." She rubbed her lips together. "But soon."

"Not nearly soon enough," he growled, closing the gap between them. She instinctively wrapped her arms around him as he leaned in to kiss her. Neither of them was interested in starting slow, and soon she gasped for breath. Her heart beat in her ears as she became aware of a strange tingle in her lower stomach. His lips trailed kisses along her jaw and then dipped lower as his hands fell from her shoulders to the front of her gown.

She released the sweetest sigh as his hands grazed her breasts for the second time.

"You like that?" Aiden asked, with a wholly masculine smile spread across his face. She bit her lip and groaned as his hands made another pass, unable to respond. Leaning back in, he teased the tender skin at her nape, her curls tickling his forehead. Then his eyes drifted down the back of her gown, and he reconsidered their positioning. "You'll need to sit." He urged her to the chaise as he loosened her laces. Lynette, caught in a haze of desire, didn't have the capacity to question his intentions even when she felt the heat of his breath on her chest.

Her jaw dropped when her breasts were engulfed, one by a hand and the other by his mouth. She arched her back and pushed further into his caress, but it still wasn't enough. The throbbing beneath her skirts only intensified with each pass of his tongue. Similarly unsatisfied, he reached his free hand to the hem of her gown. Once there, it made the climb, stopping only to quickly massage the cheeks of her backside before returning to the object of his desire: her front and her core.

She was just as he imagined. He ran a finger along her slit, coating it in her desire. Shivering, he rested his head on her bounty, shut his eyes, and tried to rein in his hunger. After a few deep breaths he straightened, but when his eyes found her face, he nearly lost it all over again. Her cheeks were pink, and her lips were parted. It would have been easy to lift up her skirts, sink himself into her heat, and give them both the relief they sought. But he knew she deserved so much more than just something quick on a library chaise; she deserved a warm bed and a night full of passion. Still, in her state, he also believed she deserved completion.

Lynette opened her eyes to find Aiden staring at her. "Everything all right?"

He exhaled shakily. "Just checking to make sure you're all right."

"I believe so," she said and tried to sit up, thinking their interlude had reached its conclusion.

"Not yet." He halted her movement. Staring straight into her eyes, he cupped her mound, and her mouth fell open with a gasp. Their eyes remained transfixed on each other as he bent his head to her breast and suckled it teasingly while his finger found the nub that contained a woman's greatest pleasure.

"Aiden . . ." she moaned, slightly louder than she should have.

"Shh, you can't scream . . . not yet," he said as his fingers continued to rub her core.

"But . . . Aiden . . ." She tried to keep her voice soft, but her body was aflame, and she felt as though she was going to internally combust.

"I promise, when we're married, you can scream as loud and as much as you want, but here and now, you must stay quiet," he whispered frantically in her ear before covering her mouth with his. He rejoiced in the discovery that she was an enthusiastic lover and regretted the need to keep her silent. A smile spread across his face when he thought of the day he could revel in the noises he wrought from her. But until then, he kept his mouth on Lynette's, who was so lost in her pleasure that she couldn't even kiss him back. Not that it mattered. He kept thrusting his fingers and swallowing her cries until she reached her climax.

After what felt like both an eternity and not long enough, she lay sedately in his arms. Aiden, for his part, hated the thought of ending their moment alone, but even as an engaged couple, they couldn't risk being found together as they were. "Come here." He helped her to stand and right her dress by retying her laces. "We must get back."

She nodded, a blush brightening her cheeks. "We must."

Aiden couldn't resist pulling her back in for another kiss. His lovely wanton from a moment before had morphed back into an innocent miss, and he didn't know which one he preferred. Both roused something in him that made him feel warm. Ending the kiss, he rested his forehead on hers. "In four weeks' time, we won't have to sneak around like this anymore."

"And until then?" Lynette asked, wanting to know how many more interludes they would have before they married.

"I'll continue to trample your flounces and offer to take you on tours of my house," he replied with a devilish smirk. He might have decided to wait the four weeks of their engagement to bed her properly, but he didn't feel the need to make the same concessions in regard to moments like the one they'd just shared. She'd been too lush in his arms for him to feel satisfied by their most recent encounter, so they would need to continue to toe the line of Society's dictates.

When they rejoined their family in the drawing room, it seemed the wedding talk had continued through their absence. The conversation washed over Lynette, who had to make a special effort to listen and be a part of the plans being made, since her body still hummed while her mind raced. What had happened in the library was the single most exhilarating experience of her life, and she found it hard to concentrate on anything else.

"How does that sound, Miss Elphinstone?" someone asked, which brought her out of her reverie. Embarrassingly, she couldn't ascertain who had posed the question and what it had been regarding, which left her staring doe-eyed at the group.

"Yes, that sounds lovely," Lynette replied, taking a gamble by responding in the affirmative.

"Excellent! We shall pick you up tomorrow afternoon and go to Bond Street together then!" Rowena said, seemingly happy with Lynette's response, while Lady Keith gave her daughter a reproachful look, obviously aware that she had been woolgathering again.

But it couldn't be helped, Lynette thought to herself. One could not experience what she had in the library and then be expected to participate in polite conversation. She dared to look at Aiden, who sat in conversation with her father. He didn't seem to have the same difficulty paying attention. The idea gave her pause; did their tryst not affect him in the way it did her? Was it because she loved him, but he didn't love her? No, she rationalized, what they'd just done in the library was lust, which had nothing to do with love. So then how could he look so unaffected?

It must be because the sensations were so new to her, she concluded, by the time she and her family were ready to return home. She wasn't fanciful enough to believe she was the first woman he'd had trysts with before. It was just another way women were treated differently in Society; their virtue was deemed important, whereas men's virtue wasn't. Furthermore, despite her obvious lack of experience, she believed he was very skilled in passion. It was evident in his touch and kisses. He could anticipate her every need before she was able to consider it herself, and she was sure such a talent only came from experience.

However, her revelations didn't make her feel any better. Instead, she found herself wanting to affect him the way he affected her despite her inexperience. If their marriage needed to be bound by duty, then there could at least be lust within it. It might not equate to the love match she'd originally wanted, but it was more than a simple marriage of convenience. Lust could be the middle ground between duty and love. Aiden wanted duty; Lynette wanted love, but lust could bridge the gap between both of their wants.

Chapter Fourteen

As arranged the night prior, the Elliots' carriage arrived outside the Keiths' town house in the afternoon to convey the two families to the modiste's salon. Lynette peered out of the window the entire way to Bond Street, counting the people they passed by. The clouds in the sky threatened rain, and she would have preferred to curl up with her novel. But instead, her afternoon would consist of her filling out her trousseau. She pursed her lips. If only a trousseau included books she could put in her new library.

The rain held out during the short ride, and Adele Cote, the preferred modiste of the *haut ton*, welcomed the group when they arrived. "Your Graces." She curtsied in greeting to Rowena and Eleanor. "And milady." She repeated the gesture, but not as low, to Lady Keith. Then finally, she came upon Lynette. "And this must be our bride." She smiled and bobbed once more.

"And her attendant," Kathleen said, clearly wanting to be recognized.

"Of course." Adele greeted her with another customary curtsy and then turned back to Lynette. "Shall we talk of the fabric first?" She motioned toward the fabrics she'd set out. "What color were you looking for?"

Lynette took a moment to admire the feel of the fabrics before her. There were silks, satins, and lace. "I like this one." She pointed to a shimmering gold satin.

Adele nodded. "That would make an excellent choice."

"I feel as though the silver would suit your complexion better, my dear," Lady Keith said.

Lynette breathed deeply, resisting the urge to disagree with her mother yet again.

"May we see them both laid upon her?" Rowena requested with a thump of her cane.

Adele led Lynette to the tailoring platform and laid the silver fabric on one shoulder and the gold on the other. The matrons looked Lynette over as she stood awkwardly awaiting their decree.

"The gold for the wedding, I believe," Rowena said after a few minutes, overruling Lady Keith. "It brings out the gold in her eyes."

"The gold it is then." Adele set the fabric aside.

Lynette blinked at the Dowager, a silent thank you on the tip of her tongue.

"Are you interested in any lace or embroidery?" Adele asked next, and Lynette agreed to some of both.

"She shall need another dress for the engagement ball," Rowena said once they finished discussing lace and embroidery. "Gloves and stockings as well."

"Are you drawn to any other color?" Adele gestured to the fabrics again. Lynette perused the selection before landing on a blue one, the color of sapphire. The shade was light enough to remind Lynette of Aiden's eyes, leading her to recall what happened the last time she wore a similar-colored dress.

"This one." Lynette reached for the fabric, her mouth

suddenly dry.

Blue fabric agreed to, Adele consulted Lynette on the style of dress she would like and then moved to take her measurements. "I should have the lining completed by next week if you can return for a fitting," the seamstress said.

Lynette nodded. "Of course."

"That was a successful shop," Rowena said as they took their leave. "Next, the shoe shop." She led the way despite her need for a cane. With all the shops Rowena insisted they visit, the entire outing lasted a few hours, which resulted in the Keiths arriving home in only enough time to prepare for their evening entertainment.

Since Aiden and Lynette's engagement had been announced in the *Gazette* that morning, the Countess of Chester's ball would be Lynette's first appearance as an affianced woman. Wearing what she deemed her best dress, which was emerald green in color, she entered the ballroom on Aiden's arm. He'd sent a note while she'd been out to inform her that he intended to escort her to the ball. Despite feeling self-conscious as a hush descended the ballroom, she kept her head held high. She expected to become the object of the *ton*'s gossip due to nothing more than their unbearable jealousy in regard to her engagement. Therefore, the best thing she could do was weather the storm and hope for someone to either make a better match than her or commit a terrible faux pas.

"I hope my granny wasn't too overbearing this afternoon," Aiden said softly once they had entered.

Lynette shook her head. "She was actually rather helpful."

He arched an eyebrow. "My granny, helpful?"

"'Tis true!" She nodded. "You were all very helpful

yesterday and today. I would never have been able to disagree with my mama without your support. Then I would be forced to walk down the aisle in a silver dress with pink roses."

He laughed. "As long as you're happy."

She smiled wider, her heartbeat doubling its usual pace. They promenaded the ballroom, stopping here and there to accept felicitations on their recent engagement. "What made you decide to escort me tonight?" she asked after a while.

"I had to see with my own eyes that you made it out of Bond Street alive," he replied in a falsely serious tone.

"I'm alive and well, Aiden, as you can see," she said, continuing the banter that flowed easily between them. The whispers had died down since their arrival, and she was starting to feel more comfortable in the crush.

"Just so." He smiled but still feared the possibility of his grandmother scaring her off. If he had a hard time not succumbing to Rowena's whims, then what chance did she stand?

The first strands of a waltz began playing, and Aiden offered Lynette his hand. "I hope you do not tire too easily tonight because I plan to dance with you as much as I can." He pulled her into an embrace. He'd been yearning to feel her body on his all day and appreciated the opportunity the waltz presented him. But if he was being at all honest, the waltz regrettably involved far too many layers of clothing, and nothing could be done about it.

"Be careful, or Society may believe that we are a love match," she warned as he whirled her to the music. Love matches were becoming popular, and everyone wanted one, including her. Or she had, she reminded herself, before she accepted Aiden's proposal.

His mouth fell open. "What, I can't dance with my fiancée as much as I want?"

She squinted at him. "I hadn't realized you were such a fan of dancing."

He wasn't, he wanted to reply, but he was a fan of *her*. So what if Society dubbed them a love match? He'd never given much thought to Society's whims and was less inclined to now that he happily held Lynette in his arms. So discarding her concerns on the propriety of it, Aiden danced with her two more times.

Chapter Fifteen

Two weeks later, it was the night of Aiden and Lynette's engagement ball. Elliot House had been decorated for the occasion with flowers, candles, and fabrics, none of which mattered to Aiden, who was simply ready for their engagement to be at its end.

"Two more weeks," he said to himself as he stood next to Lynette in the receiving line.

"What did you say?" she asked with a tilt of her head.

"Two more weeks until we are man and wife." He smiled at her. Lynette radiated beauty, dressed in a gorgeous sapphire dress that accentuated her every curve. The color of it made her skin and hair glisten, and Aiden was humble enough to recognize that he was indeed a lucky man. Two more weeks until she could be in his bed, and he probably wouldn't let her leave for another two weeks after that.

She nodded but didn't share his smile. "It will be here soon."

"Not nearly soon enough," Aiden bent to whisper in her ear.

She gasped and was filled with heat despite the seemingly innocuous statement.

The first two weeks of their engagement had been a whirlwind for Lynette. Her invitations had doubled since the announcement because everyone wanted to hear from her how she'd managed to ensnare Lord Elliot in matrimony. Lady Keith had never felt more in her element than when she described how Lord Elliot had been courting her daughter since the start of the Season. Kathleen was even made to feel special since she had matrons telling her that she would have many more opportunities to make a match once her sister became a duchess.

None of the talk bothered Lynette because she was sensible enough to know it was a necessary evil of Society. What began to irk her was everyone's opinion that Aiden was in love with her. She'd tried to put a stop to the offhanded comments as soon as they began by insisting that the arrangement between Aiden and herself was purely conventional. Hopeless romantics refused to agree, noting how often he danced with her and escorted her on outings. They were inconsequential reasons to Lynette, who thought he was merely being an attentive fiancé. Surely he wasn't doing anything special, was he?

Aiden seemed oblivious to being the object of gossip and remained unfazed as the festivities began. However, Lynette wasn't so lucky. She felt as though she heard every whisper uttered in her vicinity, which caused her to overthink her position. Aiden didn't love her, did he? Surely he would have declared it if it was true. And what did it matter to her anyway? She'd decided to accept him as he was, not with the intention of changing his mind. One did not change their mind in regard to love, she believed, so if Aiden hadn't loved her when he proposed, it was impossible for him to love her now.

"Are you all right?" Aiden asked, bringing her out of her reverie.

Lynette studied his features and noted his knitted brows. "Fine, milord." She forced a smile. She then tried to put her thoughts and feelings to the side since the crush of a ball was not the best place for a crisis.

Unfortunately, she couldn't get away from the whispers. As Aiden led her through a waltz, an activity she'd previously enjoyed, she could hear the comments regarding how close he held her. Wanting to put a stop to the gossip, she tried to correct their position but only succeeded in guiding him to step on her toe. She reeled back, the pain radiating throughout her foot.

"I need a minute," Lynette said, excusing herself from the dance. Her intention had been to dismiss him in order to garner some time alone to collect her thoughts, but instead, he stayed hot on her heels as she strode out onto the balcony.

"What is troubling you?" Aiden asked. She'd been acting strangely for several days but had been even more distraught since the beginning of the ball. He'd attributed it to the anticipation of their impending nuptials but then, given her outburst in the ballroom, felt as though there could be another underlying issue.

"They think us a love match!" She turned and spat, tears accumulating in her eyes.

He reached for her. "Who?"

She shook him off. "Society."

"Why do you care what they think?"

"Why don't you?" She turned the question back onto him. He had to live in the same world she did, so why wasn't he affected as much as her? "Why are you marrying me?"

He threaded his fingers through his hair. "You know why."

She nodded stiffly. "For duty." It was just as she'd thought; he didn't love her. So then why did hearing him say it hurt so much?

"You agreed to the marriage." It was Aiden's turn to accuse. Why was this suddenly becoming an issue? He thought the two of them were getting on splendidly, so what had changed to make her question their agreement?

She rolled her eyes. "I know I did, milord."

"Do not *milord* me," he said through gritted teeth. It was then he realized they were having their discussion in the public eye. Some of their guests might believe they were having a tryst on the darkened balcony, but if anyone decided to inspect further, they would see it was an argument instead. For someone so concerned with Society, Lynette was surely inviting its censure. He grabbed her by the elbow and pulled her down the balcony's steps and into the garden. There, he ushered her back into the house via a garden door, which led into a sitting room on the ground floor. "Now, explain to me, calmly, why it is you suddenly feel this way," he said once they were safely hidden away.

Lynette paced the darkened room. "I feel as though our entire relationship is a lie!"

"How is it a lie?"

"Weren't you just listening? Everyone believes that we are a love match." Her arms swung around her wildly. "They see us dance in the ballroom and have declared it love when that couldn't be further from the truth."

"Simply don't listen to them," he said. "They'll soon grow tired of us." It seemed like a logical solution; if the gossip was upsetting her, she'd be better off not listening to it.

"It's not as simple as that." She huffed. "As long as we are in the public eye, someone will have something to say about our love match."

His jaw clenched. "And that would be so terrible?" *Is loving me such a terrible idea?* he wanted to ask. The whole conversation was ludicrous, but it made Aiden wonder what Lynette thought of him. Why did she agree to marry him if she hated the idea of them being in love? Wasn't a love match what she'd always wanted? Shouldn't she be happy that Society thought of their relationship in that way?

She whirled around to face him. "Yes, because it is a lie."

Aiden stepped toward her, closing the space between them with a single stride. "This is a lie?" he demanded softly but didn't wait for a response. Instead, he covered her mouth with his and pulled her into a searing kiss to prove to himself that she wanted him. What Society saw might have been a lie, but what they had in private was real, raw, and full of passion. It didn't need to be defined by Society's dictates as long as they had each other.

His kisses were all heat and ardor, and as much as Lynette was loath to admit it, she welcomed his lips on hers. She was powerless in the face of his lust, her heart clinging to the physical aspect of their relationship. Because without the fervor, what was she left with? Duty. She'd never wanted to be used for such a function and hated the part she'd agreed to play. So she embraced his desire for her, believing it was the lesser of the two evils.

Not getting any resistance, Aiden continued his kisses and only tore himself away from her lips in order to place his mouth on her breasts. His hands loosened her laces, and the neckline of her gown widened to expose the creamy silk skin that was her bosom. With one hand, he massaged the aching flesh as her moans spurred him on. He then led her backward to a settee, where he laid her down before him. He set his lips to a single rigid nipple and worked it with his tongue. She arched into the sensation, and her mews of pleasure filled the space. But it wasn't enough, he wanted more. Tearing his hands away from her breasts, he reached for the hem of her skirts and roughly peeled them up and away from her body.

His fingers traced a path up her leg and stroked the satin skin of her inner thighs before he reached even higher to find the source of her pleasure. A cry escaped her, loud and echoing through the room, but he was past the point of caring. He stroked the bundle of nerves just above her molten center, and her body grew tense as it yearned for its release. He released her nipple with a pop, eliciting a soft moan of regret before his head ducked under her skirts to find another bud to play with. Lynette's eyes shot open, shocked at the indecency of Aiden's movements but couldn't deny the pleasure it brought her. His lips played, and his fingers moved, then with a shriek, she accepted her pleasure.

Aiden rose from beneath Lynette's skirts and instantly met her eyes. Her chest heaved, not having been long enough since her climax to slow. Still, her eyes stared at him, looked into him, saw through him. He knew what he'd done and had the decency to feel ashamed. He'd just tried to prove to her that their relationship was not a lie, and the only way he thought to do it was to give her physical pleasure.

"That was not a lie, milord. It was simply lust,"

Lynette said after she regained her mental faculties. He'd just given her the most exquisite pleasure, and all she wanted to do was cry because he'd succeeded in proving to her that their relationship contained nothing more than lust and duty. There was simply no love between them despite what Society might think. Not wanting him to see her tears, she stood and righted her dress as quickly as she could, and then without another word to Aiden, who still sat dumbfounded on the settee, she left.

Chapter Sixteen

Lynette knocked softly on her father's office door the morning following her engagement ball. "Papa?"

"Lynette, my dear, how are you faring?" Lord Keith asked his eldest daughter with a hopeful smile. After her interlude with Aiden, she'd cried in the withdrawing room for some time before she attempted to keep a brave face for the rest of the ball. In the end, she had to feign a megrim and insist her family leave early, much to her mother's dismay.

"Better," she said because she knew it was the answer her father was looking for. The fact of the matter was that she was heartbroken, and she only had herself to blame. She'd thought loving Aiden would be enough, that it wouldn't matter if he didn't return her affection because she could love enough for the both of them. Short of love, she'd thought lust could be enough for her, or at least something that could soften the sharp lines of duty. However, their latest tryst proved even lust wasn't enough because, even after the spectacular pleasure he wrought from her, she still felt hollow.

How innocent she'd been! That was why the *ton*'s gossip bothered her so much. It had tantalized her with a love that would never come to pass. The hurtful truth was that she was merely Aiden's means to an end: a hostess for his parties, a mother to his heir. Lynette didn't want to only be those things. She wanted more, always had and always would.

Lord Keith put down his quill to give her his full attention. "Is everything all right?"

"I would like to break off my engagement," she said in a rush. It was the main reason she'd sought out her father in his office. He was the only one who had the power to do such a thing, but she had planned to suggest it with a little more tact.

"Break it off?" Lord Keith asked, his eyebrows disappearing behind his hair. "Whyever for? It is most assuredly a fine match between you two. What cause do you have to break it off? He hasn't offended you, has he?"

"No, no, I just don't want to marry him anymore," Lynette replied but knew then and there that her reasons wouldn't be enough. It wouldn't matter to her father that she was just a means to an end since her parents married for the same reasons Aiden wanted to marry her.

Her father released a breathy chuckle. "I'm sorry, my dear, but we do not just call off engagements because of a lover's quarrel."

Lynette pursed her lips, loathing the insinuation that she and Aiden were lovers when they were merely two people who wanted vastly different things. "It's been done before."

"Not without scandal." Lord Keith shook his head. "No, this marriage shall go through unless you give me a real reason it cannot. If he has caused you some offense, then I shall have to call him out—"

"No, Papa, he has not," Lynette said because despite no

longer wanting to marry Aiden, she also did not want him to die in a duel with her father. "I don't mind a scandal. I am six and twenty. I think it is time for me to retire to the country."

"And what of your sister? If your reputation is tainted by scandal, so is hers. No, you will not rusticate in the country when you are engaged to a perfectly respectable gentleman."

"But Papa—"

"No, my decision is final." He turned back to his paperwork, but Lynette remained rooted in her place, her mouth open, ready to argue; however nothing came out. She slowly backed away, having no fight left in her. What was the point when her father made his opposition quite clear?

Lynette left his office with her head hung low, unsure what to do next. She surely couldn't marry Aiden, not now, with her heart aching as it was. There had been a time when she believed it was better to love than be loved, but now, she thought it would have been better for her to not love at all. Withdrawing to her room, she cried on her pillow, ruing the day she'd agreed to his courtship of her. She'd wanted to feel special, which was exactly how he made her feel, so much so that she fell in love with him. It would have been easier if she hadn't requested a true courtship. If he hadn't taken the time to court her, her heart would have remained protected.

After a while, her tears dried, and she tried to plot her next move. She could run away, take a mail coach to some country town. But where would she live? And how? She didn't have nearly enough pin money to see her settled anywhere, and what skills did she possess in order to get a job? Tossing that idea aside, she contemplated more before finding her answer. Only one other person could release her from her engagement, and that was the man she was engaged to.

The door to Elliot House opened as Lynette stepped out of her carriage with the aid of a footman. The butler welcomed her in and instructed her to wait in the reception room while he went to inform his master of her arrival. She played with the lace on her gloves and reminded herself of the reason for her visit. She hadn't wanted to see Aiden again after their most recent interlude. If her father had allowed her to break off their engagement, he would have been the one to inform Aiden. Regretfully, that hadn't gone according to her plan, thus her visit to Elliot House. She could only hope she'd garner more success with Aiden than she had with her father.

"Lord Elliot will see you now, Miss Elphinstone," Carson said upon his return. "In his study."

She gulped. Meeting Aiden in the study made her mission infinitely harder since it spoke to him, his title, and his masculinity. She dreaded another confrontation in a man's place of business, but it wasn't as if she could request a different location, so she followed Carson up to the first floor, where the office was. He opened the door before ushering her in. Aiden, who'd been sitting at his desk, stood for her arrival.

"Would you like some tea brought up?" he asked.

She shook her head. "No, it's not necessary."

"Then that will be all, Carson," Aiden dismissed his butler. "Lynette." He breathed her name, a whisper of an apology on his lips. He knew he'd severely misstepped the night before when he'd been unable to control his demons. He hoped her visit meant she wished to reconcile their disagreement in an effort to settle the tension between them prior to their wedding.

She squared her shoulders to begin. "I am sorry to interrupt your morning, milord, but there is something that I wish to discuss."

"By all means." He motioned for her to continue. Her use of *milord* unsettled him but he tried to remain open-minded.

Lynette took a deep breath. "I would like to be released from our engagement."

Desperate to shackle his emotions, Aiden turned away from her and stared out of the window. *She can't possibly believe that I would break off our engagement, could she?* He turned back to her. "Why?"

"I simply don't wish to marry you," she replied, a lump forming in her throat. She couldn't tell him the real reason she no longer wanted to marry him, because the thought of confessing her love to him when he didn't love her in return made her feel sick.

"You did two weeks ago!" He threw his hands in the air. "What has changed?"

"I am not satisfied with our arrangement, milord," she said by way of explanation, her chin lifted in defiance.

"I was completely upfront with you at the time of my proposal, was I not?" he asked, his speech clipped.

"Yes, but you also said I could deny you and you would accept it."

"At the time of our proposal!" Aiden shouted, a hailstorm of emotions flowing through him. "Not now, not when our wedding is less than two weeks away."

But Lynette didn't even flinch. "I accepted you under false pretenses, milord."

He rolled his eyes. "And what pretenses were those,

dare I ask?"

"That I could have a marriage without love," she replied and hated herself for it. She'd told herself that she wouldn't speak of love, the loathsome emotion, but he hadn't given her much choice.

Aiden stood perfectly still; his jaw clenched with his fists in the same state at his sides. It had been bad enough to think that she couldn't love him, but to hear her say the words out loud . . . he didn't wish the pain he felt on his worst enemy. But now it was out in the open, what was he to do? Release her from their engagement as she had requested, or force her into the union against her will?

"There will be societal repercussions if we terminate our arrangement." He tried to appeal to her sensible side. Surely if she was all obsessed with Society's opinion of her, she wouldn't willingly invite their censure.

"I'm aware and prepared to withdraw to the country."

It was as if she had it all planned out. She would leave him and live out the rest of her life on some country estate, he thought bitterly. "And what of me?" he asked, his voice breaking. "My reputation will also be in tatters, and I don't have the luxury of being able to retire to the country as you do. I must wed!"

Lynette squinted at him. "I thought you didn't care about Society's ideas."

"I don't, but I also cannot willingly encourage their criticism," Aiden said. "My family requires me to wed, so wed I must."

She sighed. It all came back to his need to marry. Sucking in her lips, she looked him dead in the eye. "Be that as it may, I feel that I can no longer marry you willingly, and you said that you would not marry an unwilling bride."

He drew a hand down his face. All his good intentions were coming back to bite him. "That was before, when it was only your refusal I would have had to accept." There was no way he could release her from their engagement; the fallout would be too great. He wouldn't have a leg to stand on in securing another bride during the current Season. And while it was true he didn't want to marry someone unwilling, whom did he have the greater duty to, Lynette or his family? His family, of course, since blood bonded them. Therefore, he would marry her; her present wishes be damned.

"So you will not end our engagement?" she asked incredulously. As if she truly believed he would let her go so easily.

"No, I shall not," he replied with finality.

She lifted her chin even higher and looked at him over her nose. "You cannot force me to marry you."

"Perhaps not, but I also cannot release you from our engagement."

"Because of duty?"

Because I don't want to, Aiden almost said. While duty remained the dominating justification, he also couldn't deny he wanted her. He wanted her in his bed as much as he wanted her smiles and banter. What confused him was how he could continue to want her in spite of her obvious disdain for him. It made no rational sense, so he simply nodded and allowed Lynette to believe whatever she wished. And in return, she turned on her heel and strode out of the room.

Chapter Seventeen

To Lynette's surprise, Aiden continued to escort her to balls for the remaining two weeks of their engagement. She said as much to him the evening after she requested to end their understanding, and his response was that they should continue as they had been, as if nothing had changed between them.

But everything had changed. While he'd continued to escort her to events and dance with only her every night, he did so only to keep up appearances with Society. Moreover, his demeanor had altered quite immensely; he no longer lingered when touching her or held her too close while they waltzed. He'd also given up trampling her flounces to secure a moment alone with her. All in all, their relationship had become quite chaste, which Lynette decided she was grateful for. Not only had it put an end to the whispers in regard to their love match, but it also allowed her to realize she'd been wrong in thinking that lust was the lesser of two evils. At least with duty she knew where she stood, whereas lust tricked her into believing there could be more.

While Lynette continued to play with the idea of running away in the days leading up to her wedding, she ultimately decided against it. As much as Aiden had hurt her, she didn't wish him ill, which is what she would be doing if she caused him any embarrassment. So without any further uproar or scandal, the Honorable Miss Lynette Elphinstone went to St. George's Church in Hanover Square and became Lady Lynette Elliot, Countess Elliot, and the future Duchess of Northumberland.

The wedding itself was a widely attended affair. The church was packed with well-wishers, and anybody who couldn't fit inside opted to wait outside to celebrate the nuptials of such a noble couple. After the ceremony, the newlywed's carriage conducted them through the streets of Mayfair until they reached Elliot House, where the wedding festivities would be held. The first event was the wedding breakfast where Lynette was formally introduced to the extended Elliot family, including Aiden's aunts, uncles, and cousins. The wedding ball, held after the wedding breakfast, turned out to be an absolute crush. Attended by members of the aristocracy, the Elliot family, and their connections, everyone assumed no other ball would be held in competition. And despite Aiden and Lynette only sharing one waltz, their first as a married couple, it was still agreed by all in attendance that the couple was hopelessly in love.

When the party reached its conclusion, Lynette retired to the bedroom that had been prepared for her. With help from Milly, who had decided to stay on as her lady's maid through her marriage, she prepared for her wedding night. First she removed her dress and replaced it with new lingerie from her trousseau. Then Milly unpinned her hair and brushed it, so her brown curls hung to frame her heart-shaped face. Before she left, Milly sprayed her with a perfume she insisted would entice her new husband. Left alone in her room, all Lynette had left to do was wait.

And wait she did. She sat by the fire, waiting for what had to have been hours. Finally, when the candles melted down and the fire was nothing but ash, she decided she'd waited long enough. She stood and shrugged on her night robe before marching the short distance to what she knew to be Aiden's bedroom. She knocked but received no response, so she knocked again, only harder. Still garnering no reply, she tried the handle, which turned easily. She walked into his bedroom with her head held high, but to her great dismay, her new husband was not there.

With a sigh, Lynette reassessed the situation. If he wasn't in his bedroom, there was only one other place he could be. With new intent, she left the bedchamber and padded farther down the hall to the study. Once there, she didn't even attempt to knock, deciding instead to simply open the door and step inside.

"I thought I sent you to bed, Carson," Aiden said, not turning to look at who had entered his study.

"I see you are mistaken, milord," Lynette said, her tone short and clipped. Upon not finding her husband in his bedroom, she assumed he was hard at work, finalizing plans for their estate tour, where they would visit the dukedom's estates to secure their roles as lord and lady. She'd never imagined he would be relaxing by a fire in a comfortable armchair, sipping on a glass of brandy.

"Lynette." Aiden stood immediately, unprepared for his wife to find him in his study. He'd been waiting for her to go to bed so he could do the same and therefore hadn't foreseen a scenario where she sought him out in his study, dressed only in her night robe.

"Are you attending to work, milord?" she asked, even though it was obvious to them both he wasn't.

"Not presently," he replied, unable to meet her eye.

"Then is there a reason you are in your study, milord?" She surveyed the room for any sign of wrongdoing. Was it possible he had a mistress? Would he consort with her on their wedding night?

Aiden sighed and ran his fingers through his hair. "I was waiting for you to go to sleep." It had been the only way he could think of to force himself to keep his hands off her that night. He hadn't expected her to wait up for him, though he realized he probably should have since it was their wedding night. But he'd just assumed she would be so exhausted from the day's events that she would fall asleep without a thought for him and what they could be doing. While he, on the other hand, had thought extensively about what they could be doing, hence the need for a stiff drink.

She pursed her lips. "I may be new to this, milord, but isn't there something that needs to be done before I go to sleep?"

"No, not tonight." Aiden shook his head slowly. Her consistency in calling him *milord* signified her annoyance with their present situation, which was just as well since he shared the emotion. He shouldn't have married her and had wanted to call it off that morning but had been too afraid to. Afraid of what would happen if he did: afraid for his family, himself, and Lynette. Now he felt like a cad for forcing her into a marriage she didn't want. It didn't matter that he wanted her or that he'd fantasized about having her since the moment they'd met. He couldn't bring himself to touch her because of the overwhelming amount of regret he felt regarding how he secured her hand.

Not to mention he couldn't bear the thought of having her in his arms and not being wanted in the same way he wanted her. The memory of their engagement ball and the passion he'd thought they shared was still fresh in his mind. He couldn't endure her rejecting him again because it would surely be his demise.

Lynette frowned. "We will not be consummating our marriage?"

"Not tonight." *Possibly not ever*, he wanted to add. If the marriage was never consummated, maybe she could get an annulment, then he could be free of his regret.

"Surely even a marriage based on duty needs to be consummated." She rubbed her chest, trying to soothe the tingling within it. He'd spent weeks arranging moments alone with her, but now that they were free to do whatever they liked, he decided to balk. So what was stopping him from doing his husbandly duty?

"Because while I have forced you into a marriage, I will not force myself upon you in bed!" Aiden said through clenched teeth. She was trying his patience, and if she had any sense of self-preservation, she would leave him.

"Don't we have a duty to beget an heir?" she asked, her voice trembling as much as her hands.

"I do," Aiden replied since it was his duty to extend the Elliot dynasty, his cross to bear.

Lynette's eyes began to burn, and she tried to swallow the lump that had settled in her throat. "And who will beget him with you?" *Did he intend to sire a bastard with a mistress?* Logically, it made no sense. What was the point of marrying her then? Still, as overwrought as she was, she was incapable of being even slightly logical.

"We can talk about my heir at a later date," Aiden

said with a sigh. It was taking every fiber of his being to refuse her. The belt of her dressing gown had loosened from her movements, and her long brown locks cascaded down her shoulders, stopping abruptly at the gentle swell of her breasts. It was the first time he'd ever seen her hair undone, long tresses made for his fingers, made to be splayed upon his bed. But he couldn't take her as it would surely lead to another regret.

She stood with her mouth agape and leered at him from the corner of her eye. "So you'll marry me for duty but won't bed me for the same reason?"

"Not tonight," he repeated for the third time. He had no other response, or at least none he could give her until he came to terms with his own thoughts and feelings. Maybe they could reconcile and come to some sort of agreement, but it would have to be another time. He yearned to reach for her but knew he didn't deserve her touch, so he stayed where he stood.

Lynette wanted to scream and rail against him until she forced words from him. If he was so insistent on wedding her, why wasn't he just as insistent on bedding her? It was the primary goal, was it not? Not to mention that, considering the way he'd once desired her, she'd been made to believe he wouldn't find any hardship in it. Still the silence reigned, and since there was nothing else left to be said, she turned and went to bed, where she cried for the remainder of the night.

Chapter Eighteen

After a very restless night, Aiden rose early and began preparations to withdraw from London. He had no plans to return to Town until the following Season when he likely took up his seat in the House of Lords. His parents and granny would travel to and retire at St. James Park in North Yorkshire while he and Lynette would take a more scenic route, first stopping at Elberry Park in Surrey and then continuing the journey north to Yorkshire and Northumberland. The estate tour was for the benefit of them both. He would be able to visit the estates and meet the tenants as the new heir. At the same time, she would be introduced as the new countess and future Duchess of Northumberland while also seeing the lands and estates she'd married into.

His only hope was that they could remain civil while traveling and spending time at each estate. He knew he wasn't in his new wife's good graces, and if there was a chance for him to rectify the situation, he planned to take it. In the light of day, he knew he didn't want to annul their marriage and would much rather fix it instead. Time away from societal and familial expectations was just what they needed to set their relationship to right. He hoped it would rekindle the connection they'd made and remind her why she accepted him in the first place. Yes, some time alone together would be most welcome, Aiden was certain.

So he busied himself with instructing servants on their duties. Carson would have to shut down Elliot House, which he was more than capable of doing. Lynette's maid and Aiden's valet, Claude, would travel with them, along with a footman and two coachmen. Eleanor and Rowena would also travel with their maids and Seymour with his valet, two footmen who could help with his condition, and two coachmen to drive the carriages. Throughout the madness, Aiden stood in the foyer and watched as footmen carried boxes and trunks through the house and loaded them onto the carriages. Finally at roughly midmorning, the packing was complete, and everyone was ready to travel, so the family of five stood outside Elliot House to bid each other adieu.

Lynette rubbed cheeks with Eleanor and Rowena before she shook Seymour's hand. She couldn't help but take note of how pale he was and how he had to be helped into his carriage by a footman ahead of his wife and mother. It didn't take a leap of imagination to conclude that his health was faltering. Suddenly Aiden's rushed proposal made sense to her. How he had seemed content to lengthen their courtship until he couldn't any longer. Despite their recent differences, she couldn't help but understand the pressure he was under, first in losing his brother and then having to come to terms with his father's condition. She accepted that it would have been enough for anyone to reevaluate their duty as he had.

Aiden helped Lynette into their carriage and then stepped into it himself. He rapped on the ceiling, and they started to move as the coachman navigated through London's busy streets. Surrey was just a short carriage ride away, and they would arrive at Elberry Park by midday. There they would spend at least the next week at the estate, Aiden tending to business, Lynette tending to other things. She wasn't entirely sure what those things were but assumed she would be in charge of managing the servants and being a hostess. But since they would only be in residence for such a short amount of time, she didn't think there would be much need.

Lynette watched through the carriage window as they traveled farther and farther away from London. She and Aiden hadn't spoken all morning except for simple questions and answers in relation to their travels. Even though she didn't want to be, she was still angry with him. She'd thought that having a relationship defined by duty meant she would know where she stood. But by his refusal to bed her, her only clear purpose—that of begetting an heir—had been taken away. This purpose seemed entirely urgent to her, given the duke's condition, and yet Aiden was somehow intent on keeping her from fulfilling it. She couldn't help but wonder again if he had a mistress, someone he lusted over more than her. Surely that was the only rational explanation for his actions; he simply didn't desire her as much as she originally thought.

"Penny for your thoughts?" Aiden broke the silence. Lynette looked at him, her big brown eyes full of emotion. "I know you saw my father."

"Is he . . ." she didn't know how to phrase the delicate question.

"He is likely dying a slow death." He nodded, needing no prompt. Lynette was to be the Duchess of

Northumberland, and it was past time she learned just how soon that day could come. "He is usually very weak and fatigued. It used to just be in the mornings, but it's getting increasingly worse throughout the day. The doctors say there is fluid in his chest, which makes it hard for him to breathe."

"Aiden, I am truly sorry," she said, taking his hands in hers. It was the first time they had willingly touched since their engagement ball, and it didn't go above either of their notice.

He swallowed. "It was hard to find out at first, but I've come to terms with it now."

"How horrible it must have been to return because of your brother's death and then find out your father is also likely dying."

Aiden cleared his throat. "My father's condition caused my brother's death." It was the first time he'd acknowledged the succession of events, the first time he'd spoken them aloud. "My parents kept my father's illness from my brother until last September," he said, which caused Lynette to gasp, not needing to be told the connection. "My brother decided to drink at a village pub and then crashed his curricle while driving back to the castle." He stared out of the carriage window, his eyes burning. "Ferdy had always had a temper."

She shook her head. "Still, he should have been more careful."

If only he'd been more careful. Aiden released a bitter laugh. He'd still likely be on the Continent then, still undercover, still a second son. Ferdy would still be alive and possibly sire a son with Matilda. Lynette could have married Thornburn. How different things would have been if Ferdy had simply been more careful.

She took a deep breath. "I do not resent you for needing to marry me."

"Lynette—"

"No, Aiden, let me say this." She forced herself to meet his eye. "While I am not ultimately happy with how our situation has transpired, I do not resent the fact that it was necessary. Thus I urge you to allow me to help you fulfill the rest of your duty. You are your father's heir, so you will need one as well."

He patted her hand. "There will be time for that." Once their relationship was on solid ground again, and he could be sure she wouldn't reject him.

"You cannot take this from me; it is the only way I can help," she said, her voice wavering.

Aiden was about to assure her that there were many ways she could help, but he never got the chance.

"Do you have a mistress?" Lynette asked, the words pouring from her mouth.

"What?" he sputtered, caught off guard.

"Do you have someone warming your bed?" she asked more forcefully. "We never discussed it before."

"And you thought now would be the best time?"

"It's as good a time as any." She shrugged, needing to put the matter to bed.

"The answer is no, I do not have a mistress," Aiden replied, still incredulous at their current conversation.

"Do you plan to take one?"

"Now?"

Lynette rubbed her lips together. "At any time in the future."

"I had not considered it," he said, which was the truth. Since meeting her, no other woman moved him the way she did. She was the only woman who interested him and the only one he yearned for in his bed.

She raised her chin. "Then I don't see any reason why you shouldn't come to me this evening."

Aiden looked at her: straight back, jaw clenched, inviting him to her bed in a far from seductive manner. Her demeanor spoke to her opinion of him having a mistress, which seemed like a sore topic indeed. But why? Lynette had recoiled the last time he was passionate with her, so why would it matter if he took a mistress? "Sharing a bed doesn't only have to do with begetting an heir."

"I understand there is a fair bit of lust involved." She sniffed and waited for him to tell her that he didn't desire her enough to take her to bed.

"I want you to enjoy it." He looked at her through his eyelashes and held his breath.

"I can enjoy it?" Lynette asked with a furrowed brow. She'd never been told the bedding was enjoyable. In all her wisdom, her mother instructed her to allow Aiden to do what he needed to get her with child. What he needed, she was still not sure; she assumed he needed her body but didn't know any of the explicit details.

"Of course you can." He released a nervous chuckle. Never in his adult life had he been made to question his abilities in the bedroom. On the contrary, all of his mistresses had seemed wholly satisfied after a night of shared pleasure, and he'd always thought that Lynette had enjoyed their previous encounters. At least, all except their most recent one, he conceded.

"Can you show me?" she asked softly.

Aiden was at a loss. Did she really want him to show her how she could enjoy intimacy, or was she still only set on them begetting an heir to fulfill his duty? He reassessed his wife; she wasn't sitting nearly as rigid as she had been when they were discussing his potential mistress. Her face also looked warmer and more welcoming, not the strict, harsh lines that had been present when she clenched her jaw. He felt incapable of deciding until Lynette's voice called to him once more.

"Please, Aiden, show me." She hadn't realized until they were alone together how much she'd missed his touch—missed his lips, his hands, and their warmth. She wanted nothing more than for him to admit that he missed hers too, but short of saying the words, she wanted his body on hers.

Succumbing to her temptation, he glanced out of the window at his surroundings and determined they had more than enough time before they reached Elberry Park. So throwing caution to the wind, he placed his lips on hers and kissed her until their breaths mingled and their tongues dueled.

They moved closer to each other, and she received a hint of contact with his chest. She stroked her hands up his arms to his shoulders and wrapped them around his neck before threading them through his hair. In response, he teasingly drew his fingers down her neck and took her bosom in his hand. He held it steady, simply relishing the weight of it before massaging it purposefully through her dress. The movement rewarded him with a soft moan, making him wish they were not in a carriage but a bed. He rued the fabric that covered her breasts and longed to suckle her nipples. But Lynette wanted more than that, so he decided to focus his attention elsewhere.

"Remember the evening we became engaged, and I showed you the library?" Aiden asked, not wanting to refer to their engagement ball. His hand dipped low and slipped underneath her skirts. He began slowly, giving her time to pull away if she decided to. Inch by inch, he tickled the delicate skin between her thighs, his eyes never leaving hers as his hand journeyed ever higher until it reached its ultimate goal.

She nodded jerkily, unable to speak as his hand cupped her. The pressure he exerted was too much but too little at the exact same time.

"It'll be similar to that." His finger finally found the spot that made her burn. "I shall touch you just like this. Can you feel the pleasure?" he asked, needing to hear her response.

But Lynette was past the point of being able to reply, and the only sound she was able to muster was a sigh as he began to rub her with long and steady strokes. She grasped the lapels of his coat and held them in her fists as if her life depended on it.

"And then I shall enter you here." He illustrated his words by mimicking the motion with his finger. "Only it will be bigger and will make you feel fuller." He watched her face as varying levels of pleasure struck her. He eased a second finger inside and continued his movements. "And then the pleasure you feel will reach a precipice."

Her eyes were half shut, and her head had fallen back. She felt like she would fall off a cliff but didn't want to embrace the imminent death. He'd made her feel like this in his library and during their engagement ball, but he'd never explained the sensations or what caused them. The carriage's movement underneath them only added to the effects, making her want to scream.

"When we share a bed, we shall reach that precipice together, but today, take it, my dear, take your pleasure. Lynette, look at me and take your pleasure," he commanded, wanting to see his effect on her. It had been the first time he had felt in control in at least a fortnight, and he was drunk on the power.

Finding the strength, she opened her eyes and looked at Aiden to find his passion mirrored hers. Then the dam broke, and he kissed her just in time to smother the earth-shattering scream.

He wrapped his arm around her and stroked her shoulder affectionately as she slowly drifted back down to earth. "That is what the bedding will feel like," he said after a few moments of silence. "Only better."

Chapter Nineteen

Better . . . Lynette couldn't believe that pleasure could get much better than what she'd already experienced. She and Aiden had arrived at Elberry Park not long after they'd finished their interlude, and she still barely had the capacity to think of much else. She stood in the duchess's bedroom, directing Milly on which dresses she'd like removed from her trunks. They wouldn't remain long at Elberry Park, perhaps a week, maybe more if duty retained them, but she still felt the need to arrange her things to her liking. She reasoned that it would keep her busy until dinner if nothing else. Regrettably in this instance, Milly had sorted all of her mistress's belongings well in advance of dinner time since she was extremely efficient at her duties. Knowing it was inconsiderate to keep the young maid detained for no reason, Lynette dismissed Milly to see to her own settling in.

Faced with hours of free time, she retrieved *Sense and Sensibility*, determined to read it after not having had enough time to devote to the endeavor since becoming engaged. While the narrative still intrigued her, and she wanted nothing more than to find out what business necessitated Colonel Brandon's departure from Barton

Park, she couldn't entirely focus on the text, her mind straying to Aiden and the passion they'd recently shared. Since the carriage ride, she was more determined to experience the bedding, but not in the interest of duty or begetting an heir. She simply wanted to know how much better the pleasure could get between them and was thus still skeptical of the possibility.

How to get past Aiden's reluctance to bed her, though, she wondered. Surely he wasn't so averse to touching her as she'd thought the previous night during their altercation. Once he'd been convinced to pleasure her in the carriage, he'd seemed satisfied with the activity. She would simply need to convince him again, she decided, then she would feel wholly informed on the intricacies of pleasure.

Lost in her thoughts for longer than she cared to be, Lynette only realized the time when there was a soft knock on her door. "Are you dressing for dinner, milady?" Milly asked, peeking her head inside.

"I'm sorry, Milly. I lost track of time." She set her novel aside. It felt odd being called *milady*, especially by Milly, who had served as her lady's maid since her debutante year. She was then struck with the thought that it would only get worse when she became *Your Grace*.

Setting herself to the task at hand, Lynette asked her maid to prepare a simple evening gown since it would only be her and Aiden that night. Milly quickly retrieved a plain red dress for her mistress, helped her put it on, and then re-pinned her hair. Once she was ready, Lynette dismissed Milly and sent her to her own dinner. Exiting her room, Lynette retraced her steps to the front of the house where she'd entered earlier in the day. She hadn't had much of a tour of the house yet and wasn't sure of the dining room's location. That was when she caught sight of Aiden ambling down the steps she'd just descended, dressed in his black tailcoat. When they were on the same level, he offered her his arm.

"I shall have Totty give you a proper tour of the estate. Until then, I would be happy to escort you to the dining room."

Lynette remembered Totty was the head housemaid from their earlier introductions. "I would appreciate that." She accepted his escort. "How often does your family reside at Elberry Park?"

"My father and mother regularly visited, usually either before or after the Season, and from my understanding, Ferdy and Matilda visited just as much," Aiden said as they reached the dining room for dinner. He took in the layout of the table, set for two, with him and Lynette sitting at opposite ends of the table. He pulled out the chair next to the head where he would sit and offered it to her. "Adams, could you please have this place set for your lady?" he asked the butler, having decided to dispense with the formalities since they were the only ones in residence and did not require a formal setting. Furthermore, he preferred to have her next to him if possible.

Adams immediately set to the task administered to him and then began serving the first course. "I've been contemplating whether to offer Matilda and her daughter Elberry Park if they are agreeable," Aiden informed Lynette as they started eating their soup. "They are currently still residing at Eldridge Castle, but since this house is largely underused throughout the year, I thought it might fit Matilda's needs."

Lynette wasn't quite sure what response she should

give. She didn't know Matilda well at all, having only met her on occasion during the Season, and she didn't know her circumstances either. However, she did know that women not holding the title did not usually reside full time at the ancestral seat, which was what Eldridge Castle was to the Elliots. "It is close enough to London that she could easily go into Town if she chose, yet far enough away so as not to reside in the city all year."

"Precisely my own thinking." Aiden nodded. "I wouldn't want to suggest that she go to St. James Park since that is where my granny and parents reside."

"Especially with your father's illness. I don't believe that would be the best environment for a young child."

"I shall broach the subject with Matilda when we reach Eldridge Castle. But if she isn't agreeable, do you mind if she continues to reside there with us?"

Lynette nearly dropped her spoon. "Surely that is not my decision to make."

"It is your home now as well," Aiden said, hiding a smirk behind his glass. He'd thought he'd discerned a way of regaining her favor while settling himself in at Elberry Park during the afternoon. He recalled her initial misgivings regarding marriage, such as filling a role any gently bred miss could. Therefore, he would return to his original objective and attempt to show her that she was special to him. He knew asking her opinion on Matilda would surprise her since it was not typical for men to share thoughts and decisions with their wives. Thus it was the perfect way to show her that she wasn't like her peers in Society.

Lynette was still at a loss for words. Never in her life had she heard her father ask her mother's opinion or vice versa. Only in *Sense and Sensibility* did Mr. John

Dashwood ask his wife's opinion on family matters, and Lynette was still dubious about how that turned out. Still, Aiden had asked her and was therefore waiting for a response. "I dare say Eldridge Castle is big enough for us all."

He nodded. "It most assuredly is."

"Then I don't foresee a problem with her staying there if that is what she prefers." She didn't intend to put the poor matron out and conceded she might change her opinion once she got to know Matilda more intimately, but as of that moment, she felt sure she'd spoken diplomatically.

He smiled again. "Excellent."

Dinner continued, and the newlyweds chatted about what they wanted to do while in residence at Elberry Park. Aiden assumed some of the local matrons would come calling the following afternoon to give their congratulations, and Lynette resolved herself to receive them. They also planned to take some horses around the estate one day to visit their tenants and properly introduce themselves.

Once dinner was complete, Aiden decided to refrain from the port, allowing them to retire to the drawing room for tea. After they settled in their respective chairs, Lynette realized she didn't know what to expect of the rest of the evening. Was she to entertain her husband? There was a pianoforte in the room; did he expect her to play? She remembered telling him that she was rubbish at the piano, but still, wasn't that what wives did for their husbands in the evening? It had to have been why her mother was so insistent that she practiced.

Aiden, unaware of his wife's misgivings, picked up the day's paper that Adams had left out for him since he hadn't had time to read it in its entirety yet. He'd been too busy settling in and then sorting through the pile of paperwork he'd brought with him from London and thus looked forward to a quiet evening. It felt as though since returning to England, he hadn't had any time to himself because he'd been required to go out and socialize. While he didn't mind the idea of socializing regularly, he also appreciated the notion of having time alone with his wife.

"Did you want me to play the piano?" Lynette finally found the courage to ask.

Aiden dipped the paper to look at her over it. "I thought you didn't enjoy the pianoforte."

"I don't."

He looked at her sideways. "Then why offer to play it?"

She shrugged. "Because I assumed that you would want some entertainment."

"I'm content with reading my newspaper," Aiden said and then turned back to it.

Lynette shifted in her seat, her eyes darting around the room.

Sensing her continued discomfort, he lowered the paper again. "You can participate in a pastime you enjoy as well."

"I spent all afternoon reading," she lied, knowing full well she'd spent the entire afternoon looking at the same page while mulling over the complexity of passion.

"Did you finish your novel then?"

"No."

"Then continue reading it now," Aiden suggested, unsure how it could be a new concept for her.

"I apologize." She looked down and pulled at her fingers. "I'm just unsure of what is expected of me."

Aiden folded his newspaper and put it down, giving Lynette his full attention. "What do you mean?"

She drew in a shaky breath. "I mean I've never been alone with a gentleman . . . like this." She waved her hand around. "I was trained to manage an estate, host parties, play the pianoforte, and dance. But never in my years in the schoolroom was I instructed on how to spend an evening with my husband."

"How do you usually spend your evenings?"

"Usually at a ball or similar gathering."

"What about in the country?" he asked. "Surely you aren't attending a ball every night in the country."

"I'm not," she replied, a small laugh escaping her lips. "I usually read if I'm allowed."

"Allowed?"

She nodded. "My mother preferred me to practice more ladylike pursuits."

"Well I won't stop you from reading in the evenings if it's what you enjoy," he said.

Lynette's lips parted, and they stared at each other.

Aiden leaned toward her. "What else do you like to do while in the country?" They had talked about so many things over the course of their acquaintance, but they had all centered around London. He knew her favorite bookshop, her preferred path through Hyde Park, and her distaste for musicales. Never once had they broached the subject of the countryside, except to acknowledge there weren't as many bookshops to visit.

"Well, I like horse riding," Lynette said. "So I usually started my mornings with a ride through the forests surrounding Dowsorrell Castle."

His eyebrows rose. "You've never told me about your proficiency in horse riding."

Her shoulders relaxed, and she released a breath. "It is something I delight in."

"You are more than able to continue that activity at this and all the other estates." Aiden reached for her hand and their fingers intertwined. "Especially at Eldridge, there's always a stable full of horses begging to be ridden."

She looked at their hands, and a smile tugged at the corners of her mouth. "I would enjoy that very much."

Once the talk of horse riding concluded, they talked about other things, such as current events Aiden noted from his newspaper and gossip from the scandal sheets. He deliberately ignored any mention of themselves in the lines because he didn't want to sour the mood. They ended up talking for so long and were so immersed in each other's company that it wasn't until Lynette stifled two yawns that he decided it was time for bed.

Aiden stood and offered Lynette his arm to escort her back through the house and up the stairs to their bedrooms. He hated the thought of leaving her and wanted to draw her into his bedroom with every fiber of his being. But he also acknowledged they had just spent an engaging evening together in the drawing room, simply talking and enjoying each other's company. He didn't want to ruin any progress he'd made with her, so he decided it was best to end their evening on a high note. "This is where I bid you good night, my dear." He leaned in, daring to kiss her.

She melted into the embrace and allowed the sensations to overwhelm her. But then all too soon, he stepped away and walked backward through his bedroom door, thus leaving her alone in the hallway.

Dumbfounded, Lynette entered her own bedroom and found her maid waiting inside. She stayed silent as Milly helped her undress and take down her hair. When Milly reached for the brush, Lynette dismissed her. Staring unseeing at her reflection, she ran long strokes through her hair. Her eyes strayed to the door that connected Aiden's bedroom to hers. Should she take a chance and enter his room? What did she have to lose? Her sanity, she decided, but she was probably bound to lose it anyway if she stayed where she was.

Once in his room, Aiden dismissed Claude directly, preferring to undress himself. He yanked his cravat off from around his neck. He wondered how many days it would take him to regain the confidence he once had with Lynette. Before their engagement ball, nothing would have kept him from bedding her, but now he questioned his every move. He wanted to believe she wanted him but accepted he'd made that error once before. Nevertheless, he found himself fighting an internal battle to stay in his own room and not enter Lynette's to take her the way his body demanded.

Suddenly, he heard the click of a door and looked up to see Lynette as she slowly walked into the bedroom. "Aiden," she whispered his name, and he nearly broke into a million pieces.

He wound his cravat around his hand and tried to focus on the tightness. "Lynette, please."

"No, I want . . . you."

He took a step toward her. She was the image of a dream standing before him. Her beautiful brown curls hung loosely around her shoulders. He could see the hard nipples of her breasts poking out through the sheer silk material of her nightdress. This time she hadn't bothered with a robe when coming to seek him out, and why should she? She only needed to leave her room to enter his. Every part of her that had been left to the imagination the night before was there before him now, and he felt powerless not to take it.

"Do you want me?" he asked, needing to hear the answer on her lips. "Or do you want to fulfill a duty?" He watched as Lynette breathed deeply, contemplating her answer. "I don't want you to just see this as a duty you need to perform."

She wet her lips. "I could say the same for you."

"I've never seen you as a duty." He frowned. "I've always been open with how much I want you. You were the one who wished to end our engagement."

"I'm sorry." Lynette lowered her head. "I shouldn't have asked to sever our connection, but I . . ." she still couldn't say the words. Her love for him burned brighter than she'd ever thought possible, but speaking the words aloud would make her feel too vulnerable. "I can't deny that I want you, Aiden."

"Are you sure?" His eyes widened, and he loosened his grip on his cravat. As much as he had wished it were true, he never let himself truly believe it until she said the words.

She held her head high. "I'm sure."

"There's no going back after this." The cravat fell to the floor, and he slowly undid the buttons of his shirt.

Lynette shook her head. "I don't want to go back."

Words ceased to exist after that. He covered her mouth with his, and their tongues mingled as passion flamed. She encircled him with her arms, felt the taut muscles in his upper back and shoulders, and reveled in their strength. He speared his fingers through her hair and held on to handfuls as he trailed kisses along her jaw up to her ear. She shivered as he drew a line down her back and stopped at her hips. Without warning, he picked her up, his hands cradling her bottom, and carried her to his bed.

Then with a smile, he stepped back to survey his work. She was just as he'd always envisioned: long brown curls splayed across his pillows, perfect upturned nipples that waited to be tasted. The hem of her negligee had even ridden up, hinting at the curls that hid the center of her pleasure.

He finished removing his shirt and then set to the task of his trousers, stockings, and shoes. Soon he was naked in all his godly glory, and Lynette received her first glimpse of what was to come. All too soon he joined her on the bed, covered her body with his, and placed his lips on hers once more. Her hands explored the newly exposed skin and caressed his shoulders, arms, and chest. When he tugged the top of her nightgown down to expose her breasts, it incited her to become bold and draw her fingers over his nipple. As a reward for her caress, he dipped his head and drew one tight, crinkled nipple into his mouth to suck and toy with. She held his head to her chest and cherished the feeling while she ran her fingers through his hair.

Loath to leave her bounty, he continued his journey south and pulled her negligee down with him. Soon it pooled around her legs, not covering much at all, and he was able to look his fill. Feeling wholly exposed, she attempted to bring him back down on top of her, but he resisted. Instead, he reached out and placed his fingers at the center of all her pleasure. She arched into the caress, and a long, loud moan escaped her lips. He continued rubbing as he returned his face to hers. "There's no need to be silent tonight, my lovely," he said, his voice oozing with desire. "I want nothing more than to hear you scream."

And scream she did. He kissed a straight line down her

body, between her breasts and over her stomach, before his lips found what his fingers had been teasing. The first touch of his tongue caught her off guard, and she almost bolted upright, but then his lips pulled that tight bud into his mouth, and he suckled fervently. His hands delved even lower, filling her with one and then two fingers, but neither felt like enough. She writhed upon the sheets, and her hands grasped for whatever she could reach. The whole time she felt like the dam would never break until it finally did, and she glimpsed stars behind her eyes.

Breathing heavily, Lynette felt Aiden hovering over her again, his kisses fluttering around her face. It took all the energy she could muster to open her eyes, and when she did, they met with his. He studied her, taking note of every blink of her eye and every breath she took. Then when he found whatever it was he was looking for, he scooped her up, raised her hips, and placed his member, hot and hard, at her entrance.

"Are you ready?" He brushed her hair from her eyes. She looked utterly divine. Skin flushed pink after finding her pleasure, her hair wild and tangled. He knew it would help for her to find completion before he took her, but it had been so hard to keep from sinking into her warm and inviting depths, and he was more than ready for the main event.

"Yes," she breathed, not fully understanding what she was supposed to be ready for. Then she felt him entering her, filling her in ways she'd never thought possible. Her head fell back of its own volition, her eyes clenched at the sensation. After what seemed like an eternity, there was a little pop of pain and then he was fully embedded within her.

He breathed deeply and tried to rein himself in. All he

wanted to do was pump fully and freely into her but was waiting for some sign she would welcome it. He did his best to stay perfectly still, not wanting to move for fear of hurting her more than he already had. Then contrary to every belief he had before that moment, she lifted her head and looked at him.

"Is that it?" she asked as if it did not meet her expectations.

He stifled a groan, his control slipping. "Are you all right?"

"Fine," she replied as if he'd just asked her about the weather. She attempted to move, which garnered a growl from him. "Are you all right?" She turned the question back on him.

He didn't know if he wanted to laugh or cry. The beguiling woman would kill him, that was for sure. He withdrew slowly as a response, and her eyes widened. She moaned at the loss of him and wrapped her legs around his hips in an attempt to pull him back. If he'd had the composure he would have chuckled, but instead he thrust his hips back to meet hers. Her mouth dropped open as her eyes fell shut. He continued his movements, slow at first, but increased the pace as time went on, and her hips met his thrust for thrust. Their passion for each other filled the room, each yearning to reach the precipice of such an act. Having felt he would soon lose his control, he slipped a finger back between them and rubbed her small bundle of nerves again. It was more than enough for her; she cried out and felt as though she was falling once more from the cliff of pleasure but found that this time, he was there to save her. He growled her name as he poured his seed and then collapsed onto the bed with her still in his arms.

They lay together, both utterly sated until Aiden's gentle breathing signified that he was asleep. Lynette, however, was wide awake and rolled over to face him. She marveled at the features of his handsome face, from his defined jaw to the point of his nose. He looked magnificent even as he slept, maybe even more so somehow. Her heart clenched at the thought.

The passion they'd just shared was sublime; she couldn't deny that. However dubious she'd been before they shared a bed, she was certain now. His desire for her had never abated, and it was as strong and virile as ever which forced her to determine which function she preferred: duty or lust.

Duty was logical because it could be defined by a set of parameters. As a wife, she had a duty to manage his household, host his events, and rear his children. Lust was a lot murkier, being closely related to love, and consisted of absurd amounts of pleasure, but it made her feel special and wanted. There had been multiple times when she'd thought she preferred one over the other but accepted that she had never been wholly convinced by the attributes of either.

But love encompassed the best of both. Love made her want to manage his estates, host his parties, and bear his children—not because she was duty bound to do so but because she *wanted* to do so. Love made her want to help him as much as it called her to his bed. Therefore love answered all of Lynette's questions. If only Aiden could love her! Maybe she could come to terms with him only lusting for her, she rationalized. While it wasn't love, it was still more than duty, and as long as he didn't lust after anyone else . . .

No, she was merely deluding herself again. Neither

lust nor duty would ever be enough. Unable to fall asleep due to her inner turmoil, she rose slowly and gently from the bed. She retrieved her nightgown from where it had been thrown on the floor and donned it. Then after one more look at Aiden sleeping peacefully, she returned to her own bedchamber in an attempt to guard her ever-fragile heart.

Chapter Twenty

A hint of sunlight streamed into Aiden's bedroom when he woke up just before dawn. He lazily rolled over, intending to pull Lynette close only to find that she was no longer beside him. His hands shook, and his heart raced as his eyes darted around the room. Unable to sit still, he rose and reached for his trousers, intending to dress and begin his day, but the door to her bedroom taunted him.

With a shake of his head, he strode to the adjoining bedroom where he found his wife asleep in her own bed. He crossed his arms and leaned against the doorframe, contemplating his next move. He could wake her up and demand to know why she left him, which was what his domineering instincts told him to do. Or he could easily slip into bed with her, which was undoubtedly the simplest option. Either way, he refused to let her be possessed by whatever daft notions made her leave his bed. Decision made, he moved farther into the bedroom. He approached the bed and slipped his hands underneath his wife, emphatically plucking her from it. Then with Lynette still in a deep sleep, he carried her back to his bedroom and placed her carefully in his bed, where he determined she truly belonged. He smiled as he wrapped his arms around her and breathed easily again.

Lynette woke several hours later to sunlight streaming into the bedroom and cursed the curtains that had never been pulled. She found it strange at first because it wasn't like Milly to forget such details when helping her prepare for bed. Then, rolling over slowly, she realized that she wasn't actually in her bedchamber but in Aiden's instead. Her brow furrowed as she finished rolling over to find him staring at her. "Why am I not in my own bed?"

Aiden hadn't known what to expect when Lynette woke. Anger, repulsion, flat-out rejection? It all seemed viable. He certainly hadn't foreseen her casualness in speaking to him, as if her main concern was the sun streaming in through the windows. "Is that where you'd prefer to be?"

Her mouth dried as she realized she'd once again rejected him in an offhanded attempt to guard her own heart. She winced but couldn't very well tell him the true reason she'd left his bed. That would involve her admitting she loved him, which would only set *her* up for rejection. "I simply thought that's where I was meant to sleep."

He blinked, his eyes relaxing. She hadn't returned to her bed as a way to dismiss him; she merely didn't understand the purpose of her staying in his. He could accept that the societal expectation of husbands and wives keeping separate bedrooms was what spurred her to leave, but despite this new insight, it still begged the question, had she *wanted* to remain in his bed? If she wanted to be different from other wives of the *ton*, then she could be unconventional in this sense.

"You thought wrong," he said as he hauled her to his side. Now that he could think clearly again, he noted how delectable she looked in the morning, fresh-faced with wide eyes and tousled hair. He'd been hard when he woke, but with each passing minute, he was becoming harder than stone. "Your room can be used to store your dresses, to wash, and to dress. It won't need to be used for sleeping . . . or for anything else." He brushed an errant lock from her face.

She rubbed her lips together and dared to meet his blue eyes. "Why?"

"Because you belong in mine," he replied without missing a beat. "You agreed to as much last night." His face dipped toward hers.

She squeaked with surprise, her body quickly hot all over. Her mind ran wild with thinking. He couldn't possibly mean to . . . it was morning, for heaven's sake!

But Aiden's intentions were nothing but clear when he placed his mouth on hers. Lynette's hesitations melted away within seconds once he began to kiss her. His mouth roamed her body, second only to his hands, which expertly touched her. It all seemed more forbidden in the light of day, which allowed her to see his every move. Their eyes locked as he spread her legs, his shaft poised to breach her entrance for a second time. She could see his face gleam with satisfaction when he embedded himself fully, and she tried not to think too deeply about what her face must look like to him.

He reached out to caress her breasts, taking one nipple between his finger and thumb to roll gently while he thrust into her. She bit her lower lip but was unable to contain her sighing moan, causing him to grin as he reveled in the reactions he could garner from her. She tried to keep some sense of decorum despite his fondling, but it wasn't long before the façade melted away. It was only the two of them anyhow, joining their bodies together in an act as old as time itself. Aiden let himself go as soon as Lynette did, his name a moan on her lips, signifying they were once again completely and utterly sated.

Despite the hour, they stayed abed for some time, celebrating their lust for each other. He persuaded her to take their breakfast alone together in his bedroom, which allowed them to sit intimately as they ate their meats and cakes. When duty could wait no longer, he dressed himself before leaving her with a searing kiss on her lips.

With Aiden gone, Lynette rose and returned to her room to ring the bellpull. Milly appeared promptly and was wise enough to not comment on the state of her mistress's hair as she brushed and styled it. Once her hair was tamed, Lynette selected a rose-colored morning gown to get her through the day. Totty, the head maid, appeared shortly after she finished dressing to offer her a tour around the house. She agreed and followed the maid out of her bedroom.

After a short perusal of the first floor, which simply consisted of bedrooms and Aiden's study-come-library, Totty led Lynette to the ground floor. The house was square in design, with various rooms surrounding an inner courtyard. Starting on the right side of the entrance hall, which was big enough to serve as a ballroom, Totty pointed out a morning room in addition to the dining room and drawing room that Aiden and Lynette had used the night before. Lynette noted how the morning room was indulgently decorated with dark-green hues and decided it could be used as her reception room if the local matrons did decide to call. In contrast, the drawing room was decorated in deep reds, with family portraits lining the walls. Totty informed Lynette that Matilda and Ferdy had used the room to receive guests for a dinner party a few times, which started the wheels turning in Lynette's mind.

A long corridor, the length of the house itself, made up the entire rear of the house. It was neutrally decorated but contained various pieces of art, such as paintings and sculptures, and Lynette thought she could have mistaken it for an art gallery. They finished their tour of the ground floor after they inspected the private family rooms, which were situated to the left of the main entrance hall and similar in size and shape to their counterparts on the opposite side. Following the inside of the house, Totty led her outside, first to the inner courtyard and then to the rear garden. The courtyard featured a fountain and perfectly trimmed hedges artfully placed around the perimeter. The rear garden was just as well kept as the inner courtyard, containing various types of flowers.

"The gardens are very well maintained," Lynette said. "Who takes care of them?"

"I do, milady." Totty beamed from her mistress's praise. "I've always had a knack for flowers and plants."

"You do it justice." Lynette nodded, complimenting her. As the two women reentered the house, she turned to the maid. "I don't want to step on any toes here since his lordship and I won't be in residence very long. It seems you run quite the tight ship, but if there's anything you need from me or anything I can do while I'm here, please simply ask."

"You won't be stepping on anyone's toes, milady. 'Tis your house, after all," Totty assured her new mistress. "It's actually quite nice to have you and his lordship in residence. Even if it is for a short amount of time, it's still a pleasure to be able to take care of you."

Totty and Lynette talked a bit more about supplies that might be needed and the types of foods she'd prefer to be served while she and Aiden were in residence. After that, Totty excused herself to attend to her duties and to talk with the chef about menus. Then deciding it was too glorious of a day to sit inside, Lynette retrieved *Sense and Sensibility* from her room to read in the inner courtyard.

As she read about the disappearance of Mr. Willoughby, Marianne's subsequent heartbreak, and Edward Ferrars's visit to Barton Cottage, she acknowledged that she enjoyed having the freedom to read without feeling the rebuke of her mother. In possession of her own household, she was finally her own mistress. While it was true she had vowed to honor and obey her husband, Aiden said he wouldn't prevent her from reading for leisure. Never again would she need to practice her needlepoint or singing. She couldn't help but laugh at the thought of her offering to play the pianoforte for him. It was just a shame her mother wasted so much money on piano lessons since it was unlikely she would ever play again.

Adams found Lynette hours later, still in the courtyard. "You have visitors, milady."

She closed her book and smiled. Rising from her chair, she followed him to the morning room, where three ladies sat waiting for her. They introduced themselves as Mrs. Beasley, Mrs. Tipton, and Mrs. Morton. Mrs. Beasley and Mrs. Morton were both wives of local landowners, whereas Mrs. Tipton was the wife of the local clergyman. Once they'd all been introduced, Lynette instructed Adams to bring refreshments while she sat down to get to know the ladies. Mrs. Beasley, Lynette estimated, was the oldest, with two daughters ages sixteen and eighteen.

Mrs. Tipton, the youngest and recently married, had borne no children yet, while Mrs. Morton was somewhere in the middle, with three young boys ages seven, five, and three. Mr. Beasley cultivated radishes, lettuce, and spinach, whereas Mr. Morton reared cattle for a dairy farm.

The ladies had been all in a tither at the prospect of visiting Elberry Park when they'd heard that someone was in residence. Mrs. Beasley and Mrs. Morton expressed their condolences regarding Ferdy's death, remarking how nice he and Matilda were the few times they stayed at Elberry Park. Knowing that Aiden had been on the Continent for nearly a decade, Lynette decided to press the matrons for any knowledge they might possess about Ferdy, Matilda, and how they had made use of the estate.

From what Lynette could glean, Ferdy and Matilda sojourned at Elberry Park during Parliament's Lenten recess every year and sometimes stayed through the autumn if they needed to go to London for a special parliamentary session.

"Many gentlemen enjoy hunting in the area," Mrs. Morton said.

"Which makes it the perfect location for a house party in the autumn, milady," Mrs. Beasley added.

Lynette pressed her lips together, getting the impression that the matron wanted more entertainment in the area, at which she could present her daughters. "I'm aware that Lady Matilda hosted dinner parties here."

Mrs. Beasley sat up straight and sipped her tea. "My husband and I enjoyed Lady Matilda's dinner parties immensely."

Mrs. Morton nodded enthusiastically. "Oh yes. The food was always divine."

"Maybe I should throw a dinner party before my husband and I quit residence." Lynette tilted her head to the side. "Just something small to allow us to meet the locals."

Mrs. Tipton clasped her hands in glee. "That's a splendid idea, milady."

Mrs. Morton leaned forward. "I'd be honored for an invitation."

"If you need any suggestions on who to invite, I'd be happy to help," Mrs. Beasley said.

Lynette smiled. "I'll gladly accept any advice you can give."

The visit concluded shortly thereafter, but not before Mrs. Beasley could extend an invitation to the assembly she planned to host the following evening in honor of both her daughters. Lynette gave her hearty agreement on behalf of herself and Aiden and then wished the matrons farewell. She received two more ladies after the departures of Mrs. Beasley, Mrs. Morton, and Mrs. Tipton. They were not the last, though, and Lynette received nine ladies in total by the end of the day. All were wives of the local gentry, and all were extremely pleased to have the Elliots in residence.

As busy as she was with callers, Lynette didn't see Aiden until they met for dinner. After escorting her into the dining room, he pulled out the chair next to his for her to sit in and then instructed Adams to start serving.

"What do you think of the house?" he asked as they began eating.

"It's a lovely house," she replied truthfully. She couldn't help but note that he'd kept their sitting arrangement from the night before, with her next to him instead of at the other end of the table. It felt very intimate to her, just the two of them eating side by side. Their knees touched underneath the table, and they could hold hands between courses. "Would you mind if I proposed some improvements, though?" she asked, continuing the conversation about the house.

His eyes met hers. "And what improvements might those be?"

"Firstly, one of the private family rooms could be converted into a small library."

Aiden stifled a laugh and realized he should have foreseen such a proposition from Lynette; if she had any input, there would be a library at each of his estates. "Is the study not big enough for your purposes?"

"Oh, I'm sure it is," she said in a rush, not wishing to offend his office, but then she noted the amused look on his face. Her eyes danced as she lifted her wine glass to her lips. "I wouldn't want to overrun all your serious books with my silly novels."

"While I insist that there is more than enough room for both frivolity and solemnity, I wouldn't want to dissuade you if a personal library is your heart's desire," Aiden said. A library was such an easy gift to give to his new wife, and it would make her happy.

"I shall make the arrangements." She smiled widely, her cheeks big and round. "Which brings me to my next point," she said after pausing to enjoy her soup.

"Yes?"

"As the highest-ranking members of the community, it is our responsibility to provide entertainment. There are various young ladies in the district that will not have the opportunity of a London Season, which makes local events all that much more important," she explained, thinking about Mrs. Beasley's daughters in particular.

Aiden's eyebrows rose. "I wouldn't have imagined my wife as a champion of the London Season."

"Maybe not at first, but I am now." Lynette shrugged, feeling forced to recognize that the London Season was what had brought her and Aiden together.

"Very well. What sort of events do you suggest?"

"The house has so much potential, and we could use it for any number of events. A summer ball, perhaps, to utilize the courtyard; a dinner party for neighbors; and maybe even a house party in the autumn."

He nodded. "All fine ideas, I would say."

"I also think we should at least host a dinner before we quit Elberry Park," she said. "It's fine for us to visit our neighbors and other landowners, but I think it would be better for us to invite them to dine with us. It would feel more welcoming, I believe."

Aiden reached for her hand and moved his thumb against hers. "I shall leave that with you then, as I believe you'd know best."

"I'll arrange it then." She lifted her chin and sat up straighter. "We shall have to stay at Elberry Park for at least a week in order for me to return all the visits I received today. Oh! I nearly forgot to mention that we were invited to an assembly tomorrow."

"A week it shall be." He took a sip of his wine. "There's really no timeline we must keep to."

"Oh, but I am most excited to see Eldridge Castle," she said. "I want to know if it resembles Dowsorrell Castle at all."

His blue eyes glistened. "It shall remain where it is until we arrive there."

"Can you describe it to me?"

"I can," he replied and described his childhood home

in great detail during the second and third courses.

Once they finished eating, they took their tea in the drawing room. Lynette ordered a bath to be prepared for her to have before bed, and once it was ready, she left Aiden to see to her ablutions. He remained in the drawing room to read the newspaper until he noticed Milly walk by the door. He called out to the maid, who turned to him.

"Is your mistress finished with her bath yet?" he asked.

"Not yet, milord. She told me to return after some time to help her dry and dress," Milly replied.

"That won't be necessary tonight, Milly," he said, setting his paper aside.

The maid conceded despite her dubious nature, and he went directly to his wife's bedroom. Dispensing with the formality of knocking, he entered. She sat relaxing in the bathtub with her wet hair piled on the top of her head.

She opened her eyes when Aiden walked through the door. "Milly will be returning to help me."

"I told her she won't be needed tonight," he said, his voice low and husky, as he strode to the tub to place a searing kiss on her neck.

"I shall get you all wet," Lynette warned as he reached for her without bothering to shed his clothes first.

"Then we shall both have to dry off," he said, unconcerned with the possibility of wet clothes. He wouldn't be wearing them much longer anyway. Offering no more objections, she melted into his arms and allowed him to carry her into his bedchamber. Despite the roaring fire she felt a chill, her body dripping with water.

"You smell like flowers in a spring rain." Aiden breathed in Lynette's scent. "I simply want to drown in your skin."

And drown he did. He engulfed her body with his

own and drove her mad with his teasing touches. Every caress was either too soft or too short, never long or hard enough. He tickled her breasts with his fingers but refused to tweak the nipples. She groaned her displeasure and arched her body into his, which remained clothed. His tantalizing fingers gripped her hips mid-arch, and he bent his head to the curls that colored the apex of her thighs. Once there, he breathed deeply but refused to grant her contact with his lips. She struggled underneath him, and her hands sliced through his hair in an attempt to push him into her.

Aiden looked up at her impishly, his poor innocent wife seemingly unable to cope with his teasing. "Tell me what you want." He blew hot air at the junction of her thighs.

Lynette couldn't respond. She couldn't possibly put into words the feelings she wanted him to elicit. Instead, she wriggled manically as her body screamed for pleasure.

"I'm waiting." He hovered over her tauntingly.

"Your hands, your mouth, anything!" she screamed, and he rewarded her with everything. Lifting her legs onto his shoulders, he spread her wide and sucked her pleasure bud into his mouth. He worked her with his fingers and tongue, showing no mercy until she shrieked her pleasure. Then, barely pulling away, he released himself from the confines of his trousers and adjusted her so that one leg remained on his shoulder while he wrapped the other around his hip.

Sighing blissfully at his intrusion, she matched his thrusts, having barely recovered from her first climax before the second one threatened. Recalling the pleasure the movement provoked, she placed her hands on her own breasts and rolled her nipples between her fingers. She moaned as she pinched them, her face contorting to show her various degrees of ecstasy.

The sight of Lynette pleasuring herself as Aiden pumped into her was enough to send him over the edge. None of his previous mistresses had done what she was doing to herself and him. Burying himself to the hilt, he shot off his seed and ground his pelvis into hers. Once finished, he collapsed onto the bed beside her.

She breathed heavily and ran her eyes up and down his body. "Why are you still clothed?"

Aiden looked down at himself and noted that he was indeed still clothed in his tailcoat with his cravat, while tousled, remained tied. The most disheveled part of him was his trousers, which gaped open at his hips. "I guess I just hadn't taken the time," he replied. He'd been too concerned with touching her, and then the urgency to be inside her became too great.

"But what if I wanted to touch you?" she asked next, her usually sweet, innocent face shifted into one much more provocative in nature.

Wasting no time, he sprang from the bed and dispensed with his clothes before rejoining her. "Touch me. I'm yours," he said, once sprawled out beside her.

And touch him, she did. Lynette ran her fingers down his chest, admiring the feel of his hair crinkling beneath her nails. Within minutes, his breathing became hard and labored as he enjoyed her attention. Whether she intended them to be or not, her movements were pure torture. She plucked his nipples as he had just witnessed her do to herself and bent her head to take one into her mouth. He caressed her still-damp hair and enjoyed her enthusiastic attention. Then content with her exploration of his chest, she journeyed south.

Faced with his erection, she hesitated and wondered if

she should ask permission before she touched him there. He watched her intently, and his breath caught in his throat as she weighed her options. Finally, deciding that he'd never thought to ask her before he touched her intimately, she reached out and grasped his stiff shaft. He felt as though he would be eaten by fire as his wife inexpertly played with him, first with her hands and then her lips when she dipped her head to take him into her mouth. He couldn't decide if he preferred her inexperienced attention or if he should school her on what he truly liked. In the end, it didn't matter because he didn't think he could take either form of blissful torture.

"Lynette," he beckoned. She stopped her kisses, and he drew her body on top of his. Lifting her slightly, he positioned himself at her entrance and guided her to sit on him. "Show me your riding skills." He placed his hands on her hips.

She felt it odd at first, sitting astride him, but with his encouragement, she squeezed him with her legs and rode him as she would a horse. The pressure the position elicited pleased her to no end. She let her head fall back, and her hair framed her shoulders with the ends tickling her nipples. He reached up and clasped a breast with each hand to massage. The movement sent shockwaves from her chest to between her thighs, and she squealed in delight as her pleasure crested for the third time that night, with Aiden only shortly behind her.

Chapter Twenty-One

The next day, Lynette rose and dressed in a dark-blue riding habit with the intent of beginning her duties as Lady Elliot. When she was ready, she went to break her fast and consequently met Aiden in the dining room.

"Off for a ride?" he asked, noting his wife's attire.

"I thought I would explore the estate." She nodded as she helped herself to eggs, sausages, and bread. "In addition to returning some of the visits I received yesterday."

"Yes, of course," he acknowledged while he sipped his coffee. He considered remarking on her ability to awaken so early after their extensive activities the night before but ultimately decided against teasing his wife. Aiden was not at all tired himself; if anything, he had an extra spring in his step courtesy of his wife. "Why don't I join you?"

Her eyes widened as she sat down. "You want to pay house calls?"

"I shall have to meet the locals eventually." He shrugged. "And it'll be less tedious if we do it together."

They finished their breakfast and then withdrew to the stables. Once there, Aiden requested that his stallion and a mare for Lynette be harnessed for riding. Horses ready, he lifted her into her saddle. His hands clasped her waist, and they stood face to face, making it impossible for him to miss the hitch in her breathing. He smirked as he remembered how similar his movements were to the ones he'd made the night before when he positioned her atop him. Her lips parted, and their eyes met. He lingered a moment longer than necessary before he released her in her saddle and then watched her take great care to arrange her skirts.

With a smirk still playing on his lips, Aiden approached his horse and mounted him. "Do you mind if we call on the steward first?" he asked, bringing his horse alongside Lynette's. "I've exchanged letters with him but would like to meet him personally. Then after that, we can visit whomever you'd like."

She agreed and motioned for him to lead on. The steward's house was not far from the main house, simply down by the estate's main gate. After the short ride, he dismounted and lifted her from her horse before he went to knock on the door. A few minutes later, a man of no more than thirty with a medium build, blond hair, and blue eyes answered.

"Mr. Stanford, I presume?" Aiden asked.

"Aye, Eugene Stanford, milord." The steward bowed politely and welcomed them inside. The house was small, bearing only two reception rooms on the ground floor, three bedrooms, and an office on the first. What it lacked in size, it made up for in warmth, but it was still decorated by a man's standards.

"Please forgive our intrusion, but we are in residence and wanted to meet you personally," Aiden said.

"Yes, milord, milady, please come and sit down." Mr.

Stanford gestured to his settee. "I'd heard that you'd arrived at Elberry Park but didn't have the chance to call on you yesterday."

"That's quite all right, Mr. Stanford," Aiden said. "We don't plan to be in residence for long. We simply wanted to get a look at the estate. I haven't been here since I was a boy, and my new wife has never visited, so we thought now would be the best time."

"Yes, of course." Mr. Stanford nodded enthusiastically. "Would either of you like some tea?"

Lynette and Aiden both accepted the offer, and Mr. Stanford rang for a maid to fix it. While waiting for the tea, Aiden invited the steward to tell him about the estate, its land, and its tenants. Mr. Stanford had only been employed at Elberry for three years, having been hired by Ferdy when the estate's previous steward had retired. While partaking in the tea, Mr. Stanford took the time to express his condolences concerning Ferdy's passing, which Aiden humbly accepted. The meeting confirmed to Aiden that his brother had hired well, determining that Mr. Stanford was a hardworking man who, while young, was also skilled in his profession.

"After we quit residence here, we shall continue north, ultimately to Eldridge, until the start of next Season," Aiden said as he stood to leave. "You can direct correspondence there should you need anything."

Mr. Stanford inclined his head. "Indeed, milord."

"Mr. Stanford, I was planning to arrange a dinner for some of the local community before we leave Elberry Park. Would you be interested in attending?" Lynette asked.

"I would be honored, milady," he replied, grinning.

"Excellent. I shall send an invitation." Lynette smiled

as well, happy that plans for her dinner party were coming together nicely.

After that, Aiden and Lynette mounted their horses and took their leave. He spurred his horse down the road, noting the acres of farmland they passed on the way to their next stop.

"What is it you grow on this land?" she asked.

"Carrots mostly, but some farmers also rear lambs," he replied.

Lynette nodded, and they continued their ride. Needing to pass through the village on their way to the Mortons' house, she insisted that they stop to meet the shopkeepers, knowing that they would be the best sources of information regarding the district. Stabling their horses at a local inn, Aiden escorted her down the main street, where he was able to meet and talk with some of his tenants. He was happy to find that they were indeed content with Mr. Stanford as a steward and that while the land sometimes gave them problems, they were also mostly happy renting their farmland from the Elliots. Overall, everyone they met was simply excited to meet the new lord and lady of Elberry Park and expressed their sincere hope that they would reside there more often throughout the year.

Pleased with their findings, Aiden and Lynette returned to their horses and continued their journey to the Mortons' house, where Mrs. Morton invited them to stay for luncheon, which they accepted and enjoyed. After bidding the matron farewell an hour later, Lynette suggested they stop at the parsonage to call on Mr. and Mrs. Tipton since it was nearby. The visit agreed upon by Aiden, they rode the short distance through a field and arrived to find Mrs. Tipton caring for her garden.

The visit with the Tiptons only detained them for

another quarter hour and consisted of Lynette finding out the young vicar's needs. Aiden watched intently as his wife listened to Mr. Tipton's concerns regarding the parish and how they could encourage the community to become more involved. While departing, she assured the vicar that she would give some thought to how she could help him in his endeavor and would inform him of her conclusions before she and Aiden withdrew from Elberry Park.

Aiden couldn't stop smiling during the ride back to Elberry. Lynette was embracing her role in Society after just a few short days, and while he'd never doubted her capabilities for the position, seeing it first-hand stirred something in him. He couldn't explain it. When he watched his wife with the shopkeepers or the vicar, a warmness spread through his chest, and his heart began to race. It made him want to tell anyone who would listen that she was his wife so they too could appreciate her abilities. But she was merely doing her duty, and it seemed strange to want to celebrate something so ordinary.

The feeling didn't fade when they returned home just in time to dress for an early dinner before the Beasley ball. Aiden's eyes never strayed from his wife throughout the meal, even though she only did mundane things. He watched her hand as it brought the spoon to her lips. The gold in her brown eyes twinkled as they discussed the day. He was so enthralled with her that he nearly forgot to request the carriage to be brought around! Thankfully, Adams saved him from that embarrassment and arranged it quickly, just as they were finishing dessert. Aiden wiped his mouth with his napkin and cleared his throat as he stood. His eyes met Lynette's as he offered her his hand, and he struggled to breathe the entire way to the

Beasley ball.

"You should dance with the Beasley girls tonight," Lynette said as they walked into the assembly. Guests were already milling around, but it was nothing compared to the crushes they experienced in London. As they took a turn around the ballroom, she introduced Aiden to the ladies she knew.

"You are very good at this," Aiden said as they moved from group to group. He still hadn't been able to shake the feeling that had taken hold of him earlier in the day. If anything, it had gotten stronger. His entire body was warm, and it had nothing to do with the number of people surrounding them.

She smiled at him. "It's my duty to guide you through Society."

"Yes, I know." He squinted at her. "I'm simply in awe of how effortlessly you do it."

"Next time you see my mama, please tell her that." Lynette threw her head back and laughed. "She had me worried I wouldn't make a good wife to my husband."

"To me?"

"To any man."

Aiden struggled to swallow, his mouth suddenly dry. He didn't like the idea that what she did for him, she could do for any other man. It seemed so . . . impersonal, and Lynette was anything but. The way she smiled at him, her brown eyes dancing as she introduced him to matron upon matron. While he cared deeply for his granny, when she introduced him to people, he had to suppress a groan. But when Lynette did it, he couldn't help but share her enthusiasm.

He wanted to say as much but decided against it in the end. His lips remained closed as he followed Lynette around the ballroom and danced with the Beasley girls. His eyes never left her, whether she was next to him or across the room. And when the ball broke up well after midnight, Aiden took his wife home to his bed, where duty was the furthest thing from his mind.

Chapter Twenty-Two

Lynette woke late the following day, her eyes opening slowly in the darkened room. She'd convinced Aiden to close the curtains so the sun wouldn't wake her, but it still didn't stop him from kissing her at dawn. A slow smile tugged at her lips as she stretched across the bed. Reluctantly, she rose and went to her room to wash and dress. Once ready for the day, she descended the stairs to have her breakfast.

"Good morning, milady," Adams said when she entered the dining room.

"Good morning," she replied as she filled her plate with bacon, eggs, and sausage, her mouth watering at the sight. Content with her selections, she turned to the table and sat.

Adams cleared his throat. "If you prefer, milady, I can bring a breakfast tray to your room when you have a lie-in."

"That's all right, Adams." Lynette smiled at him. "I like to break my fast in the dining room."

"If you're sure . . . I'd just hate for you to be lonely, eating in here by yourself."

With her fork halfway to her mouth, she blushed.

"I appreciate your concern, but I assure you, I'm just fine." The butler seemed to take her at her word, but she finished everything on her plate to ensure his mind was completely at ease. She didn't want the servants to worry over her well-being, especially when she was the happiest she'd ever been. Everything was going splendidly. She was making connections with the local matrons and arranging church events for the vicar. Aiden had even complimented her!

Lynette left the dining room with her head held high, ready to get to work. Invitations for her dinner party needed to be written and sent, so she walked to one of the private family rooms where she'd spied an escritoire she could use. She began by deciding that the party should be planned for five days hence, giving her enough time to send out invitations and make the necessary arrangements for such an event. Then depending on how things transpired, she and Aiden could leave for North Yorkshire one or two days later. Content with her plans, she wrote out the invitations to twenty people, including the Beasleys, Mortons, Tiptons, and Mr. Stanford. With the quill to her lip, she recalled how Mrs. Beasley's oldest daughter flirted with Mr. Stanford at the assembly the evening prior. She flipped through the invitations until she found the one addressed to the Beasleys and added both daughters to it, hoping to spark a little romance.

When the invitations were complete, she sat back and smiled, Aiden's words from the night before ringing in her head. Eager for him to see her progress, she collected the invitations to take to him. She bounced up the stairs, humming softly, and knocked lightly on the office door.

"Come in," Aiden called, and she stepped inside. Surprisingly, it was the first time she'd been inside his study at Elberry Park. During her tour, neither she nor Totty wanted to disturb him, so they glossed over the room since Lynette was happy enough to know its location in lieu of its interior. Now given the opportunity, she took in the room. It was rather massive, featuring book-lined shelves, an enormous mahogany desk situated to the left, and French doors that opened onto a balcony overlooking the inner courtyard. It also possessed a light and airy feel, which diminished the masculinity of the decor. Lynette liked it instantly, thinking that it was probably the best room in the house.

She approached his desk. "I wrote out the invitations to the dinner party. Would you mind sealing these so they could be sent out?"

"Of course," he replied and took them from her. "What decisions have you made regarding the party?"

"We shall have twenty-two guests if they all accept. I'll talk with the chef about the menu, but I was thinking beef for the meat course."

"Sounds delicious." He licked his lips, his eyes on hers.

"Oh! And I was thinking there should be some after-dinner entertainment." Her eyes widened, and her cheeks flushed. "Maybe some musicians so our guests can dance."

"A wonderful idea," he said, taking his cues from her. He wasn't about to stand in her way if she wanted music and dancing. Not while her eyes were glistening as they were.

As Lynette continued to talk animatedly, his mouth began to water. His hands tingled with the need to touch her, and he considered persuading her to lift her skirts so that he could take her on his desk. He shifted his stance and marveled at the sheer intensity with which he wanted his wife. It seemingly didn't matter how many times he'd had her. His desire had yet to abate.

It was a new concept for Aiden, who had never wanted someone with such fervency before. He'd had his fair share of mistresses over the years, and each time he became bored with one, he'd simply move on to another. The same would have to happen to his lust for Lynette, given time. Surely he couldn't go on wanting to lift her skirts indefinitely.

"Whose books are these?" she asked, breaking his trance.

"Either my father's or Ferdy's, I would assume," he replied. "You're welcome to browse the shelves while we're here to see if you find any enticing."

She smiled at the suggestion. "I shall have to another time as I plan to take the afternoon to return some calls."

While he ached to detain her, he knew they both had duties to attend to. He would just have to wait till that evening to sate his desire. So he kissed his wife goodbye and allowed her to get on with her day, and he returned to his desk in an attempt to resume his.

But Aiden's mind had other plans and insisted that he analyze why he lusted over his wife so strongly. From the moment he'd met her, he had been attracted to her physically, which was explained easily enough. She was an undeniable beauty with alabaster skin, deep brown hair, and brown eyes that contained specks of gold. She was also passionate in the bedroom after her innocence had been overcome. Moreover, she'd learned how to derive pleasure from their encounters, which only increased his own pleasure tenfold. Together her ardor and beauty could justify his lust, but it didn't feel like enough for some reason. He'd been with alluringly passionate women before and had never once felt like he did with his wife.

He had similar sentiments the day before when he'd acknowledged his appreciation for her societal prowess, unsatisfied that it was merely about her ability to fulfill her duty to him. What did it mean that the two foundational edicts of their relationship no longer seemed like enough? What more was there for him to hope for?

And then the answer hit him like a hailstorm, essentially knocking the breath right out of him. Could he be in love? Love seemed so hard to define, and he'd never experienced its impact before. It made the puzzle fit together, though—why he no longer equated Lynette's abilities in running a household or hosting a party to duties, and why he desired more than her body but a holistic connection. Finally, after nearly thirty years, the impossible had happened: Aiden had finally succumbed to the effects of love.

His awakening, however enlightening, caused him considerable anxiety. Would she ever love him in return? He remembered her telling him when she tried to break off their engagement that she couldn't have a marriage without love, meaning that she couldn't love him. He wanted to believe that they had overcome that challenge since she at least *lusted* for him now. But could that lust transform into love? For him, it obviously had, but that didn't mean it would for her. And how would he know if it ever did? He couldn't possibly tell her that he loved her until he was sure that she returned his affection because anything prior would only set him up for rejection. Having been rejected by her previously, it was not a feeling Aiden wanted to have repeated. Thus he faced a conundrum: how to gain Lynette's love and keep his heart from breaking in the meantime.

Chapter Twenty-Three

On the night of her dinner party, Lynette chewed on her lip as she donned a pair of earrings. Earrings secured, she leaned back and stared at her reflection in the mirror, her eyes darting from her ears to her gown. She'd decided to wear the sapphire dress made for her engagement ball since it was her newest and best, but it brought up unsettling memories of Aiden and their troubled beginnings.

Things had changed considerably since that night and even more so since arriving at Elberry Park. Aiden and Lynette were ruled by duty during the day and bound by lust at night. However unsatisfied she remained with the arrangement, it seemed that she'd accepted it for what it was. And not a false acceptance like the one she'd deluded herself with when she'd agreed to his proposal. Her acceptance of duty and lust was finally true. But that didn't stop her from doubting the dress and the emotions she recalled feeling the first time she wore it.

Lynette's expectations for the evening certainly didn't help her anxiety. She'd been preparing for the occasion for nearly a week. She'd worked with the chef on the menu, had personally picked out the flowers from the florist, and had arranged for a string quartet. If the weather held, she anticipated inviting the guests into the inner courtyard after dinner for the music, but if not, they had the drawing room. Either way, it was her plan, her party, truly her first moment as Lady Elliot, Society hostess. It was the first of her duties that she could fulfill in its entirety, and she did not want to imagine letting Aiden down.

"Our guests will be arriving shortly, my dear." Aiden's voice shook her out of her reverie. He leaned against the doorframe that connected their rooms and exuded masculinity as he filled it.

"I'm ready," she announced and stood, her hands unconsciously moving to smooth her skirts.

He smiled and stepped in to meet her. "Hmm . . . not quite." He brought his hands out from behind his back and presented her with a jewelry box.

"Aiden!" she gasped as she opened it. Inside was a silver necklace adorned by a rectangular-shaped sapphire, which was the exact color of her dress, and was accompanied by matching earrings.

"I coerced Milly into telling me what dress you planned to wear tonight." He drew the necklace from the box as he motioned for her to remove the necklace and earrings she currently wore. Once her jewelry was switched, she turned and faced him, and he admired his gifts hanging from her ears and neck. The necklace in particular was stunning and offset the low-cut bodice of her gown, just as he'd anticipated.

The dress roused similar emotions in Aiden as it did in Lynette. A heaviness settled in his stomach when he recalled the fight they had the first time she wore it, how he rucked up her skirts to try to please her into submission, and her rejection of him afterward. Seeing her wear the dress again was like rubbing salt in a healing wound, especially since he'd only recently realized his love for her. So he decided to give her jewelry, to serve as a peace offering of sorts. As if the necklace and earrings would make the dress new again and wipe their slates clean. It didn't hurt that she looked ravishing while she wore them. Her original selections were not poor in any way; they simply couldn't compare to the sapphire gems.

"Now you are ready." Aiden smiled. Among his other reasons, he wanted the jewelry to be his first step in securing Lynette's returned affections, his rationale being that all women enjoyed jewelry and receiving presents. It was as if he needed to court her all over again, he acknowledged. He had already secured her hand in marriage, albeit through some coercion, but now he had to secure her love.

He bent to capture her lips in what he had intended to be a chaste kiss. A mistake, undoubtedly, since there was nothing chaste regarding his feelings for his wife. As soon as his lips were on hers, he wanted to beg off the dinner party that she'd painstakingly arranged in order to spend the evening alone together.

She breathed steadily as their eyes met. "We shall be late to our own dinner party."

He almost did the right thing and stepped away, but seeing her in her dress and the jewelry he lavished upon her did him in. The woman did things to him, things that made him forget himself. There would be no looking at her without undressing her with his eyes, so there would be no way of getting through the evening without first slaking his desire. "I can be quick." He took her hand and guided her to his bedroom.

"Aiden!" Lynette squeaked but didn't pull away.

"Tell me you don't want this as much as I do," he said, knowing that one word would silence him forever.

But she didn't say anything because she couldn't deny her desire for him any more than he could deny his desire for her.

Lynette's silence was enough for him. He positioned her at the foot of his bed and urged her to bend over with her hands holding on to a bedpost. Being careful not to wrinkle her skirts, he flipped them up and out of his way. His hand then found her hot, wet, and waiting.

"I can feel how much you want me," Aiden growled, hungry for a taste of her, but he'd promised them both that he would be quick, so quick he needed to be. There was no telling when Adams would come to find them to announce that their guests had begun arriving, so his only goal was to slate their hunger enough to get them through the evening. Then in the dead of night, he could lay her down upon his pillows clad only in her sapphire necklace and worship her properly.

He released himself from his breeches and entered her easily. They both groaned at the contact, and she flushed red with passion as he gave her long, delicious strokes. Her hands clenched the bedpost, and her head fell forward with a cry upon her lips. He gave her all he could give. His fingers rubbed while his hips ground into her, allowing his member to massage her in the most spectacular ways. It was all too much, and too soon, she broke on a scream, unable to believe that she had crested the climb so quickly. Only holding out until she'd found her release, he accepted his pleasure and emptied himself into her. Their breathing still heavy; they stayed as they were a moment longer, his head falling onto her back to kiss her shoulder.

After regaining his faculties, he stood and did up his breeches while Lynette smoothed her skirts. She did so with the haughty air of a satisfied female, and he smirked as he offered her his arm. "Milady," he said teasingly.

"Milord," she responded in kind and accepted his arm. It did not escape his notice that it was a rare time she'd called him *milord* playfully, as she usually reserved the title for when she was annoyed with him. Happy to have secured a brand-new memory of her in the sapphire dress, Aiden escorted her down to the drawing room, where they awaited their guests.

They needn't wait long for people to arrive. Within minutes, Mr. Stanford appeared, with the Mortons not far behind him. Next came the Beasleys—the mister, the missus, and their two daughters. Finally, the Tiptons arrived later with the rest of the guests. The party was well attended since everyone who received an invitation had accepted.

As the evening wore on, Mrs. Tipton gushed over the floral arrangements, and Mrs. Morton prattled on about the meal. The gentlemen talked about the harvest and if it was worth introducing a new crop to the fields. Once the dinner had concluded, the women withdrew to the drawing room and left the gentlemen to their port. Lynette called for tea, and the ladies sat and gossiped while waiting for their husbands to rejoin them.

Mrs. Beasley doted on Lynette in particular. "I am just so happy we could meet you and his lordship, even if it is just for a short amount of time." She smiled over her teacup. "How soon do you plan to return?"

"The soonest we'd return is prior to the next social Season," Lynette said, hoping to placate the matron.

However, with the duke's health as it was, it was hard to anticipate too far in advance. She knew that Aiden was prepared to take his father's seat in Parliament if and when necessary, but it was simply too uncertain when that time would come.

"Indeed! Why, that's the best news yet!" Mrs. Beasley beamed. They sipped their tea in silence for a few minutes until she thought of a new topic. "I must say, milady, I can only hope that my girls make at least half as good a match as you and his lordship have made."

"I daresay they will," Lynette assured her. "Why, they are both very beautiful, so any gentleman would be happy to have either of them to wife." Her compliments were all completely true. Both girls looked like younger versions of their mother, with honey-colored hair and vibrant blue eyes. She'd made sure to sit the eldest Beasley daughter next to Mr. Stanford during dinner in the hopes that they could share in conversation.

"Yes, I have to agree," Mrs. Beasley said. "But what I mean is that I hope they find at least half as much love in their marriages as you have found in yours."

Lynette's smile faltered slightly as her heart began to race. She hadn't had to think about the societal view of her marriage since she and Aiden had left London, but Mrs. Beasley's words brought it back to the forefront of her mind.

"Oh, but you don't agree." The astute lady met her eye. "Pardon me if I speak out of turn, but it is very apparent that you and his lordship are very much in love."

Lynette smiled tightly. "I thank you for your view, Mrs. Beasley." She knew that the woman was only trying to pay her a compliment, but she remained unsettled. It reminded her of London, where Society thought they understood her relationship with Aiden better than she did. "We are well matched indeed," she said, hoping it would be the end of the conversation. Her eyes darted to the door. For some reason, it suddenly felt like the gentlemen were taking an inordinate amount of time with the port. She willed them to make an appearance so she could have an excuse to walk away, but sadly no one appeared to save her.

"Better than well matched, milady—truly made for each other." Mrs. Beasley patted her hand. "You may be too close to see it, I daresay. But truly, it is so wonderful to see, as love matches are rare indeed."

Finally, the gentlemen entered the drawing room, giving Lynette the excuse she needed to leave Mrs. Beasley without a reply. The woman had stirred emotions in her that she'd thought were settled. But settled or not, her party was not the venue in which to sort through them. This was her crowning moment as Aiden's hostess in Society, and she was going to relish it, not allow the viewpoints of a matron to invade her person as she had weeks before at her engagement ball. She reminded herself that she and Aiden had come a long way since then and that they were happy with only duty and lust. At least, that's what she told herself.

Lynette continued to ponder the thought as she invited her guests out into the courtyard and instructed the string quartet to begin playing. The fountain was illuminated by candles and served as a topic of many conversations. She watched as Mr. Stanford bowed to the elder Beasley girl and asked her to dance. The sight made her smile, happy to have been the spark to ignite the young couple's love affair.

"You outdid yourself, my dear." Aiden appeared at her

side to congratulate her. "This shall be the highlight of the Season in Surrey."

She chuckled. "At least until we return and I have the opportunity to throw another party."

Whatever emotions Mrs. Beasley had unearthed within Lynette, anger was not one of them. It was easy to banter with Aiden, and her heart soared when he pulled her into a waltz. Maybe they had overcome the challenges they had faced at their engagement ball. Maybe she really had accepted their relationship for what it was. It surely felt like she had. If Mrs. Beasley's chatter had brought anything to light, it was how much she loved Aiden and how much she wished he loved her in return. But the thought that he didn't no longer angered her. Instead, Lynette was simply happy that he wanted her by his side at a party and in his bed at night.

Chapter Twenty-Four

Two days after the dinner party at Elberry Park, Aiden and Lynette departed the county via the Surrey Docks where they would set sail to St. James Park in North Yorkshire. The first leg of their journey was by carriage to the dockyard where they would board *The Aether*, which would then carry them to North Yorkshire in twelve hours. At first Lynette was shocked at the idea of sailing up the eastern coast of England, but once Aiden explained that it was much more time effective than traveling by carriage for four days or more to St. James Park or Eldridge Castle, she came around to the idea.

Upon arrival at the Surrey Docks, Aiden went to speak with *The Aether*'s captain while the servants loaded the luggage onto the ship. The Elliots weren't the only ones eager to set sail, so the dockyard was a hive of activity, with sailors and merchants moving in every direction. All of Aiden's servants worked very efficiently, though, and the captain was able to set sail before noon.

The ship itself was a beautiful piece of craftsmanship with three fully rigged masts and was big enough to carry far more than their current party. Overwhelmed by its sheer magnitude, Lynette stood at the bow and looked out as it navigated through the River Thames. It wasn't until sometime later, when she felt rather than heard Aiden come up behind her, that she allowed herself to melt into his embrace.

She looked at him out of the corner of her eye. "How are you feeling about seeing your father again?"

Aiden had been asking himself the same question since they had begun preparing to travel to St. James. Unfortunately, it was hard to put his thoughts and feelings into words when it came to his father. "I shall feel better being closer to him," he replied. "My biggest worry was that he should pass on with me being more than a day's journey away."

"Do you think we should reside at St. James Park for a while then? So that you can be near him?" she asked.

He shook his head. "No, we shall be close enough at Eldridge Castle." While St. James was big enough to accommodate them all, he didn't want to be at the same residence as his parents and granny, especially while his relationship with Lynette was so new. He felt secure in his business affairs, but his relationship with his wife was still foreign to him. The last thing they needed was interference, which was exactly what he expected from his granny. "We shall spend no more than a week at St. James. We'll do the same as we did at Elberry, only I am more familiar with St. James and its management."

For as long as he could remember, St. James Park had been his granny's permanent residence. She always joined the family in London every Season since it was the only time of year she got to see most of her friends in Town, but the rest of her time was spent at St. James. Thus, Ferdy and Aiden had spent a lot of time there growing up before they went off to Eton.

Lynette tilted her chin up. "Shall I host another dinner party?"

"My granny would love that." He ran the backs of his fingers along her jaw.

She shivered. "I shall take it up with her then."

The Aether sailed easily up the coast, the wind propelling them along. Aiden and Lynette relaxed most of the journey, taking a small meal of cold meats and cheeses in the middle of it, enough to tide them over until they reached their destination. They watched the sunset port side and arrived at the Port of Middlesbrough at nearly midnight.

"We shall rest at an inn tonight, and I will send for carriages in the morning," Aiden informed Lynette as he helped her disembark. He then led her, Milly, and Claude, the only two servants who traveled with them, through the dockyard and to the inn his family usually stayed at when arriving in North Yorkshire. It was a reputable establishment, hosting mostly merchants coming and going from the docks. He ushered his wife and their servants inside before ringing the bell for service. "Good evening, sir. I require rooms for myself, my wife, and our servants," he said when the innkeeper appeared.

"Aye, good evening, milord," Mr. Wallace greeted him. "I've got three rooms for you."

The men haggled and settled the price for the rooms, and Aiden requested some food be brought up to them since they hadn't eaten much during their journey. Mrs. Wallace, knowing that her customers arrived at odd hours during the day or night, assured them that she had some stew still warm from dinner.

With everything settled, Aiden and Lynette made their way to their room and waited for supper. They ate the delicious beef stew and crusty bread when it arrived and were instantly satisfied. Ready for bed, they undressed each other and curled up underneath the blankets, her head on his chest. He stroked her hair and then her arm, his eyes blinking at the ceiling. Lynette's breathing was slow and even, but as tired as Aiden was, he simply couldn't fall asleep.

When they woke the next day, they would complete their journey to St. James, putting them at the center of familial expectations once more. Familial expectations had ruined their relationship in London, causing him to marry her more or less against her will. Despite how well things had turned out for them since then, his stomach soured when he thought about how he would be subjecting Lynette to such a dreadful environment yet again.

He knew that as soon as they arrived, his granny would inquire about their success in begetting an heir. Yet despite how important Aiden knew the task to be, the thought of begetting an heir hadn't crossed his mind since leaving London. He didn't think of duty when he took Lynette to his bed; he only thought of the pleasure they could share. But he knew his grandmother wouldn't understand because the only thought in her mind was securing the next generation of the dukedom. How could he protect Lynette from that? And how could he get her to love him in the face of it?

After a restless night, for Aiden at least, he and Lynette both dressed and went down to the inn's pub to break their fast. Just when they were finishing their eggs, meats, and cakes, two Elliot carriages arrived for them and their belongings, and they were on their way to St. James Park within the hour. Lynette felt at home in the northern English countryside, as it reminded her of the lands surrounding Dowsorrell Castle in Scotland. Her lips parted, and she peered out of the window for the entire carriage ride.

As the carriages rolled up the drive of St. James Park, she took in the architecture, which denoted an English Venetian design. They were greeted immediately by the butler and two footmen, who wasted no time unloading the carriages once they stopped in front of the house.

"Good morning, milord." The butler bowed. "It's good to have you here, hail and whole."

"I appreciate that, Phillips," Aiden said. "This is my wife." He gestured to Lynette, who stood by his side. "Is my family up and about yet?"

"Not yet. They take their breakfast in their rooms, but I expect your grandmother to go for her morning constitutional within the next half hour or so."

"And my parents?" Aiden asked about their after-breakfast routine.

"They tend to stay in their rooms for much longer in the mornings and inform me when they are ready to take some air so that I may send a footman for assistance if necessary," Phillips replied.

Aiden nodded and noted, to his immense relief, that his father's illness had neither changed nor worsened in the week since he'd last seen him. He squeezed Lynette's hand and escorted her inside, with Phillips following closely behind.

"Mrs. Hubert has readied your old chamber but was unsure which one to assign milady," the butler said.

"We won't need any other chamber, Phillips." Aiden waved his hand, dismissing the servant.

"Very well, milord. Will you both be in need of anything

else before luncheon?"

"No, thank you." Aiden shook his head, dismissing the butler once more before turning to his wife. "Would you like a tour of the house?" he asked, wanting to ensure she was settled before becoming reacquainted with his family.

Excited by the prospect, Lynette agreed and allowed him to escort her through the country house. The entrance hall featured two separate staircases leading to the house's two wings. He explained that the east wing was used for entertaining while the west wing was reserved for the family. On the ground floor, the east wing consisted of two reception rooms, a large dining room, a drawing room, and a ballroom, while a morning room, a smaller dining room, and a study made up the rooms on the west side. In addition, the family bedchambers and a library occupied the west side of the first floor, while guest bedrooms were reserved for the east side.

They concluded their tour in the garden, where five massive glasshouses stood. Aiden ushered Lynette through the door of one, and they walked down the aisles lined with exotic plants and fruits.

"We are known in the area for our nectarines." He plucked a rather ripe one from a stem and then offered it to her.

"But not peaches." She smirked, accepting the nectarine.

"Nectarines are a St. James specialty," Aiden said with a glint in his eye. He watched her as she bit into the fruit, not in need of any further encouragement.

A drop of juice escaped the corner of Lynette's mouth, and her tongue darted out to catch it. Her eyes closed as she savored the taste before bringing the fruit to her lips for another bite. But the sight was too much for him. He leaned in and kissed her. The nectarine fell from her hand as she wrapped her arms around his neck to pull him even closer. He relished the fruit's sweetness combined with her own intoxicating flavor as the kiss grew even more heated. The only sound in the glasshouse was their heavy breathing as they fought to rein in their mutual desire.

As one they slowly parted, as if daring the other to pull them back. Aiden swallowed hard, and Lynette blinked up at him. "So what do you think?" he asked. "Of the nectarines."

"Not quite as juicy as Lady Paxton's peaches," she replied, unable to resist an opportunity to tease him. "But just as sweet." She ran her tongue over her swollen lips.

"I shall leave cultivating the nectarines to your expertise then, my dear." He squeezed her hand as they continued their walk. "Since you are such an expert on exotic fruit."

Lynette laughed loudly at the idea that she was an expert in anything but eating the exotic fruits, and Aiden savored her laugh. His heart clenched with the knowledge that he could be the only one to make her laugh as she did.

After their perusal of the glasshouses, they returned to the garden, where they found Rowena sitting on a bench, bent on instructing a maid on the proper way of tending to the flowers. Upon seeing them, she waved them over and gave the maid a reprieve.

Aiden approached and kissed his grandmother on the cheek to greet her while Lynette curtsied appropriately.

Rowena invited Lynette to sit next to her. "I trust Elberry Park was accommodating."

"Indeed, it was." Lynette nodded. "The staff is all very well trained, and we had the opportunity to socialize with the local gentry."

"I'm happy to hear that," Rowena said, looking genuinely pleased. "You shall need to reacquaint yourself with your peers in this district as well, Aiden." She turned to Lynette and patted her hand. "My dear, you may join me on my visits this afternoon as it'll be an excellent opportunity to meet people."

Lynette agreed, knowing that with or without the Dowager she would need to make her rounds, but with her, it would be vastly easier to get to know people quickly.

"What of my mother?" Aiden asked.

Rowena shifted on the bench. "She hasn't joined me for several afternoons, eschewing Society for the time being."

"And my father?"

"The same," she said but didn't meet his eye. Clearing her throat, she turned to Lynette. "We shall be needing that heir soon, my dear."

"Granny!" Aiden exclaimed at the indecent remark, and Lynette couldn't stop herself from turning three shades of red.

"I trust you have work to tend to?" Rowena asked, her lips thin lines on her face.

After her most recent remark, Aiden hesitated, toying with the idea of answering negatively and staying with Lynette to act as a buffer between her and his grandmother.

"Best to get it done now as we have a ball at Audley Hall," Rowena continued before Aiden could decide. "Your old friend Marcus has decided to abstain from the Season again, so his mother has been hosting a house party."

Aiden didn't want to comment on his friend's choice to forgo a London Season in the inane hope that it would keep the matchmaking mothers away. "I shall take my leave of you ladies then?" Aiden's eyes met Lynette's.

She smiled. "I shall see you at dinner."

Lynette stayed in the garden with Rowena until they needed to change for their afternoon visits. Once dressed and ready, they departed from St. James to visit the Caldwell residence for luncheon and tea. On the way, Rowena advised her of the local gentry and aristocracy in the area. In addition to the Marquess of Zetland, whose property bordered the Elliots' on the south side, there was also Viscount Ecclestone, whose property bordered Zetland's to the east. Rowena expressed her disdain that the two peers, who were alike in age to her grandsons, had yet to marry or even show an interest in the state. Besides the peers of the realm, there were also the Caldwells and Nortons, who were part of the landed gentry, and Mr. Upton, who was the vicar.

Upon arrival at the Caldwell estate, Rowena introduced her new granddaughter-in-law to those in attendance. Mrs. Caldwell, Lynette's first introduction, was a middle-aged matron with a son- and daughter-in-law of her own that were in Bath for the Season. Next, they came upon Viscountess Ecclestone, mother to the current viscount. She was extremely pleased to meet Lynette and congratulated her on swaying Lord Elliot into matrimony.

"It was simply time for him to marry, and I happened to be available," Lynette offered her usual response.

"Oh, but my dear, it has been time for my Wesley to wed for some years, and he continues to put it off. I can only hope that a lady will persuade him into matrimony as you have with Lord Elliot," Lady Ecclestone insisted.

Rowena and Lynette continued interacting with the other ladies in attendance, and once they'd made their rounds, Rowena decided it was time to sit and enjoy their luncheon.

"I had thought to host an event at St. James while Aiden and I are in residence." Lynette broached the subject carefully, unknowing how the Dowager would react. "I hosted a dinner party at Elberry Park while there, and I believe it went well."

"Indeed?" Rowena set her inquisitive gaze on her granddaughter-in-law. "I agree, an event is a necessity, and as the de facto Duchess of Northumberland, it should be up to you to host it."

Lynette shifted in her chair. "Your Grace, I hardly wish to step on any toes."

"Nonsense, you know as well as I that Eleanor's days of hosting are over. You are the duchess in everything bar name and should act like it." Rowena punctuated her statement with a thud of her cane. "What type of event were you planning to host here?"

"I thought to ask your opinion, frankly," she replied. "A dinner party was enough at Elberry Park—"

"Indeed, most, if not all, near Elberry go to London for the Season. A house party there after the Season never went amiss, but during the Season, there aren't nearly enough in their country homes."

Lynette nodded. "Yes, I did think that as well."

"I would say a ball would not go amiss here, though. Some of the gentries do not go all the way down to London or Bath for a Season, so the events here are quite popular," Rowena said. "You could invite those from at least fifteen miles away, which would surely amount to a substantial party."

"A ball it is then."

Rowena met Lynette's eye. "I must say, I appreciate

you taking up the mantle as a Society hostess. I was quite afraid since Aiden wasn't trained for it."

Lynette swallowed to keep her mouth from falling open. How could anyone, especially family, think of Aiden as anything but capable? On the contrary, she thought he was the most capable man she'd ever known. But if the Dowager's statement was anything to go by, Lynette's sentiments were not shared. It was clear that Rowena didn't believe her grandson could succeed as heir.

After getting over her initial shock, Lynette considered the concept. Aiden had been born a second son, something that she found trivial given that he'd still been born to a wealthy, influential, aristocratic family. His family's standing in Society should have given him some respite from the uncertainty that typically befell a second son, but it obviously hadn't. Thus, he bought a military commission to secure his future.

Becoming heir had changed everything for him. He no longer needed to rely on his military service to provide him a future since he had one, ready-made, that was cast in stone. But it hadn't originally been cast for Aiden; it had been allotted to his brother. Ferdy had been raised with the intention of succeeding his father, while Aiden had been raised . . . for what? At that moment, Lynette didn't know, but for whatever it was, the Dowager obviously didn't seem to believe that the skills were transferable. Or that Aiden was competent enough to prevail despite the lack of formal training. No, Rowena still thought of her grandson as the spare and was blind to his capabilities, unable to accept that even as a second son, he was more than worthy.

This newfound realization also shed new light on another one of Aiden's attributes: his aversion to rejection. Granted, nobody liked rejection, Lynette realized, but he seemed to loathe it more than most. Multiple times, he mistakenly took her attempts to guard her own heart as a dismissal, as if it were to be expected. She soured at the thought of Aiden's opinion of himself being so low that he had to guard himself against rebuff. Her handsome, virile husband should have felt secure in both his body and mind. If there was anyone who needed to worry about being unworthy, she thought it surely should have been her.

"Maybe he wasn't, but I was." Lynette tilted her chin upward, hoping to put Rowena's reservations to bed. But then she recognized the meaning in her own words. She'd been a firstborn, a daughter, yes, but firstborn no less. She'd been trained in much the same way Ferdy had. Her purpose had always been to carry her family's mantle as a wife, mother, and Society hostess, which put her above Aiden in some respects. Those born second, like her husband and sister, felt they had to fight for recognition, as evidenced in the way Aiden bought his commission and Kathleen's determination to marry a lofty-titled gentleman. Lynette was living out her birthright, whereas Aiden was fulfilling his brother's.

"I see that you are." Rowena nodded before turning to engage someone else in conversation.

Lynette sat back and sipped her tea, but it didn't ease the heaviness in her chest. Surely Aiden no longer doubted how much she wanted him. He couldn't possibly still see himself as anything but worthy of her affections. But what about in regard to his family? She recognized that he might have continued cause to doubt himself there, but it wasn't right. Family was supposed to support each other, and if his own family wasn't going to take up the mantle, then she would.

Chapter Twenty-Five

For Lynette, the week at St. James Park consisted of social engagements and planning her own ball. With Rowena and Eleanor's help, she wrote invitations for seventy guests and arranged the music, decorations, and supper menu. Then on the night of the ball, she stood in her bedroom once more, only this time it was the one she shared with Aiden. He'd deemed it unnecessary that she have a separate room for dressing and bathing while they were at St. James. They would quit the residence in just a few days to travel to Eldridge Castle, the ultimate end of their estate tour. As enjoyable as it had been, she was relieved it would soon be over since she'd been feeling more fatigued and thought the travel was affecting her. She'd previously traveled only twice a year but had now changed counties three times in a few months. So Eldridge Castle called to her, if for nothing else than for the stability it offered.

"My grandmother is simply beside herself," Aiden said, making his presence known.

Lynette's eyes widened as she turned to her husband. "Whatever for?"

"There's nothing for her to do," Aiden replied with

a smile. "You've arranged it all, which means she has nothing to adjust."

She smirked. "That was the point, was it not?"

"Indeed, it just shows that in the few weeks we've been wed, you've become one of the foremost Society hostesses." Aiden couldn't enumerate his wife's virtues enough. She really had exceeded his expectations during their stay at St. James Park. He remembered thinking she would need his help to manage his grandmother, but it seemed that the Dowager had finally met *her* match. Lynette consistently remained two steps ahead of Rowena and therefore anticipated her every move. At some points during the week, it had even looked like Lynette was directing Rowena on what to do. A smile pulled at the corners of his mouth every time he thought of his grandmother, the general, being outflanked by his wife.

Yes, Aiden had worried in vain about the need to protect Lynette and should have directed his concern to his father. It turned out that he had indeed worsened since leaving London. The eleventh Duke of Northumberland could barely leave his room anymore, thus seemingly reaching the end of his affliction. His complexion had become even paler, his physique slimmer, and his breathing more labored. Two footmen carried Seymour down the stairs every morning for a bit of fresh air and then carried him back to his room a few hours later. Aiden had heard his mother crying in her room more than a couple of times, leading him to believe that the end was near.

The only silver lining in the entire ordeal was Lynette. She was Aiden's ray of sunshine, illuminating his darkest time.

Lynette smiled at Aiden, her brown eyes glistening.

She knew he was complimenting her to make her feel good, and she did, albeit slightly. Her emotions had been all over the place, as if she could either laugh or cry at the drop of a hat. She attributed it to her fatigue from traveling since, as Aiden had said, she'd succeeded by leaps and bounds in the realm of duty, and the lust they shared was as strong as ever. But every time she looked at Aiden, a lump formed in her throat. His pained expressions, usually visible after visiting with his father, didn't help. They made her want to cry and wrap him in her love. Love could conquer death, could it not? If nothing else, it could at least conquer the despair death brought. But as much as she wanted to say those three little words, she couldn't bring herself to do it. It was her turn to fear the sting of rejection, and with her emotions as they were, she couldn't take the chance.

As the ball began, Aiden and Lynette received their guests. It was a heavily attended affair, with attendants from all over North Yorkshire. When the strands of the evening's first waltz were strung, he pulled her close despite her insistence that it was their duty to dance with their guests and not with each other. But he would hear nothing of it since surely a single dance between husband and wife wouldn't cause an uproar.

The action did indeed cause a frenzy, though. Whispers remarked at how the couple looked so lovingly at each other, how Lord Elliot held his wife almost too close, and how Lady Elliot was surely the luckiest woman in all of Britain. Lynette assumed that Aiden would once again remain oblivious to the gossip, just as he had leading up to their wedding, and therefore decided she, too, would do her best to feign disinterest and simply enjoy the dance. She presumed wrong, though. This time Aiden was fully aware of what was being said as he twirled her around the ballroom.

At first he was aghast. Were his feelings so easily discernible for the entire assembly? Did Lynette hear the whispers too? He looked at his wife and noted her composure. Surely if she'd heard the gossip, she'd react differently, so he thought his emotions were at least hidden from her. What would happen if or when she did hear it, though? Would she confront him and demand to know the truth? Or would she simply pull back from him, given that she couldn't return his love?

He felt as though he was trying to swim on dry land; he didn't know where he stood in his wife's affections. He'd spent the better part of two weeks courting her in an attempt to secure her love but hadn't seen evidence that it was working. Overall, everything felt the same. Lynette still smiled at him, held him affectionately, and was passionate with him every morning and night, so what more could he possibly want? The answer was simple: Aiden wanted love. But now he was in a race to get it, to ensure it, before she got wind of the gossip surrounding them. Because even if he didn't, the whispers would definitely show his hand.

After their waltz, Lynette renewed her urging that they needed to dance with their guests, and Aiden obliged her. One by one he led eager young ladies onto the dance floor and listened to them prattle on about nothing in particular. His eyes met Lynette's across the ballroom as she danced with Lord Zetland. She never prattled, simpered, or did any other silly things ladies were known for. He shook his head and looked upward, mentally adding it to the list of things he was thankful for.

Needing a reprieve from the dance floor, he stood out

a cotillion with a glass of wine in his hand. He watched Lynette as she danced with Mr. Upton, her smile lighting up the entire room. Even though the longer he stared the more likely his feelings for her would be found out, he couldn't take his eyes off her.

"You entered the lion's den and came out alive," Marcus Dunn, Lord Zetland, said as he came upon Aiden. He was followed closely by Lord Wesley Ecclestone.

Aiden tore his eyes away from his wife. "Come now, London's not that bad." He smirked. "Compared to the Continent, that is." He'd grown up with Marcus and Wesley, having played together when he and Ferdy visited their grandmother in North Yorkshire. Despite being similar in age to Aiden, they were both first sons who had yet to feel the call of duty to wed and sire an heir.

"It wasn't London I was referring to, but in any event, I went down last Season and told myself never again." Marcus shook his head. "If I hadn't had my mother nagging me, I wouldn't have gone down at all."

"My mother may nag all she wants, but she will never get me to succumb to a Season. The closest I'll get to London is Ascot or Newmarket," Wesley vowed. "Elliot is simply the exception to the rule."

"And what exception would that be?" Aiden asked, his eyebrows raised.

"That one can be both happy and married," Wesley replied. "It is quite unusual to find happiness in the state of matrimony."

"That's because of who he found as his wife," Marcus said. "I just danced with her and she's lovely. I wouldn't be so averse to the Season if there were more like her in London."

Aiden stood still, his heart hammering in his ears. He couldn't deny his friend's claim since he'd just been enumerating Lynette's virtues. He remembered feeling like his friends; that marriage was a necessary evil. And maybe it would have been, he conceded, if he hadn't found Lynette. He couldn't imagine feeling as he did with any other woman as his wife. Maybe that was why he'd been so adamant about marrying her; he had somehow foreseen that she would be his eternal happiness.

He arched a brow at his friends. "I have a mind to wager that you gentlemen will find your own exceptions to the rule."

"How much are you willing to bet, Elliot?" Wesley asked, thinking he had nothing to lose.

"Five shillings," Aiden replied, offering a friendly wager. "I bet you both that I'll be dancing at your weddings."

"Five apiece?" Marcus scratched his chin. "And what's the time frame on this wager?"

Aiden smirked. "There is none since you both have said that nothing and no one will tempt you into matrimony."

"But when can we collect on the debt?" Wesley asked. "On our deathbeds?"

The idea gained a chuckle out of all three gentlemen, but then after a moment of thinking, Aiden reached into his coin purse and extracted ten shillings. "You'll return it to me at your weddings."

"Bet accepted," Marcus and Wesley agreed.

"There are far too many ladies without partners for the likes of you gentlemen to be wagering in a corner." Lynette appeared, her eyes narrowed and lips pursed. "If your grandmother would have seen, she'd have swooned."

My Duty To You

"There, there, it's simply a wager among friends." Aiden entwined her arm with his and patted her hand.

Lord Zetland and Lord Ecclestone had enough sense to excuse themselves and find partners for the next waltz, leaving Aiden to pull his wife into the dance.

Lynette looked at him pointedly. "We have already danced together once this evening."

"We are no longer courting, so there is nothing for anybody to be scandalized by if we dance more than once," Aiden said as he pulled his wife closer to relish her smell and softness. This time, he knew he was inviting the whispers that followed them but was past the point of caring.

Lynette's lips remained pursed, but the muscles in her back relaxed under his hand. "It's up to us to ensure our guests enjoy themselves."

"'Tis your ball; you should be able to enjoy it as well." Aiden refused to let her go. Her wide eyes blinked up at him, and he thought he saw tears pooling in the corners. "Are you all right?"

"Just fine." She forced a smile. "A bit tired is all."

He began to pull away. "We don't have to dance—"

"No, no, I want to dance with you." She pulled him back and held him even tighter.

They resumed dancing, but Aiden couldn't take his eyes off his wife for a different reason now. What could have upset her? Had his grandmother been more of a trial than he'd known? Whatever it was, he wanted to fix it. He would take on anyone and anything that upset his wife.

Lynette seemed better by the end of their waltz, but a fire still burned in his veins. He considered complimenting her on the ball again, anything to put a smile on her face, but it no longer felt like enough. Then his eyes widened, and his heart began to race when he realized what *would* be enough: he could give her the love match she'd always longed for. Ideas for how he would do it flitted through his mind. When they reached Eldridge Castle, he could take her on a picnic on the bank of the River Eld, line the path with candles and roses, and then lay her down on a blanket bathed in nothing but moonlight. After they made sweet, passionate love, he would profess his undying affection for her, and she would return the emotion in kind.

The fantasy aroused Aiden like no other, but it would only work if Lynette shared his affections. If she didn't, then neither of them would be happy in the end. He sighed. Would there ever come a time when he was confident enough not to fear rejection? He didn't know but decided that if it ever did, he would keep the vision of Lynette and him on the bank of the Eld in the back of his mind.

Chapter Twenty-Six

Two mornings after the ball, Aiden and Lynette quit St. James Park, saying farewell to the Dowager, Duchess, and Duke of Northumberland. It was an especially difficult goodbye for Aiden since there was no way of knowing if he'd ever see his father alive again. Seymour sensed it as well and hugged his son ever more tightly. Once the goodbyes were said, Aiden and Lynette returned to the Port of Middlesbrough, where they sailed north to Eldridge Castle. It only took them a few hours on the water this time, the journey between St. James and Eldridge being much shorter than the one between them and London. By midmorning, they were docking on the River Eld, which lay just north of Eldridge Castle and was part of Elliot land.

As Aiden helped her down from the ship, Lynette took in the castle. It was an impressive Norman structure: an imposing fortress that still consisted of the main building, an inner bailey, and a barbican.

"What do you think?" Aiden asked as they walked from the river to the gateway.

"It's certainly a magnificent building," Lynette replied, unable to tear her eyes away. It was three times the size of Dowsorrell Castle, but this was her house now, and she was going to have to run and take care of it with the help of her servants.

He wrapped an arm around her shoulders. "Just think of the events you can hold here."

"Hmm... let's not get ahead of ourselves. It'll likely be a project for me to simply learn my way to the breakfast room every morning."

He laughed, and they walked through the barbican and to the front door, where the butler stood waiting with a spaniel at his side. Aiden greeted his dog and introduced her as Winnie before presenting the butler as Jameson and then moving on to introduce the rest of the staff. After introductions were made, Aiden inquired as to where his sister-in-law, Matilda, was. Jameson directed them to the duchess's private room, which was situated to the left of the main entrance hall.

Lynette's hands trembled as Aiden led her down the hall, his dog beside him. It felt as though she was encroaching on Matilda's territory by meeting her in the duchess's private room. She loathed the thought of being brought in as Matilda's replacement but acknowledged how it underscored the interchangeability of women in the aristocracy. She looked at Aiden out of the corner of her eye. There was once a time when she'd felt interchangeable with other young ladies in Society. She'd insisted she didn't want to fill a role any woman could, yet she had by marrying Aiden. But was it truly a role any woman could fill? Would any woman love him as she did? She'd like to think it was impossible but was ultimately unsure.

She swallowed the lump in her throat and plastered a smile on her face as Aiden led her through the doors.

Matilda, dressed in black widow's weeds, sat in the middle of it, staring intently at her embroidery.

"Matilda," Aiden said and was rewarded with her attention. She smiled widely when she saw him and cast her embroidery to the side.

"I missed a stitch somewhere." She waved her hand in explanation. Then, embroidery forgotten, she stood, and Aiden stepped toward her to pull her into a hug. The pair greeted each other warmly, and Lynette could tell that they were as close as siblings.

"Matilda, this is my wife, Lynette." Aiden introduced the two women.

"So you did get married then." Matilda looked over the pair. "Wasn't such a hardship after all." Turning from Aiden without warning, she rubbed cheeks with Lynette before pulling back to smile at her.

Given the opportunity, Lynette regarded Matilda. She'd always thought of her as beautiful, with shiny black hair, sky-blue eyes, and porcelain skin. Lynette thought that not even her widow's weeds could diminish her allure and suddenly felt plain in comparison.

"It seems marriage agrees with me more than I thought it would," Aiden said and met Lynette's eyes. As usual, he became lost in their inviting depths until Matilda's voice broke the spell.

"His granny essentially had to drag him away to London." She smirked at Lynette, and the ladies laughed at the thought of Aiden being dragged to London by his grandmother. "I'm glad you've returned; it has been quite lonely all by myself. I would have thought your parents would return after your wedding."

"They decided to reside at St. James." A knot formed in Aiden's stomach. He'd forgotten all about poor Matilda in mourning at Eldridge Castle. He knew it would've been impossible for her to attend his wedding while in mourning, but it didn't make him wish any less that she had been there. She was a sister to him, and it felt wrong that she hadn't been included in his nuptials.

Matilda's eyes shifted before finding his. "Your father's health is still poor then, is it?"

Aiden stared at her, unblinking, as he tried to make sense of the words she'd just said. "Aye." He swallowed, and his cravat suddenly felt too tight. Matilda had obviously known of his father's illness before he had. Why else would she inquire? That meant his parents had found it more fit to inform their daughter-in-law than their second son.

Through the haze, Aiden tried to find reason. It was likely Matilda was told after Ferdy's death. She'd also lived with his parents for a lot longer than he recently had. Both were good reasons as to why she'd found out before him. And even without the reasons, he concluded, the blame couldn't lie at her feet. It hadn't been her responsibility to tell him; that rested solely with his parents and maybe even his grandmother.

"Nevertheless, I'm happy you're both here," Matilda said in an attempt to change the subject, aware of the shift in Aiden's demeanor. "And I'm truly happy to get to know you better as I've never had a sister." She reached for Lynette's hand.

"The feeling is mutual, only I have a sister, and I can only hope you're more agreeable than her," Lynette said, and the ladies laughed together.

"Lynette needs a tour of the castle if you'd like to take her around and get properly acquainted," Aiden said, needing some time to himself. "I assume we can expect a quiet evening, just us before the wolves get wind of my residence and decide to descend."

"Oh bother, they have only just stopped visiting to express their condolences regarding Ferdy's death." Matilda rolled her eyes. "My only saving grace is I haven't been expected to return the visits while in full mourning."

"Right, I shall leave you both to it and see you at dinner." Aiden gave Lynette a chaste kiss before he and Winnie left the two women alone together.

"Well then, we shall start here." Matilda extended her hands to the room. "This is the private room of the duchess and therefore now belongs to you."

"Please, no." Lynette shook her head. "I am not even the duchess yet."

"Neither was I," Matilda reminded her. "Eleanor and I shared it when she was in residence here because she insisted, but I've only been using it myself since the family went to London."

"Then I suggest we share it just the same." Lynette met her eye. She didn't want to put the woman out of a room that felt more rightfully hers. She'd been married to Ferdy for longer than Lynette had been married to Aiden, and neither of them was truly the Duchess of Northumberland.

"If you insist, but I am truly not that attached to it." Matilda shrugged and looked away. "Come, let me show you the rest of the castle." She cleared her throat and linked arms with Lynette. They followed the hall around the castle, and Matilda pointed out the different rooms and their various purposes. There were two state bedrooms on the main floor, a chapel, a gaming room, a library, a drawing room, an anteroom, and the dining hall. In the center of all the rooms on the main floor was the grand staircase, which led to the first and second floors that contained Aiden's office, bedrooms, a nursery, and a schoolroom. Lynette had the pleasure of meeting Matilda's daughter before they continued the tour of the castle grounds, which consisted of the inner bailey, the stables, and the gardens.

Lynette slowly shook her head as they walked through the gardens. "I shall surely get lost."

"There are so many servants that you're sure to run into someone all the time." Matilda patted her arm. "They'll always be able to point you in the right direction."

"How did you get on when you first came here?" Lynette asked, unaware of how Matilda and Ferdy became matched.

"My father is Earl Ravensworth. He lives just down the road to the west, so I grew up around this castle," Matilda replied, her gaze straying to one of the turrets.

"This is your home then," Lynette said, thinking back to Aiden's idea of offering Matilda Elberry Park. However, after meeting and talking to her, Lynette was unsure if it was still a good idea even if Aiden had the best intentions when suggesting it.

"It always was," Matilda said, an errant tear spilling from one eye. "Now, it's more a reminder of the past and of a future that never will be."

"I know it may not be my place to say . . . and I only bring it up because of what you just told me . . ."

Matilda leaned toward her. "Yes?"

"Would you consider leaving Eldridge?" Lynette asked quickly before she lost her nerve. "Not that you have to—or that Aiden wants you to—it's just if this place holds such painful memories . . ."

"But where would I go?" Matilda asked, her bottom lip quivering.

"To Elberry Park, of course," Lynette replied, her head falling to the side. "Aiden wouldn't suggest St. James due to his family being there, but Elberry is only used once or twice a year," she explained further. "It's completely up to you; you are more than welcome to stay here at Eldridge with us or run Elberry as your own."

Unable to hold them back any longer, Matilda burst into tears. Lynette wrapped an arm around Matilda and rubbed her back as a lump formed in her own throat. She chewed on her lip while Matilda cried and only spoke again when she thought it was safe to do so. "I am sorry if I upset you, Matilda."

"No, no, it's not you." Matilda forced a smile. "Well, maybe a little," she conceded after a while. "Aiden had told me I'd always have a place within the Elliot family, but when you asked if I'd be willing to leave—"

"I broached the subject horribly," Lynette said, her head downcast. "Please forgive me because that was not my intention."

"I know." Matilda bent to meet her eye. "I can't say it hasn't been hard living here without Ferdy, especially by myself. I see Ferdy everywhere—in the stables, in the library, even in my room at night."

Lynette reached out to Matilda, clasping her hands in hers. "You love Ferdy." She knew it was true based on the look in the woman's eyes. There was so much hurt there now that her loved one was gone.

"With all my heart." Matilda nodded. "For all my life."

Lynette listened closely as Matilda went on to tell her all about her love affair with Ferdy. For many years Matilda had thought that he'd only seen her as a little sister, but they continued to correspond even while he was at Eton. When Ferdy returned home after graduation, Matilda was preparing for her first London Season where Ferdy seemed to play the role of a protective older brother.

"I ended up telling him to either offer for me or leave me alone," Matilda said with a far-away look in her eye.

"So he offered for you?" Lynette asked with bated breath.

"No, he left London and returned here." Matilda shook her head. "It wasn't until I returned to Northumberland after the Season that he finally plucked up the courage to ask me." Despite the innocuous conclusion to her story, she blushed heavily, remembering exactly what her proposal entailed.

Lynette sighed deeply. "It sounds like something out of a novel."

Matilda continued to blush. "I will admit, it was all very romantic."

"It's everything I've ever wanted . . . if only Aiden loved me as Ferdy—"

"Oh, but he surely does love you. One only needs to see how he looks at you."

"That's what everyone says." Lynette rolled her eyes. "I believe that it's only lust being confused with love."

"There is a fine line between lust and love," Matilda said thoughtfully. "But truly, from the little I've seen of you two so far, he loves you. He's just too much of a man to admit it."

Could it be possible? Were all the gossips of London, Mrs. Beasley, and Matilda, right? Did Aiden love her? Out of all the people who were of the same opinion, Matilda's judgment was the one Lynette put the most stock in. She knew Aiden better than anyone else since they had grown up together. Surely that meant she had an understanding of his heart and mind. If that was the case, Lynette could take Matilda's assessment as truth. Aiden did love her and was simply unable to tell her for whatever reason.

But what reason could that be? Surely it was not Aiden's fear of rejection or the pressure he felt to prove himself—because what was left for him to prove? From what she could gauge, he'd done well in taking over as head of the family. He was managing his family's finances and investments, working with his land stewards to manage his estates, and had secured a bride. Sure, there was some underlying doubt about his abilities in the social sphere, but she was helping him there. In her estimation, the only thing left for him to prove was his ability to sire an heir.

Lynette studied Matilda, noting her undeniable beauty once more. If she and Ferdy had loved each other as much as she had described, they would have spent every night together. So then why did they only have one child after more than a decade of marriage? Lynette knew these things were inexplicable, but the blame typically fell on the woman. But what if it had been a problem with Ferdy? What if Aiden was worried that they'd have the same issues? Then his duty to his family would never be realized. Could Aiden's uncertainty about his virility be keeping him from professing his love to her?

The thought was plausible to Lynette, but she also conceded that she might be overthinking the matter. She wanted Aiden to love her so dearly that she was willing to think up any explanation for why he simply wouldn't tell her if he did. She could either believe that he didn't love her or that he did and hadn't told her so. She knew which scenario her heart would have her believe, but she also couldn't keep her mind from wanting to think logically, like Elinor in *Sense and Sensibility*.

What was there for her to do? She wasn't any more confident than Aiden when it came to the idea of confessing her love. Surely she was the one who had more to lose. She would be devastated if she showed him her heart, and it turned out that Matilda and everyone else had been wrong about his feelings for her. No, Lynette decided, she couldn't be the one to confess her feelings first. She would just wait until she was with child and see if he confessed his love once all of his duties to his family were completed.

Chapter Twenty-Seven

Just as Aiden had expected, visitors came in swarms as soon as word got around that he was in residence at Eldridge Castle with his new bride. Lynette's first few days at Eldridge consisted of her receiving the influx of callers and later returning their visits. She made herself known to the vicar so that she could lend him a listening ear or a helping hand. She visited the local school, which the estate provided for, to meet the teacher and the children, worked with the head maid to keep the estate stocked, and consulted the chef on the daily menus.

But despite the never-ending tasks, Lynette still found time for some leisure. She began horse riding in the mornings but was careful not to delve too deep into Eldridge's forests until she became more familiar with the terrain. Her love of reading was rekindled, and she cursed the heartache that Elinor and Marianne experienced at the hands of Edward Ferrars and Mr. Willoughby. She had to take a break from *Sense and Sensibility* after that, unable to cope with the fact that even in books a person could experience heartbreak. If even characters in a novel couldn't experience love and happiness, then what hope did she have?

As June faded into July, Matilda saw it fit to come out of full mourning. She started to accompany Lynette on her afternoon calls, thus reentering Society. Lynette decided to throw a summer fete in August for villagers, gentry, and peers alike. Matilda helped her organize it, and the fair was held in the castle bailey. Merchants came from all over Northumberland to sell their wares, and games were arranged for the children. Ultimately, the festival was a rousing success, and everyone believed it should become an annual event.

On the night of the fete, after all the festivalgoers had left and the bailey was empty once again, Aiden sat in his office nursing a glass of brandy. A pile of letters from his grandmother sat before him, each written with an increasing tone of urgency. The chief theme throughout all the letters was whether he had gotten his wife with child yet. Little was mentioned about his father who, for whatever it was worth, still lived. In any event, he regarded his father's continued existence as a positive since his passing would likely only increase Rowena's worry.

He didn't know how to respond to his grandmother's letters, though. He would have expected Lynette to tell him if she was with child, but since she hadn't yet, he assumed she wasn't. How did women even know if they were expecting? Surely they had a way of knowing. As for Aiden, short of being explicitly informed, he wouldn't know what symptoms to look for. Nevertheless, he trusted her to tell him when the time came, and in the absence of knowledge, he put off responding to his grandmother's letters. Thus his need for a drink. He knew his grandmother didn't like to be ignored and wondered how much longer he could do it before she demanded answers.

"I thought you had gone to bed." Matilda appeared at the office door.

"Lynette's having a bath," Aiden replied by way of explanation. Things had been odd between them since he discovered that she'd known about Seymour's illness before he had. He'd been trying to convince himself that it wasn't her fault, but that didn't ease his resentment.

"So you're having a drink." Matilda nodded at his glass. "Penny for your thoughts?" She'd been on her way to bed when she noticed the candles were still lit in his office. Wanting to clear the air between them, she'd decided to peek her head in. Now she stepped fully into the office and awaited his response.

Aiden took a long swig of his brandy. Could he confide in her regarding Rowena's letters? Maybe she would have insight as to how he could put off his grandmother. He contemplated the idea but ultimately decided that it wasn't his grandmother's letters or Lynette's fertility that weighed heaviest on his mind. "When did you find out about my father's illness?"

"I wondered when you would bring that up." Matilda took a seat next to him. "I guess the real question is, when did your parents finally find it fit to inform you?"

"While in London," Aiden replied. "My father struggled to get out of bed one morning, and they couldn't hide it any longer."

"I feared that's what had happened." She sighed. "I found out shortly before you all went to London, but it isn't how you think." She paused and looked at her hands, which were folded in her lap. "You know how distraught I was after Ferdy's death. I was like you and couldn't make sense as to why he was even in his carriage that night. But

I was offered no explanation by anyone in the family, not your parents and certainly not your grandmother. Rumors started flying, though, since some sailors had seen Ferdy drinking late into the evening at a pub in the village. I decided if no one would give me the answers I sought, I'd find them out myself. So I went to the pub Ferdy had been seen at and told the barkeep to inform me if the sailors that had been there the night of his death ever returned."

Aiden's eyes widened. "And did they?"

"They did." She nodded. "I went to the pub to meet them and ask about Ferdy's disposition that night. They described him as troubled and after sharing a few drinks, he confided in them that he was to inherit the dukedom sooner than expected. He continued by saying that even though he was the heir, his family thought to keep the knowledge of his imminent inheritance from him for nigh on two years."

Aiden sat back, stunned by the retelling. Not the contents of the story per se, but how she had to find out such a thing from sailors she'd barely known.

"I confronted your parents with the information the next day," she said. "It's an argument I'm not proud of and I think it's likely the reason they decided to retire to St. James rather than return here." Her eyes returned to her hands. "I should have told you, Aiden, I know, but I truly didn't think they would make the same mistake again . . . and I was just beside myself with the information. I needed time to process it myself, and by the time I had, you were already in London." She burst into tears at the end of her recitation, and he reached to pull her into his arms.

"No, Matilda, I am sorry for resenting your knowledge of it. I hadn't fully considered how it was you came to know," Aiden consoled her, his hand moving soothingly

My Duty To You

across her back.

They stayed that way until her tears began to evaporate. Then as she pulled away from his embrace, she noticed the letters strewn across the table. "What's this?" she asked, reaching for one.

Given their conversation Aiden didn't even try to stop Matilda from viewing the letters, feeling that there should be no more secrets between them. Matilda was mostly silent as she perused the missives and waited until the end to speak. "Rowena sent similar letters to Ferdy, though I must admit they were never this desperate."

He ran his fingers through his hair. "I haven't issued a reply since I simply don't know what to say."

"Oh, Aiden!" Matilda's hands flew to her mouth. "That's not the best way to handle this. Your grandmother will come here and cause a scene in her attempt to gain a response."

"Well then, what would you suggest?" he asked, open to ideas. "How did Ferdy deal with her overbearing ways?"

"Now that you ask, I don't honestly know," Matilda replied. "She did come here, though, before I had Rosie, demanding to know why I wasn't with child. Ferdy roared right back at her and sent her away, saying she had no business knowing what went on in our bed."

"As he should have!" A fire erupted within him. If his grandmother thought she could come to Eldridge and strong-arm Lynette, she had another thing coming.

"Are you ever going to tell her?"

Aiden's eyes darted around the room, refusing to meet Matilda's knowing gaze. "Tell her . . . ?"

She pursed her lips. "Are you ever going to tell Lynette that you love her?"

"I've considered it," he replied, hesitantly meeting her eye. "But what if she doesn't return my affection?"

"Aiden!" She swatted him lightly. "Of course she does!"

"She's rejected me once before, Matilda. I was born a second son, and if Ferdy hadn't died, I'd still be on the Continent proving myself and Lynette could have married for love like she always wanted."

She shook her head. "She married you because she loves you."

"No, she only married me because I forced her hand," he said. "And now, what if I'm impotent and can't give her children?" He motioned to the stack of letters again. "Lynette wants nothing more than to fulfill her duty and bear me an heir. I can barely look at myself in the mirror, let alone tell her how I feel."

"Aiden." She reached for him, forcing him to look at her. "The reason your self-esteem is low escapes me, but I can assure you that you are just as worthy of love as a first son. So despite whatever troubles you have or have had in the past, I am certain that Lynette loves you as much as you love her. You only need to tell her to find out."

"And how did Ferdy profess his love for you?" he asked, yet again looking for suggestions.

She blinked, her eyes red from unshed tears. "He never did."

The thought was a blow to the heart; Aiden's older, smarter, stronger brother hadn't had the sense to tell the woman he loved how he felt.

"I knew how he felt, though," she said with a sad smile. "I'm sure he loved me as much as I loved him, but I will forever regret not saying the words and hearing them said."

All of Aiden's reasons seemed silly after Matilda's proclamation. How horrid it would be if anything were to happen to either him or Lynette before he plucked up the courage to tell her how he felt. He would wait no longer, not a moment more. He stood, his heart hammering in his chest. "I must tell her."

Matilda rose as well and leveled her gaze on him. "Yes, you must."

He looked out of the window, recalling his vision of Lynette bathed in moonlight on the bank of the Eld. Unfortunately, the moon wasn't quite full, and it was a rather cloudy night. He'd also have to rouse every servant from their beds to help him line the path to the river with candles and roses. But he decided that none of it truly mattered; the scene was inconsequential, and she only needed to hear the words spoken. But flowers . . . Aiden thought quickly as he thanked Matilda for her advice and then ran from his office. He could at least pick flowers for her, which he went to the garden to do.

Chapter Twenty-Eight

Lynette made her way downstairs after taking breakfast in her room. She had felt shattered after managing the fete the day prior and had fallen asleep directly after her bath, unable to wait for Aiden to join her in bed. Upon waking, she happily noted the bouquet of freshly picked flowers he must have left for her, but even that couldn't stir her from bed. Still tired, she opted to take breakfast alone instead of going downstairs to eat with him and Matilda. But even as she began her duties for the day, she noted that she still felt off and hoped it didn't mean she was coming down with some sort of illness. Deciding that she needed sunshine, she went to find Matilda in the garden after talking with the head maid about the shopping needed for the week.

"You're looking awfully gray this morning," Matilda said upon seeing Lynette.

She cradled her stomach and sat. "I'm still not feeling like myself."

"Fair warning then—Aiden received word during breakfast that his grandmother is coming to Eldridge and should be arriving soon."

"I wonder what has made her decide to visit." Lynette

looked upward in thought. "You said she usually stays at St. James."

Matilda swallowed her lips. "She does; she only tended to come up when there was some pressing issue that Ferdy needed to attend to."

If Lynette had been feeling more astute, she would have registered Matilda's demeanor as it pertained to the Dowager's visit, but without all her mental faculties, it went unnoticed.

Lynette's forehead creased. "I can't imagine any pressing issues for Aiden, and I've been fulfilling all of our Society duties, so she hasn't anything to complain about there."

Matilda nodded in agreement despite knowing exactly why Rowena was calling. Aiden had asked her not to inform Lynette of the reason for his grandmother's visit and to simply keep Lynette occupied while he dealt with her.

Thus, as was their morning routine, the two women sat in a companionable silence until Lynette jolted and put a hand to her mouth. She attempted to make a mad dash away from Matilda, not wishing the other woman to see her in such a state, but only made it a few feet before she had to bend over and retch up her breakfast.

Matilda approached Lynette to offer her comfort. "Your stomach pains you?"

She nodded. "I haven't felt like myself in several days, but last night and this morning have been the worst. I thought it was simply fatigue following the festival, but maybe I should have Jameson fetch the doctor."

"Where are you in your cycle?" Matilda asked, seeing the signs. She had missed them at first herself when she fell pregnant with Rose.

Lynette was taken aback by the question, her brow furrowed as she tried to think of an answer. "I honestly don't know. I forgot about my menses."

"Has it been more than a month since your last bleed?"

"It has to be," Lynette whispered as realization dawned on her.

Without missing a beat, Matilda squealed in delight. "You must be with child! That's why you're feeling so terrible. I could barely get out of bed the first month I was pregnant with Rosie. This is so exciting! You must tell Aiden because he'll be thrilled!"

Lynette waved off the comment. "He'll only be thrilled if I'm carrying his heir."

"I thought the same with Ferdy, but he was over the moon when I told him. Thought me even lovelier when I was with child." Matilda smiled, a light blush covering her nose.

Lynette wanted to reason that Ferdy had likely thought as much because he'd loved Matilda, but she decided against it, not wanting to sour the conversation.

"Please tell him soon, I'm terrible at keeping secrets," Matilda said with wide eyes.

Lynette threw her shoulders back and lifted her chin. "I shall tell him now."

Matilda didn't waylay her, thinking it would be best if Lynette told Aiden immediately. She didn't know that Rowena was already at the castle and thought that if the news of Lynette's condition reached Aiden before his grandmother did, then all the better.

Lynette took a deep breath with every step she took. While it was true Aiden needed to be informed, she was filled with mixed emotions. Would he be happy that she was with child? She reasoned that he'd likely only be disappointed if the child turned out to be a girl. But what would he think of her? Would he still lust over her body when she was heavy with his child? Or would he decide it was time to take a mistress now that they no longer needed to share a marriage bed? She knew it was common once the wife was carrying, but she didn't know where Aiden stood on the matter.

Or would he finally profess his love for her? If she was with child, then he had more or less fulfilled his duty to his family. There should be nothing left to prevent him from telling her of his feelings if he possessed them, no other question in his mind as to his worthiness of her returned feelings. As if her stomach didn't ache enough, now her heart throbbed as well. The time had come for Lynette to finally find out where she stood in regard to her husband. Was there only lust and duty between them, or was there love?

Aiden was shuffling papers on his desk when there was a knock on his study door. He was trying to keep himself busy while he awaited his grandmother or found time to talk with Lynette. She'd been asleep when he'd made it to their room, a bouquet of roses in his hand. She'd looked so delightful with a book open upon her chest, obviously having fallen asleep amidst reading it. It wasn't typical for her to fall asleep while reading or before he had a chance to join her, but he acknowledged that she'd worked so hard on the fete that she must have been tired. Suppressing the desire to kiss her awake, he simply slid into bed and let his wife sleep.

She'd still been in a dead sleep when he woke up in the morning, and instead of rousing her from it, he washed and dressed before joining Matilda for breakfast.

Upon arrival at the breakfast room, Jameson informed him that *The Aether* had left to retrieve his grandmother, who had summoned it so that she could visit. Damning the inconvenience of it, Aiden resigned himself to a confrontation with his granny. Now, the knock on his office door signified the imminence of either the opportunity to profess his love to his wife or the precursor to his grandmother's arrival. When he looked up and saw his granny's cane leading her in, he knew which event fate had bestowed upon him.

Rowena stood in the center of the room, her eyes narrowing before breaking the silence. "You have been ignoring my missives."

Aiden didn't even look up from his correspondence, thinking it would be better if he didn't engage with her. "I have not. There is simply nothing to report."

She looked at him over her nose. "Have you got your wife with child yet?"

"I have not been made aware." He shuffled some papers and continued to feign disinterest, but he already felt lost in their battle of wills. He understood her stance on the begetting of an heir and thus securing the dukedom for another generation; what he couldn't understand was her coldness in regard to it.

Rowena thumped her cane to garner his attention. "It's been nearly three months since you were wed."

Aiden looked up, his jaw clenched. "That I am aware of."

"What's taking so long then? I know she shares your bed every night—"

Unbeknownst to Aiden and the Dowager, Lynette was standing just outside the door. She'd been on her way to inform Aiden that she was with child, but their conversation gave her pause.

"It is no business of yours when or how often my wife and I share a bed," Aiden said, his speech clipped.

"I am simply concerned as to why she is not increasing if you are sharing a bed every night." Rowena sighed. "I truly hope she is not barren as she is of an age. I warned you about spinsters; maybe you would have been better off with her sister."

"That is enough!" He stood with clenched fists. "That is my wife you are speaking of, and you will only speak of her with the respect that she is due. I will not stand for it just as Ferdy hadn't."

"Aiden, it will be a great hardship on this family if she is barren." She didn't falter but was cut down once again.

"There will be no hardship on me. Hang the family and the title." He punctuated his speech by clearing his desk of all the papers that littered it.

"You cannot mean that!" Rowena shook a finger at him. "It is your duty to beget an heir."

"Be that as it may, we shall survive without one," Aiden said, his jaw set once more.

"The Elliot name will not." She thumped her cane. "I understand you may have come to care for the girl, however—"

"There is no *however* to that statement, Granny. I do care for her, and I will not allow you to speak poorly of her whether she begets an heir or not."

"But the dukedom—"

"There are more important things than the dukedom," Aiden said, finally saying the words out loud. He'd been in a similar situation when Lynette sought to break off their engagement. At the time he'd refused, partly because he inexplicably wanted her as his wife but mainly because of his duty to his family. He'd put duty before her on that day, but on this one, he wouldn't. His want for her was no longer inexplicable because it could only be defined by love. Thus by not submitting to his grandmother's whims, he'd finally corrected his greatest regret.

"Will that be all, Granny?" he asked, moving out from behind his desk. Rowena looked like she wanted to continue arguing, but he pushed past her. He had to see Lynette and tell her how he felt. She was more than simply duty and lust to him, and it was far past time that he told her exactly that. Gone were his fears of rejection, along with his fears of not being good enough. Consequently, by challenging his grandmother's wishes, Aiden had become the man he wanted to be and the man Lynette deserved. And if, for whatever reason, she didn't see it yet, he would spend every day proving to her that he was.

Aiden left his grandmother in his study and set out to find his wife. First he tried the duchess's private room, where she typically met with the head maid, but she was not there. After that, he went to the library, thinking that she might have gone to select a new novel, but she was not there either. Next he went out to the garden since he knew she liked to read out there when the weather was nice, but he only found Matilda. He asked after Lynette, and Matilda told him that his wife had gone in to find him and that was the last she'd seen of her. With a sinking feeling forming in the pit of his stomach, he continued his search.

He sought out Milly and asked if she knew where her mistress was but was told that she hadn't seen her since helping her dress earlier in the day. Then he checked Lynette's room, thinking it was the last logical place for her to be, but he still came up empty. Finally, an idea popped into his head, and he went out to the stables, where the stable master confirmed that she'd taken out a horse less than thirty minutes earlier. Despite feeling somewhat defeated, Aiden still felt satisfied that his wife had simply gone on one of her daily rides.

With nothing else to do until his wife came home, he returned to his study and collected the papers he'd strewn all over the floor. Once all the paperwork had been collected and organized, he tried to continue his correspondence but was hyperaware of the ticking clock. He promised himself he'd wait an hour, a sufficient amount of time, before he went looking for her again. Time moved at a glacial pace, and he sprung from his chair when the hour was up to return to the stables only to find that she still wasn't there.

Reasoning that there were any number of places Lynette could have gone, Aiden ordered his own horse saddled and decided to meet her rather than wait for her to return. He knew that she typically conducted her visits during the afternoon but neglected to realize that she wouldn't make them without Matilda. Nevertheless, he followed her assumed path, meeting with the vicar and his wife, who had not seen Lynette since the festival. He then rode to every house in the vicinity of Eldridge Castle but found that their neighbors hadn't seen hide nor hair of his wife either. Finally, he went to the village, thinking she could have ridden there and simply lost track of time, possibly in a bookshop or had been detained by a new acquaintance. Whatever the case, he'd waited long enough for her to return of her own accord and intended to bring her back himself.

Unfortunately for both of them, Lynette wasn't in the village buying a book or chatting with others. She was somewhere deep in the woods, lost. She'd run as soon as the Dowager Duchess mentioned her being barren and Aiden marrying her sister. She couldn't bear hearing Aiden's response, knowing it would hurt worse than his grandmother's concept of their situation. He'd chosen his family over her before, and she was convinced he would do it again. In their eyes, she'd been unable to fulfill her duty as a wife. It didn't matter that all the doubts about her abilities would vanish once she informed them she was with child. She still thought she had to face Aiden's true feelings for her.

All her worst fears had been confirmed. It had been so easy to be consumed in their desire for each other and not see it for what it was: a biological need to get her with child. That was why Aiden insisted they share a bed and why he treated her to passion every morning and every night. It had nothing to do with his forming soft feelings for her or that he enjoyed the pleasure she brought him just as much as she enjoyed the pleasure she received. The bedding was just another means to an end, a way for him to prove his worth to himself and his family.

Thus, needing to come to terms with her harsh reality, Lynette ran for privacy. She saddled a horse and gave it free rein. It wasn't until she slowed and got control over her emotions that she realized she didn't know where she was. She'd been warned about the density of the forest surrounding Eldridge and hadn't delved so deep without Aiden or Matilda by her side. She then turned the horse around in the vain hope that she would return to Eldridge Castle by going back in the same direction she'd come. However, when the sun started to lower in the distance, and she had still not returned, she realized that she must not have ridden in a straight line.

Lynette hopped off her horse and looked around. She'd had her heart broken and was now lost in the woods by herself with no idea as to how she would find her way back to the castle. As the sun started to lower beneath the treetops, Lynette fell to the ground; the only thing left for her to do was cry.

Chapter Twenty-Nine

"Lynette!" Aiden called into the night. Panic had him in its cold, steely hands. Once he'd discovered that she wasn't in the village and had never been in the village that day, he'd returned to Eldridge and mounted a search. He ordered every single manservant under his employ to search the woods surrounding the area. When informing Matilda and his granny of Lynette's sudden disappearance, he couldn't look the elderly woman in the eye. Aiden had a sick, sinking feeling that Rowena was somehow at fault for Lynette's disappearance or, at the very least, her ideas were. Unable to leave the search in another's hands, Aiden went out into the woods himself and called her name while he looked for any sign that she had passed through or was nearby. When the sun had set and Lynette had still not been found, Aiden couldn't bear to think of what had happened to her. And then to make matters worse, it started to rain.

It was a light drizzle, then a steady rain before the heavens opened, and Aiden continued his search in a torrential downpour. Then there was a flash of light before a crack of thunder, and he had to stop to calm his stallion. That was when he heard the whinny of another horse coming from his right. He turned in that direction and almost collided with it galloping away, obviously frightened by the storm. He didn't get a good look at the horse in question, but instinct told him it must have been Lynette's, so he headed in the direction from which it had come.

"Lynette!" he called again.

"Aiden!" She had been sitting on the ground, but when she heard Aiden call her name, she stood, eager to be rescued. She was cold, hungry, and tired. Her heart ached at seeing him upon his horse in front of her, but she knew that his presence was for the best. As time had wrought on, she became ashamed of running away and getting lost. She hated having to explain such things to her husband but knew that it would be necessary to get back to the castle and into the warmth.

"What were you thinking?" Aiden shouted at her and then instantly regretted it. He hopped down from his horse and pulled her into his arms. Despite being soaked through, she looked no worse for the wear, nothing a hot bath and dry clothes wouldn't be able to fix.

"I thought to go for a ride but got lost," Lynette said but couldn't bring herself to meet his eyes. "I'm sorry."

"Never mind, let's just get you home," Aiden lifted her up onto his horse and then mounted behind her. He wrapped her in his hacking jacket to keep her from getting any wetter or colder and then hurried his horse as fast as he was willing to push the beast in the storm. Twenty minutes later he halted the stallion in front of the main doors of Eldridge Castle and handed the reins off to a footman to take back to the stables. He carried her into the house and ordered a bath to be prepared and for Milly to attend to her. Then leaving his wife in the care of her maid, Aiden went and changed out of his own wet clothes.

Once dry and dressed, he paced in the hall while waiting for word on his wife's condition. A mantra repeated in his head, a constant reminder that as long as she was properly warmed, she wouldn't catch a chest infection, and all would be fine. He'd thought that all his anxiety would cease once he found her, but he was still on edge. What he needed was to be with her, to see her, touch her, anything to remind himself that she was well. Matilda's words haunted him. What if Lynette died without ever hearing how much he loved her? What if he never had the chance to hear the words returned?

Finally, Milly exited her mistress's room, and he rushed to the door. "She's having a bath, milord," Milly tried to warn him away, but Aiden would have none of it. Instead, he burst into the room and set his eyes on his wife, soaking in a steaming bathtub.

Lynette looked up when her husband entered her room. It wasn't as if he hadn't seen her taking a bath before, and she thought that it would be too much to ask for some privacy after the day she'd had. However, she also knew that he would have questions, especially since she'd been unable to stop crying since she entered her room.

"I love you," Aiden blurted, unable to keep the words within him any longer.

"Come again?" Lynette had been ready for questions and reproof. She'd thought she'd heard Aiden right, but he couldn't have possibly said what she thought he had.

"I love you." He rushed to her side. He gathered her face into his hands and placed a kiss on her lips but broke it as soon as he felt the hot tears on her cheeks. Pulling back, he saw his beautiful wife crying; her eyes were red and puffy and her face was forlorn. "What is it, my love?" He stroked her cheek, brushing the tears away. An intrusive thought told him that she was upset because she didn't know how to tell him that she didn't return his affection, but he pushed it aside. Something else had to have caused the tears, namely the ordeal she had just been through. "You are safe now. It must have been a terrible fright."

Lynette bit her cheek, hating his endearments and concern. She quickly convinced herself that his declaration merely stemmed from her absence. He had to have been worried for her welfare; she was his wife, after all. He wasn't confessing any deeper emotion; he was simply telling her what he thought she'd like to hear. She took a deep breath and decided to get it over with, once and for all. "I am with child, so you may inform your grandmother that I am not barren," she said, willing her lower lip not to quiver.

His stomach fluttered. "You're certain?"

She nodded. "I became certain this morning."

"Why, this is wonderful news!" He kissed her again in an attempt to share in the joy, but it only took him a minute to realize she hadn't ceased her sobbing. "Lynette, why aren't you happy?"

"We don't know if it's a boy yet," she said sourly. She truly hoped it was. At least then her duty would be done, and she wouldn't have to lie in his arms again. Her heart surely couldn't take the torment.

"Why would that matter?" Aiden asked with knitted eyebrows. "We are going to be parents whether it's a boy or a girl."

Lynette refused to look at him. "But you need an heir to continue the dukedom."

His eyes widened, and all the blood drained from his face. "You heard my grandmother."

"I had been coming to tell you . . ." She broke off, unable to continue her explanation.

His mouth dried, and he struggled to swallow. "That's why you took a horse into the woods?"

"I simply needed a bit of privacy." Lynette tried to rationalize her actions.

"And you got lost! You could have been injured or worse!"

"I am aware of the error of my ways, milord," she said, her bloodshot eyes narrowing at him. "I shall refrain from doing anything to bring harm to your potential heir in the future."

He grabbed her by her shoulders. "And what of yourself?"

She pushed him away. "I'm fairly certain my sister is still available."

He stared at her, his mouth agape. "At what point did you run away?"

"After the bit where your grandmother suggested my sister would have made you a better match."

Suddenly it all made sense, her running away and subsequent aversion to him. She hadn't heard his reply and simply assumed that he'd agreed with his grandmother. She'd once again reached the conclusion that she was interchangeable with any other woman who could beget him an heir, including her sister. "If you had remained at the door for a minute longer, you would have heard me dispute such a suggestion." He looked her dead in the eye. "You would have heard me say that I would rather be the end of the Elliot line than marry another."

"Aiden, you can't possibly mean that." She shook her

head, belittling his words.

"I just told you that I love you, you daft woman," Aiden pronounced ineloquently. "How much clearer can I be? Let's see, how about this: the sight of you biting into that peach in Lady Paxton's orangery is etched in my mind along with the sound you made when you realized how juicy and sweet it was." He paused to revel in the blush that heated Lynette's face and then continued. "I wanted nothing more than to cross that glasshouse and drink the juices from your lips, but then you looked at me haughtily and reminded me that we'd never met. I knew from that moment that I wanted you."

She rolled her eyes. "All you're describing is lust."

"Allow me to finish?" he asked, and his little wife pursed her lips in acquiescence.

"I won't deny that it was lust at first or that I still lust for you. My hands burn with the need to touch you, whether it be in a waltz or in our bed, and my lips still tingle every time we kiss. But lust doesn't explain how happy I am to hear about your day, even if it simply consisted of inconsequential things. Or how I feel honored to merely be in your presence. I count every smile you bestow upon me and tuck it away to remember during my darkest times."

Lynette swallowed. "What of duty then?"

Aiden took her hand and brought it to his lips. "The only duty I have is to you, my wife. I have a duty to love, comfort, honor, and keep you in sickness and health. I made those vows to you, not to my family."

She tore her hand away from him. "But you refused to release me from our engagement because of the duty to your family!"

He arched a brow at her. "And you told me you couldn't

have a marriage without love."

"That's because I thought you could never love me!"

"I was less of a man all those months ago, and I hid behind the guise of duty to my family. I didn't want to tell you that I simply wanted you as my wife because it seemed so inexplicable at the time."

She looked up at him, her eyes glistening. "And now?"

"And now I am choosing you, not duty. Do you have any idea what it did to me when I didn't know where you were? I thought I had lost you . . . before I ever had the chance to tell you what you meant to me. It wouldn't matter to me if you were barren, but I suppose that point is now moot. There could be no one else because I simply love you."

Lynette sat in the tub, utterly dumbfounded. She didn't know what to say or do. As declarations of love went, Aiden's had surpassed everything she'd ever read. She'd finally experienced the romance she'd thought only existed in novels. Realizing there was only one thing for her to do, she stood and bared herself in body, mind, and soul. "I love you. And it broke my heart to think that I was still just some means to an end for you. A way to prove yourself to your family, to run your houses, and to throw your parties."

"You were never a means to an end for me," Aiden said as he rushed to pull her into his arms. "You have always been the woman I wanted to be with, spend time with, and spend my life with. I chose you because you saw me for who I am and made me feel something. I am truly sorry it took me so long to tell you what that something is."

"Love," Lynette supplied.

"It's always been love," he agreed and kissed his wife

happily. She wrapped her arms around his neck and allowed him to pull her from the bathtub. Water dripped all over the floor but neither Aiden nor Lynette cared. He carried her the short distance to the bedroom they shared and laid her down beneath him. A full moon shone brightly into the room, illuminating her for him to worship. Their tongues mingled as their breaths grew heavier. Needing to feel his skin on hers, she tore through his shirt and then stroked her hands up and down his chest.

In an attempt to salvage his remaining clothes, he stood to remove them before covering her body with his once more. "We don't have to do this anymore, you know," she whispered between kisses just to provoke him.

He reached below to angle his shaft at her entrance, and they shared a sigh of satisfaction when he breached her folds. "I want to experience this a million more times if I can," he said as he pumped himself into her core.

She grabbed his hand, placed it on her breast, and then sought out the nub he'd once shown her. "Will you still love me even when I am heavy with child?" she asked, their eyes locked.

"Of course," Aiden replied as his forehead met hers. He wrapped Lynette in his arms, drunk on the love they shared. "It is my duty to love you."

Epilogue

November 1812

Lynette Elliot, Duchess of Northumberland, sighed contentedly as she closed *Sense and Sensibility* for the final time. She sat in the drawing room of Elliot House in London with Aiden and Matilda. It was early November, and she'd recently begun to show her condition. Aiden and Lynette had decided to settle in London for her confinement so that she could be in the care of the best doctors, and Matilda had agreed to help her sister-in-law through her time of need. A new parliamentary session had also been called, and after the death of his father in October, Aiden was due to take up his seat as the Duke of Northumberland. Thus, a new Season was about to start in London along with a new chance for people to find love.

Not for Lynette and Aiden, though, since their love had already been cast in stone. Lynette felt her eyes well up with tears recalling the year she'd had. She couldn't help feeling sentimental as of late and blamed the baby that was growing in her belly for it.

"Surely the ending is not that bad," Aiden said, noticing

his wife's tears.

"Oh, it isn't! I'm just sad that it's over." She wiped her eyes. "Though the two sisters do end up living next to each other."

"Are you distressed because you don't live next to your sister?" Matilda asked.

"Heavens no, I am quite happy where I am," Lynette replied with a laugh. The novel exceeded her expectations despite Elinor and Marianne living next to each other. With her friend Teresa Palhem's urging, she'd decided to finish the book and was happy to find that the characters had achieved the love they sought despite their sense and sensibility.

Lynette related the theme to her own romance, which was once defined by duty and lust or logic and passion. She felt as though she'd similarly attained her love as the Dashwood sisters had, and it had struck a chord with her the way the best novels do.

"You know, it's written in such a way that the second sons are characterized as respectable gentlemen who find love." Lynette waved the novel at her husband and explained. "Whereas the first sons are portrayed as treacherous scoundrels."

"I'm happy the author gives second sons their due," Aiden said. He didn't need to be reminded of the societal constraints placed on second sons, having so recently been one. He acknowledged that while second sons had more freedom to choose their own destiny, they didn't typically have the means for true independence. He'd searched for years for his means to that end, a way to raise his status, secure his future, and make his family proud. Lynette had once thought that she was his means to an end, but in actuality, she was simply his end.

"Maybe I should read it next." Matilda reached for the book. "It sounds like an interesting story."

Lynette passed it to her enthusiastically. "You shall love it, then hate it, and then love it again. I should like to meet the woman who wrote it and lecture her for causing me such emotional turmoil."

"Says the woman who will willingly buy the next novel the author writes," Aiden teased her.

"What can I say? You men love your gambling and liquor even when you lose or wake with a headache," Lynette said with a smirk. "Women love books even when they cause us emotional turmoil."

She acknowledged that sometimes, the emotional turmoil was worth the ending it wrought. So it was with the highs and lows of life. Again, she couldn't help but see the parallels between herself and the characters of the novel. If Edward Ferrars hadn't been disowned, he wouldn't have been able to marry Elinor; or if Mr. Willoughby hadn't turned out to be a cad, Marianne wouldn't have married Colonel Brandon. Similarly, if Aiden hadn't maintained their engagement when Lynette wanted to be released, where would she be now? She wouldn't be the Duchess of Northumberland or awaiting the birth of her first child, and more importantly, she wouldn't have a husband who made it his duty to love her.

Acknowledgements

Thank you to my husband, Chris for loving me and supporting my keyboard tapping.

To my friends Quivven and Lexa for listening to me talk through plots and character development.

Thank you to Gary for leading the Gothic and Romantic literature module that was a source of inspiration for this novel.

To Gillie for being the first person to read *My Duty to You*.

Finally, thank you to my editors, Ashley and Bryan, and to the team at Kingsley Publishers because, without you, none of this would be a reality.

Author Bio

Alyssa Martin developed a passion for reading at a young age and hasn't stopped since. Originally from the USA, she taught ESL in China for two years where she met her British husband. They now live in England with their ginger tabby cat, Ninja.

Connect with Alyssa on social media

Instagram: @alyssatheauthor_
TikTok: @alyssatheauthor_

Made in the USA
Middletown, DE
16 February 2025